WHEN A THUG Loves You

A Novel By

JASMINE CIERA

1

I LOOKED at the freshly painted white walls that wrapped around an empty room and stopped in the doorway to scope the new place I would call home. Looking at the unopened boxes ready to be explored and the bedroom furniture threatening to burst through my room door pissed me off even more. I couldn't believe that my life had come to this, and the fact that I had no control over this shit was even worse.

"I think this move will be perfect for us, Marcy. Just look on the bright side. We get a new start," my mom said as she placed the last box in my new bedroom. It was already hard enough, leaving my friends and family in Georgia and moving all the way to Miami, Florida with no one but my mom and twin brother and sister. Yeah, we were triplets.

My mother was a lawyer who moved to open a new office in Miami and to get away from my father since their recent divorce. Although this trip was like a saving grace to her, it was pure torture to my siblings and me, especially after all I went through. I shook the thoughts of the hurt that crowded my mind, body, and soul.

"Milan and Manuel, hurry up with those boxes! We need to get this house unpacked today!"

"She's a fucking maniac, I swear. She could've left my ass in Georgia with Dad like I said from the beginning," my brother, Manuel, who we called Mann, spoke as he sat his tall frame on my queen-size bed.

Our father was Colombian, and our mother was Black, so our mixture was deadly growing up. Although we were triplets and favored a lot, we were all very different. My style was edgy, and I sported short cuts because I didn't need my long, natural hair getting in the way of my bomb ass shape. My sister sported her natural, long hair, and her frame was identical to mine. As soon as I got enough money, I planned to get bigger breasts because this B-cup would never work with my hips and ass.

Manuel was a ladies' man. All the hoes loved him, and the fact that his light skin and good hair carried a body full of tattoos didn't help. Manuel was definitely my parents' problem child, and he loved to disappoint them. Milan did everything they asked but was also sneaky as hell, and then there was me.

I was the one who didn't give a fuck about the day I caught my father fucking his secretary or my mother fucking with one of her clients, who was a big drug dealer in our area that she had freed from prison when we all knew he committed each crime he was imprisoned for. I knew then that nothing was as it seemed, so I took shit for what it was and lived life, and I did just that. I guess my mom felt as if this move would help all of us, but I had other plans to get the fuck away from her.

"She so damn annoying, Mann. You know the only reason we couldn't stay with Dad is his new bitch won't allow it," I reminded him.

"Well, you know the real reason behind that, Marcy. Just try to make this a new start for yourself. If one of us needs this, it's definitely you," Manuel spoke, reminding me of my choices that got me here. Damn, I missed Royal. "But on the bright side, I'm about to say fuck all this shit and make my own way. I don't need their cash, and you know it, Marcy," Manuel added as we burst into laughter.

I knew he spoke the truth, which was another reason my mom

moved us all the way to Miami. The moment she found out that Manuel was selling drugs for her little boyfriend, we left, and I blamed her for all of it. It was crazy how our family was once living the American dream—two top lawyers with triplets who were now sixteen. One triplet was Manuel, who ran it on the basketball court and already had colleges looking at him. Milan was a top scholar and made straight A's the moment she walked into a schoolhouse. Then there was me, who could sing my ass off, but my parents felt singing wasn't a real career.

"Mann, as crazy as this sounds, since we are in a new state, bruh, you gotta play smart. So for now, use basketball to make your name here, and let the rest follow. Don't go looking for shit. Let it come to you," I replied, hanging up my clothes as Milan walked in.

"So y'all having conversations without me?" she asked her usual question.

"She's jealous, Mann," I replied, laughing.

"So what's new?" he asked her, referring to what Mom was talking about since she would always vent to Milan.

"She was talking about putting us in a private school."

"Oh, fuck no!" Mann and I both yelled at the same time.

"Will y'all pipe down! I talked her out of it. We're going to a public school." She laughed.

"That's my girl!" I replied, slapping my sister on the ass.

"Next time, talk to her about giving us more allowance money so I won't go back to selling drugs." We all burst into laughter at Mann's outburst.

Monday Morning...

"Here are your schedules. Should I walk you guys to class?" my mom asked as if we weren't in damn high school.

"If you take one step toward walking me to class, I will throw up right in this hallway," I replied.

"Yeah, we definitely got this," Manuel spoke.

"Have a great day at work, Mom. We got it from here," Milan added, making the conversation much better, as always.

"OK, well, have a great day, my babies, and call me if you need me. Off to work I go!" she replied, hugging Milan and waving bye to Manuel and me. She knew better than to throw any of that sensitive shit my way.

I looked down at my schedule to see that my first class was English. Of course, Milan had all honors classes, so she departed from Manuel and me as we both headed toward Ms. Zag's class.

Opening the door, the first thing we noticed was that the entire class was filled with black children, and after thinking about it, I realized I hadn't seen one white person since I set foot inside the building.

"Hello," Ms. Zag greeted as we handed her our schedules.

"Class, please welcome Marcy and Manuel Gomez, here from Atlanta, Georgia," she reassured herself, looking down at the papers we handed her.

"Y'all twins?" a black girl in the back blurted out.

"Yeah, well, actually, we're triplets. Two girls and a boy," I replied, looking her way.

"Damn, that's wassup. I never met triplets before, and your brother fine as fuck."

"Ms. Andrews, that will be enough of your outbursts for one day. Take a seat, Mr. and Ms. Gomez, and I'll make sure you get the books and materials you need to be on track with the rest of the class."

Mann and I found two seats in the back on separate rows. We took our seats, and I scoped out the classroom, noticing that there were a few cute boys, ghetto ass cheerleaders with lace fronts and loud colored nails, and others who were trying to figure us out.

Out of the corner of my eye, I noticed a pair of eyes on me. I turned to see a dark-skinned boy with a low cut looking my way. The moment I looked at him, he smiled, showing his gold teeth that covered his bottom row of teeth. I smiled back, turning around, trying not to blush. His ass was fine and thuggish just how I liked them. After what felt like forever, the bell finally rang, and we were off to our next class. My brother had math, so I had to depart from him to science.

I didn't like departing from my brother, but I was also ready to see what this new school had to offer. I knew my sister was having a heart attack since she was surrounded by a bunch of black people.

As I reached my next class, I noticed the same boy from my first class walking toward the same classroom. I walked in and quickly found a seat in the back of the class. As everyone filed in, I noticed that this science class was filled with a lot more ratchet girls than my first one. The teacher walked in and sat at his computer, never addressing the class or anything.

"Copy these notes, and after that, you're free to go," the tall, skinny, white, bald teacher stood to say.

"Mr. Henry, sit your white ass down! You know we are not doing that shit!" a black girl with a pink lace front wig yelled.

After turning beet red, the teacher took a seat and began typing on his computer. I instantly felt bad. I took out my notebook and began copying the notes on the board. The class began to get loud and obviously didn't give a fuck about doing their work.

"So where are you from?" I heard a voice ask. I looked up from my notebook to see the dark-skinned boy from my first class. His deep voice and perfect white teeth that sported a gold bottom row of teeth looked delicious.

I smiled, showing my dimples as I responded, "I'm from Atlanta."

"That's wassup. I've been there a few times. I gotta say you fine as fuck, Marcy."

I smiled, noticing that he remembered my name from the last class. "Well, thank you," I replied. That moment of excitement was short lived when the pink lace front wearing hoe approached our desk.

"Rome, why the fuck you back here talking to this half-breed bitch? So you just gon' try me like that!" she blurted out as her friends burst into laughter.

"Lacey, how many times do I have to tell you that I'm done with your ghetto ass!" Rome yelled as I joined the class in laughter. I was used to bitches trying me, and I welcomed her to take it further.

"What the fuck you laughing at? I'll slap that smile right off your ugly ass face," Lacey challenged.

"I seriously doubt that, but what you can do is turn around with your lil' minions and have a seat back at the front. Because your boy was just telling me how fine I was, and I'd like to finish this conversation and let him know I think he's kinda fly himself," I replied, smiling at Rome, who smiled back.

In an instant, Lacey slapped my books off my desk, causing my iPhone to hit the floor.

"Now what, bit—" Her words were cut short as I charged at her, making her stumble over the desk and hit the ground. Grabbing her lace from the back, I climbed on top of her and landed two punches to her face. She used her free hands to push my face back to get me off of her.

Out of nowhere, I was pulled from the back by someone as Lacey was freed and throwing punches left and right. I turned to begin hitting Lacey's friend who had just given her an advantage. I was now in a full-fledged fight with two bitches I didn't know. I pulled Lacey's friend down to the ground, beating the shit out of her. I began throwing punches everywhere since I was at a disadvantage with two on one. With Lacey's friend covering her eye, I knew I had to take Lacey down. After I scooped her, we were at the front of the class as I threw uppercut punches so I could stand straight up and go blow for blow with her. As I swung out of her grip, I felt a pair of strong arms grab me, and I was out of the classroom, in the hallway.

"This ain't over, dumb bitch!" Lacey yelled as people began coming out of their classrooms.

"Bitch, do it look like I care? Don't let this pretty face fool you! Don't nan bitch scare me! Check my record, hoe!" I yelled. Out of nowhere, I saw my brother as the school officials tried to detain me.

"Damn, on the first day, Marcy? I'd at least thought you'd wait a few weeks, and then you got the hoe leaking. Guess them boxing classes helped."

"Shut up, Mann! Get my shit and call Mom! This some bullshit!" I yelled as I was escorted to the office.

I noticed Rome watching me the entire time. I probably ruined everything with him after that incident. I was big on respect, and after my parents' divorce, they wanted all of us to go to counseling. Of course, I refused. Instead, I asked for an alternative way to release my feelings. I'd been taking boxing for over a year, and it definitely helped me release my stress.

After thirty minutes of sitting, I heard my mother's Givenchy heels clicking on the floor as she walked into the office as if she were waiting to get a call from the school.

"Oh, Marcy, you just had to find trouble. You and your brother just want me to check into a crazy house, huh!" she dramatically yelled.

Not saying a word, I stood to my feet, handing her the three-day suspension paper and walking out. I didn't have time for her uppity shit today, especially making it seem as if Mann and I were her problem children. Although we were, she didn't have to remind us of that shit all the time.

Walking to the car, I saw Rome waiting outside as if he were waiting for someone.

"Here's your things, Ms. Mayweather," Rome spoke, handing my bag and phone over.

"Let's go, Marcy!" my mother yelled, and I ignored her words.

"Your phone wasn't locked, so I put my number in it. Hit me up tonight, aight," he whispered. I smiled as I grabbed my things and went to join my mother in the car.

The car ride home was quiet until she couldn't hold her silence anymore.

"Look, Marcy, I'm trying. I don't have all the answers, but I know I love you guys with everything in me. I just want the best for you guys. Just let me help you. I know you hate me for what happened to you in Atlanta. I couldn't let you ruin your life like that, especially for a boy with no future. Just please don't hate me for that. Don't allow it to make you bitter. Marcy, just talk to me. How can we make this better between us?"

My mother now had tears in her eyes, and as much as I wanted to talk to her and tell her the real reason behind my bitterness, the words failed to escape my lips, and I just looked away. After sitting in silence for the entire ride, we pulled up to the house, and I got out. She then pulled off to return to work.

2

"WELL, I have two more days left of suspension before I go back to school, Papa," I spoke into the phone as my father tried to speak words of wisdom.

"Well, stay strong, and I love you, Marcy."

I ended the call after his words. I never disrespected my father, but I hadn't used the love word in a while, and I preferred it that way.

"Aye, get dressed! We are going to a pool party tonight!" Mann burst into my room and yelled.

"Hell no, Mann! She is on punishment. Mom will kill her!" Milan added.

"Anyways, I'll be ready in a few," I said as I pushed them both out of my room and immediately went into my large closet. I pulled out my two-piece Burberry check swimsuit with Burberry shorts and sandals to match, courtesy of my father's credit card that he gave me as an apology gift the day I caught him cheating on my mother. I walked into my bathroom and plugged up my flat iron to straighten my red, blunt-cut bob that I had just gotten done earlier today. One thing my mother didn't play about was my sister and me walking around with undone hair and messed up nails and toes. We had to keep ourselves presentable at all times. That was one quality I could honestly say I carried with me.

Two hours later...

"I can't believe you snuck out, Marcy." My sister sneered with her Chanel one piece and matching sandals. Her hair was in a high bun, and she looked great. Mann wore his Versace trunks and V-neck shirt. The house that held the pool party was a mini-mansion full of people half naked in bathing suits and some fully covered, obviously refusing to blend with the theme.

"There go my nigga Rome right there!" Mann blurted out as I changed my facial expression. How the hell did Mann know him already and acting as if they were friends or some shit?

"Wassup, Mann, thought you lost your way. Welcome to *mi casa,*" Rome greeted us.

"This is your house?" Milan questioned.

"Yeah, well, my older brother's, but I live here. This is his pool party. I just invited a few people from school," Rome answered.

I looked around, noticing a few kids from school but also checking out the thugged-out niggas and the hood rats walking around. I knew they had to be way older than us; some men looked as if they were in their late twenties.

"Come on. I'll show y'all around," Rome instructed.

We all followed suit as we were introduced to the home theater, large pool, and oversized kitchen that had more than enough food.

"Now that your tour is over, I hope y'all plan to join us in the pool," I heard a voice speak behind us. I turned around to see the finest man I thought I'd ever laid eyes on. His tall, built frame screamed 'boss nigga.' He sported dreads that fell off his shoulders onto his built frame, brown, almond-shaped eyes that went with his full lips, and brown skin. He was fine as fuck, and I couldn't help but watch him.

"We coming out right now, big bruh. These are my homies. They're new to the area," Rome spoke.

"Oh OK, well, welcome. Can I get you anything to drink?" Rome's brother asked, looking directly at me. I smiled as I declined his offer and turned away.

"Let's go by the pool," I told Milan as we walked off, leaving the boys to finish their conversation.

"You like Rome's brother," my sister said as we walked off. I smiled, realizing how obvious I was. My smile was cut short as Lacey and her crew stood on the other side of the pool, staring me down.

"Don't pay her any mind. They're nothing but a bunch of hating ass bitches," a dark-skinned girl that resembled JuJu off of *Love & Hip Hop* spoke, approaching my sister and me.

"By the way, I'm Khyrah."

"Milan and Marcy," we recited simultaneously.

"You whooped her ass, though. Glad somebody did it. Them hoes think they're the shit since she used to fuck with Rome."

"Yeah, I heard," I added.

"Y'all mind if I kick it right here with y'all tonight? I don't really fuck with many people," Khyrah said.

"Yeah, that's cool. Maybe you can tell us who is who out here," I said as my sister rolled her eyes, knowing exactly what I wanted to know.

"Cool, who are you curious about?" Khyrah asked.

"Anybody you feel the need to tell me about," I replied.

"Well, in that case, the only two people you need to be familiar with is Rome's brother, Ramel, and his crew. They run this area. Their parents were killed a few years ago, so Ramel took over from there. He runs their family business, and he's been raising Rome since they were thirteen. Ramel's much older than us. He's twenty-four, and the red guy standing to his left is his right-hand man, Jaq."

In the middle of Khyrah's dick riding, I tuned her out to watch a slim-thick red girl with long, black, straight hair, sporting the new Louis Vuitton bathing suit that I had my eye on the other day. The crazy part was the damn bathing suit wouldn't be released for purchase until next month. How the fuck did this hoe get it so soon?

She approached Ramel and placed a kiss on his lips, making her presence known to not only him but to all the gawking bitches looking his way as well. He pulled away and wrapped his arm around her neck as he finished talking with friends. As much as I wanted to turn away and focus my attention elsewhere, it was something about him that my seventeen-year-old eyes couldn't shake. In an instant, I watched as his eyes met mine. For a moment, it felt as if we were the only two people in the room. A smile crept upon his face as he winked his eye and turned away. I smiled, focusing back on the conversation at hand.

"Other than that, you guys will love Miami," I heard Khyrah say, wrapping up her little speech.

"Oh, I plan to," I spoke.

"Well, who wants to take some shots?" Khyrah asked as we followed her to the kitchen where everyone was.

3

"BITCH, HE WAS FINE AS FUCK!" I screamed into the phone.

"But I thought you wanted his brother, Rome?" my best friend, Kelsey, reminded me as I went on my rant about Rome's brother, Ramel.

"I mean, he's cute, but Ramel is more my speed," I replied.

"No, he's not. Your ass is too young for him; that's a grown ass man. Don't start this shit again, Marcy, with these old ass boys. We are seventeen for a reason," Kelsey lectured.

"Yeah, whatever, bitch. If I wanted a lecture, I would've expressed this to my sister, not my hot in the pussy bestie who's all of a sudden throwing salt," I spat back.

"Damn, you're right. Let me take my hot pussy ass the hell on. All I will say is be careful, Marcy. Them Miami niggas not like these Georgia boys. They're dangerous. I just don't want you to go through that shit again." With that, my iPhone displayed call ended. I didn't see what the big deal was. He was fine, and I could definitely see us being more than friends.

～

Monday Morning

"Welcome back," Rome greeted as I walked the hallway to class.

"Well, thank you. Missed me?" I replied as we walked into class.

"Damn right, but you never used that number I placed in your phone, so I don't know what to think about that," Rome said.

I smiled as Manuel walked in just in time. I turned away and focused my attention on the board as the class filed in.

The day went by slow as hell, and before I knew it, I was walking off of campus during lunch. As I made it halfway off campus, about to catch the city bus to South Beach, someone yelled my name.

"Marcy, where you running off to so fast!" Khyrah yelled, running up to me. I looked around before answering her. Out of all days, she would choose today to interrupt my attempt to skip school.

"Look, if you are going to skip school, at least ride with me. They pay people to catch students skipping school on the city bus. Here, follow me," Khyrah insisted. Pondering for a second, I followed her to her black 2014 Nissan Altima. Opening the door, I climbed in, buckling my seat belt, ready to leave. Khyrah pressed the push start button, and we were off.

"I see you're a modern day badass, Marcy," Khyrah spoke, starting conversation.

"Not at all. I just don't give a fuck, but on a serious note, where the real niggas at? The ballers?" I asked, cutting to the chase. I was bored with this Miami shit. I needed some fun.

"My kind of girl. Hang tight, hot girl." Khyrah laughed as she hit a U-turn.

Fifteen minutes later, we were pulling up to a red brick house. I immediately noticed the niggas hanging around on the porch and the females walking past and trying to be noticed.

"Where are we?" I blurted out while fixing my Nike tights and half shirt that I tied a knot in around my belly button area.

"This is the trap. You wanted hood niggas? Well, here they are! All flavors from the broke to the boss niggas. Take your pick. Well, pick anyone but that one standing in front of the door. His name is D-boy, and he's mine," Khyrah spoke, claiming one of the finest men standing up there. She was lucky that redbones weren't my thing, because if they were, he would definitely be on my list. We both exited the car and walked to the porch that held a few men. Khyrah immediately went to D-boy, kissing his lips as he stuck his tongue down her throat. I rolled my eyes at the public display of hood love.

"Aye, Ky Ky, who this?" a dark-skinned man asked with a mouthful of gold teeth. Looking around, I noticed that most of the men in Miami sported big, chunky dreads and gold teeth.

"Oh, wassup, Amp? That's my girl Marcy from Atlanta," Khyrah replied, turning everyone's attention to me now. I smiled and waved as they undressed me with their eyes.

"Well, I'mma be the first to say you fine as fuck, lil' mama."

I smiled at Amp's comment.

"Come on in. It's hot out here," D-boy spoke, leading us into the trap. When we walked into the house, there was one couch where two young boys about my age were playing the video game. There was one kitchen table, and other than that, the house appeared empty.

D-boy disappeared into the kitchen as Khyrah and I stood by the kitchen table. With two boxes of cereal in his hand, he turned the boxes over, dumping money onto the table.

"Y'all count that for me while a nigga cook up. Each stack you count, dump that shit to the side and put these rubber bands around them. When you done, I have more for y'all to count," D-boy spoke, grabbing a fork and Pyrex bowl from the cabinet by the table. Looking at Khyrah, I shrugged and took a seat to begin counting the money. Truth was, I wasn't a rookie to this type of thing. Little did they know, I'd counted so much money that I could damn near eyeball the amount of cash on the table.

Khyrah finally took a seat and began counting. I scammed the money, sorting the stacks out and putting rubber bands on each stack.

"Damn, Marcy, you might want to slow down with this money. You can easily miscount. Trust me, I do it all the time, and D-boy gets pissed," Khyrah added.

"Naw, I got it," I replied, tying a rubber band around my last stack.

"That's five bands right there," I spoke loud enough for D-boy to hear me.

Coming around the corner, he looked at me with a confused look on his face. "You might want to recount that, sweetheart. Ain't no way your ass finished that fast unless you a damn money-counting machine," D-boy said, laughing at his own joke.

"No need. That's five stacks. Count it if you don't believe me!" I challenged.

"Aye, Lil' Tony, come count this shit. Shawty saying this five stacks. She counted that shit way too fast. If that's five stacks on the head, I'mma give shawty $200 and hire her as our personal money counter," D-boy spoke, making a joke. Little did he know, that $200 was about to be mine.

Lil' Tony made his way to the table. As he reached for the money, I stopped him.

"Better yet, bet $500 if that's five stacks, and if it isn't, I'll owe you five hundred," I challenged again.

"Aight, bet!" D-boy accepted.

Lil' Tony began counting the money. I began scrolling through my phone since his ass was taking so long. I looked over to see Khyrah still counting her half as well, which I already figured to be about $3,500 from just eyeballing.

"Aye, lil' mama was right. D-boy, that's five stacks," Lil' Tony assured his boss.

"Told ya, and what Khyrah's counting is about $3,500, so can I get my $500 since I made you a believer?" I asked, holding my hand out. Reaching into his pocket, D-boy pulled out and handed me five hundred-dollar bills. I smiled, folding the money in my hand.

"Not only is she pretty, but I see she's smart as hell," I heard a voice say behind me. I turned around to be greeted by Ramel.

"Damn, brah, you saw that shit? We might need to hire lil' mama." D-boy laughed, dapping Ramel up.

I blushed as I took a seat back at the table. Not only was I excited to see Ramel, but he was looking fine as hell today too. I crossed my legs to contain myself as I looked away toward Khyrah, who had a smirk on her face.

"Aye, shut this shit down!" Ramel said out loud as if everyone were listening. Three men in the back and the two boys playing the game all exited the house. I stood to my feet with Khyrah, ready to leave.

"Naw, y'all stay. All these niggas standing around here need to go," Ramel said as I sat back down.

"So you go to school with my lil' brother, Rome? I'm guessing your sixteen or seventeen, right?" Ramel asked, looking directly in my eyes, which happened to be a turn on for me. There was nothing I loved more than having a man's full attention.

"Yes, but is that a problem?" I spat back, matching his look.

"I mean, you're a little young for a girl in this game, but we can definitely use your wits, and the pay will be good. I just need you to keep up with the count at this trap location. When the money hits, count and leave. That's all. Think you can handle that?" Ramel spoke, getting straight to the point.

I stood, feeling defeated. What I thought was him possibly trying to get to know me on another level was just business. Not being one to allow defeat to get the best of me, I returned his offer with a simple smile.

"I'll do it, but I'm only coming two days out the week. Whichever days that happens to be, you guys just let me know. I would also like to be paid upfront, and three thousand a month should be good for my services." I had just set the bar on my own terms. If it was just business, then I planned to be well taken care of.

"Three grand just to count money twice a week?" D-boy questioned as he laughed to himself.

"Three grand, huh? I guess you have a deal, beautiful," Ramel accepted.

I returned his gratitude with a smile. My life was about to get the action I had been craving since the moment I set foot in Miami.

"Oh, I'm glad you're happy because I planned on paying you five stacks for your service. You just saved me some money. Be quick to listen and slow to speak, beautiful. You can start by counting that bag I bought in the house," Ramel directed again. I felt defeated and somewhat embarrassed.

"We are not lil' boys, sweetie. The cash is never an issue," D-boy added.

"No worries, beautiful. Imma teach you a lot," Ramel spoke, obviously seeing my beet-red face full of embarrassment.

"D-boy, get this beauty situated. I'll be back to pick up my cut later." With that, Ramel picked up his ringing phone and was out the door.

I directed my attention to D-boy and Khyrah, who had obviously decided to finish their makeout session from earlier.

I decided to grab the black duffle bag Ramel left and start counting. I couldn't help but think about the fact that, for the first time in my life, I had been at a loss for words from a boy—no, scratch that. A man.

4

ONE MONTH LATER...

"ALL I WANT to know is where the cash came from. You haven't swiped your credit card one time since we've been in the mall," my sister, Milan, spoke as I paid damn near $700 on a pair of Gucci flip flops for her and me.

"Milan, just chill. I met someone, and he hooks me up with cash from time to time! That's all!" I damn near yelled, annoyed with her nosy ass.

"The only men I know giving a sixteen-year-old enough money to buy designer are grown ass drug dealers, and after the shit you went through back home, I pray to God that's not the case, Marcy."

"Well, long as you're praying, I guess that answers your damn question!" I replied, grabbing my bags and walking off.

"Wassup, Marcy?" a group of boys I knew from the trap spoke as they walked past us in the mall.

"Sup, fellas," I replied as I kept walking.

"What the fuck! OK, when did you become so popular with thugs? Marcy, I swear if you're into something crazy I'm telling Mom. Your ass will be shipped to that boarding school so fast," Milan threatened.

"This why I can't stand your crybaby ass now. Why does it matter?

Y'all don't give a fuck about me—you or mom—and truth be told, y'all never have! Do what the fuck you have to do, Milan, because it won't change shit. Your ass don't complain when I'm spending a grip on your designer shit and giving you money, but the moment I told you no about that ugly ass Gucci purse, you want to act like a bitch! Well, here! Take your broke ass in there and buy the ugly ass purse!" I yelled, throwing a stack of twenties and fifties in her face as the crowd that gathered around us looked on, ready for a show.

I walked off, pissed, dialing Khyrah to pick me up from the mall since I rode here with Milan. I didn't even wait to see her reaction.

"Just come get me, Khyrah. I'm at Sawgrass mall," I spoke into my iPhone.

I waited outside the mall, texting my brother about the incident with our sister.

"You're too beautiful to be getting that upset, especially with family," I heard someone say behind me. I turned around to be greeted by Ramel and his girlfriend that I saw at the party the night I met him.

"Baby, head to the car. Lemme holla at my lil' worker," Ramel spoke, dismissing his girl as she rolled her eyes and snatched the keys to his BMW X6 truck.

"You might want to tend to your woman. She don't look to happy," I insisted.

"Naw, I'm checking on you. I see you got a lil' fight in you. I like that." Ramel smiled.

"But if this shit becomes too much to handle, and your family tripping like that, then I would understand if you needed to quit."

"Trust me, I have no problem telling you if I needed time off. I'm good," I replied with an annoyed expression. I was over this conversation already.

"My bad. I didn't mean to question your ability to keep it real, and for that, I'll go ahead and pay you the five stacks a month for your help. That works for you?" Ramel questioned.

"Thanks," I simply replied, but on the inside, I was happy as hell.

Ramel stood and stared at me for a second longer before leaving as if his thoughts were running wild.

"For you to be young, you're cool as fuck. Don't let no one change that, beautiful." With that, Ramel walked off to tend to his upset girlfriend.

Ten minutes later, Khyrah was pulling up. I opened the door and hopped in, ready to fill her in on today's events. Khyrah also assisted me in counting money at the trap. She didn't make as much as I did, but I knew she basically did it to keep an eye on D-boy.

"Well, I hope you have something to wear because D-boy's birthday party is tonight at the club, and we have to be bad," Khyrah interrupted my story to say as we pulled off.

Six Hours Later...

"I'm getting dressed as we speak! Let me call you back!" I yelled at Khyrah as I spruced up my bun on the top of my head. I ran my hands down the back of my shaved head, making sure my hair was laying down. My latest cut I rocked was the back of my head shaved with designs in the cut and the rest of my hair growing back to its long, natural length.

I pulled out my one-shoulder, cranberry-colored Herve Leger Brianne dress from my closet. I ran my hand over the sequins on the shoulder and grabbed my black and gold non-designer toe seal heels from my closet.

I opened my room door to check around for my mom. When I didn't see her in her room, I knew she was working late. Getting suddenly excited since I didn't have to lie or sneak out, I ran to my brother's room to make sure he was getting ready. Manuel had been hanging with Rome a lot lately, so I knew he would be present at this party as well.

"Marcy, you not dressed yet? A nigga not waiting all day for your slow ass! Hurry up!" Manuel yelled as I hurriedly returned to my room to finish getting ready.

I applied my Jimmy Choo lotion before I slipped my tight-fitting dress up my body. This dress hugged every curve just the way I liked it.

"Swear I hate my small ass titties," I spoke aloud as my B-cups rested in my dress.

Satisfied with my look, I applied a little makeup and grabbed my matching clutch, heading toward the door.

Walking in the hallway, I bumped into Milan coming out of the bathroom. I looked at her with disgust as she returned my glare. Without speaking one word, I walked past her and out the door with Manuel. Khyrah was picking me up, and Rome was coming for Manuel. As they both pulled up at the same time, I said my goodbyes to Mann and hopped in the car with Khyrah.

As soon as I entered the car, I checked to see Khyrah's blunt-cut bob looking silky and gorgeous. She sported a multicolored Versace dress and heels.

"You look gorgeous for your man's little birthday party," I spoke, breaking the silence.

"Thanks, but I have something to tell you first," Khyrah spoke, turning the music down, looking nervous as hell.

"OK, we are going to the party, but D-boy's wife will be in attendance tonight, so there won't be much interaction with us as usual. Before you say anything, let me explain. D-boy, whose real name is Dante, is twenty-five. He got married a year and a half ago because he got the hoe pregnant, and her family wouldn't let her keep the baby unless they were married. I've been dealing with him for a year, and he's in love with me. The day I turn eighteen, he plans to leave her and be with me, so right now, this is what we have to deal with. Please don't judge me, Marcy. I don't allow many to know about my situation with Dante," Khyrah explained.

I shook the thought of wanting to tell her she was crazy for believing in a happily ever after with a thug, but I did before. I wanted to tell her she deserved so much more, and this situation wouldn't end good, but I was once a believer in this type of love before. I wanted to say so much and tell her how my past directed my future, and not in a good way. I wanted to say the reason I could count money so fast and carry the street smarts of a modern thug was that I was once taught by whom I thought would be the love of my life. However, tonight, Khyrah did not need a mother like I did when I went through my shit. She needed a rider, and I was here for all the bullshit tonight may carry.

"Fuck her. We are having fun tonight," I replied, putting my pride to the side. She smiled, satisfied with my response, but I knew this night was just beginning. I also knew that, as naïve as Khyrah was at the moment, D-boy's wife knew more than she thought.

Pulling up to the club, I noticed how thick it was. I saw Manuel and Rome waiting for us by the front so we could get in with them since we were all underage. Ramel paid the security extra to let us in. I checked my makeup while Khyrah parked, and we exited her car. Walking to the front, I scanned the long ass line and noticed the hoes I beat up on my first day of school. I rolled my eyes, grabbing Rome's hand in plain sight as we entered the club. To the looking eyes, you would think we were more than friends, and I planned to use that to my advantage tonight. In reality, we were just homies who liked to have fun—nothing more or less.

We entered the club as Rome held my hand, escorting us to the VIP area his brother held down. Walking in the section, I immediately noticed all the dudes from the trap standing around, popping bottles. It didn't take long to notice D-boy and his wife, who stood next to her man as if she owned the club. Checking for Khyrah, I noticed she stood close to my brother for support.

We walked further into the big VIP section, away front the birthday boy, toward the back where Ramel was standing with his girl by his side. Still holding my hand, Rome dapped his brother and crew up. I noticed Ramel's eyes immediately scan my body as if I were a piece of steak on a silver platter. His eyes quickly diverted to my and Rome's hands. Looking up to match his gaze, I smirked and whispered in Rome's ear.

Standing a few feet away from Ramel, I began to dance on Rome as Meek Mill's "Dreams and Nightmares" song came on. The club went crazy as everyone rapped the lyrics. Khyrah had a drink in her hand, loosening up with my brother next to her. Rome handed me a cup of Patrón and pineapple juice. The atmosphere was crunk, and I was honestly having a great time.

Rome wrapped one of his arms around my waist as he bounced to the music. The DJ gave D-boy a thousand shout outs as he switched the track to Dej Loaf featuring Future "Hey There." With the mood slowing down, I took the chance to grind my body on Rome.

"*I still taste you on my lips, yeah, yeah, I do,*" I recited as I stood face to face with Rome, grinding my body on his. He gripped my waist tighter. I looked up to see Ramel burning a hole in his brother and me with his eyes. We finally locked eyes as I allowed the liquor to take over my body. I kept eye contact with Ramel as I continued to grind on Rome.

With eyes on us, I turned around and bent over, giving Rome a perfect view of my apple ass in my dress. I continued to move my ass and hips until the song ended. I even noticed Ramel's boring ass bitch watching when she should've been entertaining her nigga.

Khyrah handed me another shot as I continued to grind on Rome. Taking the shot straight to my head, I was feeling better than ever. It had been so long since I felt free and drunk. I was in the prime of my life right now—young, sexy, making my own money, and almost grown. As the song changed, I grabbed another shot from Rome, allowing the liquor to burn my throat. With the liquor taking advantage, I began to feel horny.

Knowing my limit, I needed a breather. I grabbed Khyrah's hand and pulled her to the bathroom in VIP. On the way out the section toward the bathroom, we passed D-boy's wife, who stopped and stared at us, indicating what I already knew. She wasn't very fond of Khyrah fucking her man. At this point, I knew I had to regain my composure because shit would go left in the blink of an eye.

Walking to the VIP bathroom, I held onto the wall for support because my ass was drunk, and I wasn't a drinker, so I knew it wouldn't be long. I rushed down the little hallway and burst in the bathroom, going straight to the stall, leaving Khyrah. Squatting over the toilet, I pulled up my dress, exposing my pantiless bottom, and allowed the urine to pour out of me.

Trying to focus my thoughts, I couldn't help but laugh. I felt damn good. Holding my balance in these heels, praying I didn't fall into this nasty ass toilet, I hurried up. Wiping myself, I straightened my dress back out, flushed the toilet, and leaned up against the stall door with my eyes closed for a second. I heard a loud thump that came from the men's bathroom next to ours. Jumping back to reality, I gained my composure and went to wash my hands.

"Khyrah!" I yelled, looking around, noticing that she wasn't out here waiting on me.

A few women that I thought were Khyrah walked in the restroom.

I walked into the hallway to look for her, but I was pulled into the dark corner where you couldn't see anyone unless you walked back there.

Immediately getting scared but too drunk to react, I felt a pair of lips crash into mine. Not being able to stop myself, I kissed backed, hoping it was Ramel. Their hands touched my face, and as I traveled my hands to the person's chest, I pulled away and slapped the shit out of my attacker.

"What the fuck are you doing? Do I look fucking gay to you, bitch!" I yelled as Ramel's girlfriend smiled.

"Normally, I would kick your ass for hitting me, but that shit turned me on. I can't help it, Marcy. You bad as fuck. I know it, and my nigga do to," she replied.

"You or your nigga don't have shit to do with me. If you put your fucking lips on me or even touch me, I will kill you," I spoke, ready to beat her ass.

"From where I was standing, looks like you enjoyed it. Honestly, I don't want to fight. I just like what I see, and I went for it. I'mma let you enjoy the rest of your night," she spoke as she got ready to walk back to the VIP. The men's bathroom door opened, and out walked D-boy's wife and some dude I'd never seen before. Should've known she was a hoe. The two ladies slapped hands as they retired back to their thrones. My mind went into overdrive as I rushed back into the women's bathroom. I burst every stall door open and still couldn't find Khyrah.

I grabbed my phone and texted my brother to see if she was back up there with them. After his immediate reply, I knew something had happened. I began to panic.

@Mann: I can't find Khyrah meet me by the bathroom, something's not right.

I knew he was on his way with Rome, so I tried to keep calm. I tried to collect my thoughts, and I realized I never heard anyone come in the bathroom until after I came out of the stall. Thinking harder, I looked at the men's bathroom, instantly bursting through the door. Seeing a few men's stalls with doors, I burst through them all to find Khyrah's unconscious and beaten body in one of them. Her dress was ripped, and blood leaked between her thighs.

"Marcy!" I heard Manuel yell.

"I'm in here!" I cried, grabbing Khyrah into my arms.

"What the fuck!" Rome yelled as they both ran to assist me.

"Call 9-1-1 right now!" I yelled, pulling her dress down.

"Hold on, Khyrah. You're going to be OK. I got you! Please, just hold on!" I recited as held onto her. I was glad she still had a pulse.

Ramel and D-boy burst through the door. I rolled my eyes, annoyed that Rome would even call them.

"Oh shit, who the fuck did this!" D-boy yelled, dropping to his knees to assist me with taking care of Khyrah.

"Lock that fucking door, and don't let anyone in!" Ramel yelled.

"Don't fucking touch her! Just call the fucking police!" I yelled.

"We can't do that, sweetheart. Y'all underage. We gon' have to take her to the hospital. You gon' have to hold it down on the rest and let us handle who did this shit. Just tell them y'all were at a party, and she was drugged and raped. Make some shit up. Say you found her in an alley or some shit. We will handle the rest," Ramel recited.

I looked at my brother to confirm what I was already thinking as he shook his head in disgust. "Fuck y'all, just get me to a hospital!" I replied as I turned my attention back to Khyrah.

After five minutes of silence and D-boy making threats, two men came in and carried Khyrah to a truck. They drove us around to Khyrah's car where they placed her in the back seat. I took her keys, popped the trunk, and changed into some sweats and a t-shirt with a hat I found. From there, I started the car as I drove us to the hospital. I noticed Rome and my brother in the rearview mirror behind me. I found a pack of gum and stuffed my mouth to mask the liquor smell.

After riding for fifteen minutes, I pulled into the parking lot and ran to the front to yell for a nurse to help. Someone rushed out of the hospital with a wheelchair, and we put her in the chair. I held back the tears, feeling horrible for what I was about to do, but it had to be done. As the other nurses ran out to assist, they finally asked the one question that I dreaded.

"Ma'am, do you know this victim? Can you tell us her name? Age? Or anything?"

Looking in their eyes, I replied, "Sorry, I don't. I just found her in an alley as I walked out the store. I just want to make sure she's OK. I saw she had a pulse, so I drove her here. I knew the ambulance would take too long."

"OK, well thank you. Can I get you to stay for a statement with the officer?" the nurse asked.

"Well, actually, I'm underage, and I can't speak with an officer without my mother being present, so could I leave my number and you contact me when he gets here? I'm willing to help in anyway, but right now, my mother is expecting me home," I said. It honestly paid off to have two lawyer parents.

As the nurse's pager began to buzz, she became distracted. I knew I had a chance to leave, but I had to think quick.

"Sounds like you need to handle that. Here's my number. Please contact me if you need me," I spoke, giving her a fake number as she accepted and rushed off to assist with her emergency.

After that shit she just pulled, she could lose her job easily. She didn't even get my name. I hopped in the car and drove off to park it by an alley and wipe it down. I knew I was the worst person in the world for what I was assisting with, but I had plans of my own.

5

"I CAN'T BELIEVE someone would do that to Khyrah. She doesn't bother anyone," I heard someone walking by my locker say.

The gossip in school had already started, and as if I didn't feel horrible enough, now it was worse.

Khyrah still hadn't woken up from what happened two weeks ago. I knew she wouldn't remember anything. Her mother was a mess, and lying to Ms. Keisha made it worse. I told her I never went out with Khyrah that night because I didn't feel good. I couldn't go visit her for the fear of the nurses recognizing me, so I sent messages and checked on her daily.

I still went to work for Ramel and D-boy. I just switched locations that I counted money at. I didn't want to see any of their faces. I just wanted my money. I hadn't even spoken two words to Rome or my brother. The police came to the school, looking for answers, and even questioned me since I was known for hanging with her. They found her car but no evidence. To everyone, this would seem like an unsolved situation, but little did they know, it would be far from that.

I entered class as all eyes shifted to me. I couldn't take the fact that people acted as if it were my fault. I turned around and walked out of class to skip school like I'd done numerous times with Khyrah. I walked straight off campus. I didn't give a fuck who saw me or who even tried to stop me. I was tired of school anyway.

Walking to the nearest bus stop down the road, I took a seat and made a mental note to get a car soon. It was hot, and I was dressed in True Religion jeans, a hoodie to match, and my black Huaraches. I took a seat at the bus stop and pulled my earphones out, playing any song to get my mind off of things.

I missed the hell out of Royal. He would know exactly what to do right now. He taught my young ass a lot, and to know the real reason he was in prison made me realize the truth—that I was bad luck.

"Why you look so down, pretty lady?" I heard someone ask before I had the chance to hit play on my phone to drown the world out.

I looked up to see Ramel sitting high in a new Ram truck.

I didn't even bother to reply. I focused my attention back toward my phone. All I needed was my payment for my services and nothing else from him or his wack ass crew.

"Don't be like that, Marcy. Come take a ride with me. Let's talk," Ramel said.

I stood to my feet and walked past his truck. I was annoyed with his tone and ready to get far away from him. I started walking toward another bus stop a couple of miles away. Throwing the car in park, Ramel jumped out the car. I looked back to see him jogging to catch up to me.

"Marcy, wait! A nigga don't like this silent treatment you been giving all of us lately. You know I'm fucked up about your lil' young ass. What a nigga gotta do to make this shit right? Whatever it is, I'll do it. That shit was fucked up what happened to your girl, and I know you know who did it, so if you thinking about handling that, let me help you," Ramel pleaded.

I looked into his eyes to see the sincerity, but I needed more than that, and the fact that his grimy ass friends had everything to do with the situation made him untrustworthy.

"Thanks, but I can handle my own," I replied as I walked away.

"Fuck it. I tried to do it your way, so fuck it," I heard Ramel say as I heard his feet as he walked away.

Without warning, I was scooped in the air and tossed over Ramel's shoulder.

"What the fuck are you doing! Come on, Ramel! Put me down," I demanded as my body stayed upside down. I didn't even have enough energy to put up a fight with his dumb ass. I just really wanted to lie down and smoke the rest of my blunt I rolled at home.

Walking back to the truck, Ramel opened the passenger door and tossed me inside. Making sure I was all the way inside, he shut the passenger side door and jogged to the driver side.

"Where the hell are we going, Ramel?" I asked with an obvious attitude.

"Naw, don't ask questions now. You just had an attitude a few minutes ago."

I rolled my eyes and crossed my arms like a child. I was annoyed and turned on at the same time. I watched out the window at the houses and trees we passed. I couldn't do anything but think of Khyrah.

"Look, if I'm in this truck, it better mean one thing... that you're allowing me the ability to handle what your friends started. I know you know who did that to my girl. All y'all bitches know," I spoke, breaking the silence.

"What makes you think I know anything, sweetheart? I don't roll like that. I don't hurt women; I love them. You're talking like you a killer, and if you 'bout that life, let me find out." Ramel chuckled to himself as if I were a joke.

"You think I'm a joke, then try me!" I argued.

Sitting in silence, we pulled up to an outside movie place. He parked the car in front of the big screen and looked at me.

"We gon' see what you really about, sweetie," Ramel said.

"Ramel, let's be real for a second. I'm seventeen, about to be eighteen in a few months. But please understand I'm not young and dumb. This little game you playing won't work with me. I've been through a lot just to see seventeen. I've seen it and done it; don't play with me. What the fuck do you want, and why the fuck are we here?"

He sat quietly, looking into my eyes, debating if he should answer or not. Just as I was about to open the door and start walking, he began to speak.

"Truthfully, I don't fucking know, but I do know you're young as fuck, and it don't seem like it. Whoever groomed your ass did a damn good job. The night I seen you at the pool party, I felt some shit I never felt before. Then to find out that your sexy ass knew a little street shit and wasn't young and dumb like these other hoes, that shit drove me insane. Bitches throw ass at me every day, and that shit is annoying. I know it's an attraction between us, but you stay in your lane and play it cool. Your ass been working for us for about two months now, and I haven't heard shit. You not out here running your mouth and showing off. It's just something about you, Marcy, and I backed off because you're too young, but it don't hurt to let you know how a nigga feel," Ramel blurted out as if he couldn't hold it in any longer.

"Regardless of how you feel, Ramel, I can't rock with you and your crew like that. Y'all too grimy. Khyrah was a part of your crew. She counted money just as I do. She fucked up and messed with D-boy, but that's life, but when you can't control your bitches, I can't deal with that. And nigga, you got a girlfriend, so all this is irrelevant. Do I look like a side chick?" I spat back.

"Who in my crew did the shit!" Ramel yelled with visible anger.

"Do I look like a fool?" I answered quickly.

Opening the glove compartment, Ramel reached in and handed me a small pistol. "Whoever did it, I hope you handle it properly," he said as I looked at the gun.

"Fuck you want me to do with this?" I questioned.

"Thought you would know, lil' killer." He laughed.

"Any bodies on it?" I asked, inspecting the weapon.

"Nope, clean and unregistered. Anything else?" he asked.

"Yeah, what do you do?" I asked without looking up, making sure the weapon was on safety and tucking it in my bag.

"What you mean? Career wise? I buy and sell cars and houses. Since my dad passed, I've been keeping the business going," he responded.

"No, I know that, but what else? I know you don't do what D-boy does. I pay attention. All you do is collect and bring cash?"

Ramel laughed before he answered. "Well, it's simple, I don't sell drugs like D-boy. My crew I just invest. I do fraud, sweetheart, and I also supply the connection for Jaq and D-boy. So I get a cut off of all the money they touch, and if they fuck up, I invest my money. They work it off and pay me back double. My business alone brings in good profit but not enough to be a millionaire, so shit, I make moves. Just found a way to do less work and get more money. Plus, I promised my parents I would never sell drugs, so this is my way of keeping my promise," he stated.

"So when you come to the trap, that's your way of checking on your money and work?"

"Hell yeah! Well, to check on my money. That's their work once it hits the states," he confirmed.

I sat and thought to myself. Never had I ever seen a man that did fraud with such a thug appeal as a drug dealer. It was sexy but a whole new hustle that I wanted to know more about. I didn't know how to feel about Ramel at the moment, but I planned to find out.

I finally arrived home after spending a few hours with Ramel and collecting his money from the trap. We talked about a lot of shit, and he was actually cool. Of course, I didn't open up, but I listened to his words, and that was all I needed at the moment.

I walked into the house to see Manuel and Milan talking. Of course, my mother was nowhere in sight. I walked past them and up to my room. I had enough talking for one day.

"Khyrah is awake and asking for you!" Manuel spoke as he burst through my room door. "Her mom called here since you weren't answering your phone," he added.

"That's great." I smiled, excited to hear some good news finally. "But you know I can't go see her," I reminded Mann.

"I know, but I figured it would make you feel better to know. And I'll go check on her and let her know you'll catch her when she leaves the hospital."

"Thanks, brother. That shit means a lot," I said, turning to lay back on my bed. I had a lot to take care of tonight, and I just received the boost I needed to get this shit done.

I lay on my bed, thinking about the fucked up situations I'd been in to be so young, and the fact that my mother was missing in action yet another time I needed her the most pissed me off. If she wasn't at work, she was spending the day with Milan's ass, never bothering to ask me to do shit.

Setting my alarm clock to midnight, I turned on my side and dozed off.

"The fact that you thought it was OK to disrespect the woman I love baffles me," Royal stated as the man spat blood after Royal's last blow to the head.

"And your pussy ass had the nerve to try and take what I slide my dick into every night. Your faggot ass like to take things, I see. Aye, babe, come here," Royal spoke, motioning for me to stand at his side and look his best friend in the eyes.

"Grab the gun and rock this nigga to sleep," Royal said.

"Wait, what? I can't do that, Royal!" I whispered, instantly becoming scared.

"You can, and you will. This nigga tried to rape you. If I hadn't walked in, you could've been dead, baby. I'm going to teach you how to handle yourself whether I'm here or not. I couldn't live with myself if something happened to you," Royal said.

Grabbing my hand and placing the gun between both of our hands, he placed my finger on the trigger, and I closed my eyes and pulled it.

...

Hitting my alarm clock on my phone, I looked to see it was finally midnight. I sat up on the edge of my bed, thinking about the last time I'd been in this position. I shook my thoughts and went to my bathroom. Wiping my face, I grabbed my black hoodie, black tights, and black combat boots. I tightened my bun on the top of my head and grabbed the gun Ramel gave me hours earlier. I checked the address to make sure I was heading in the right direction.

As I walked out of my room, the house was dark and quiet. I knew my brother and sister were sleep; that was if Manuel was even home. I crept down the stairs and out the front door. I jogged up the road to the old Honda parked on the corner. I grabbed the keys out of my pocket and put my gloves on. I jumped in the car. After starting the ignition, I was off. My mind was on one thing. I knew that the day I caught my first body, I would never be the same, but the thought never crossed my mind to do it again until now.

I didn't think, I didn't blink, and I didn't allow anything to deter me from this moment. I rode in complete silence. I powered my phone off as well as taking the location app off. Without a thought, I arrived at the address given to me. Parking a block away, I hopped out the car and jogged to the address. My adrenaline began to pump as I came closer to the little house. Taking a moment to scope out my surroundings, I proceeded to the back gate.

I entered through to see a back door that led to the kitchen. I hurriedly walked to the door and twisted the handle. It was unlocked, as promised. I smiled to myself then let myself in with a gun in hand. I was ready for war. There were two things I didn't play about in this world, and that was killing children and raping women. I walked up the small stairs that led to the master bedroom. Opening the door slowly, I watched as they lay sound asleep in her bed. Walking over to her side of the bed, I watched as she slept like she didn't have a care in the world. With the gun on safety, I smacked her across the face with the pistol.

"Wake up, bitch!" I yelled.

Immediately grabbing her face, she attempted to yell in horror and pain.

"Shut the fuck up!" I yelled again as Ramel opened his eyes and looked my way.

"What do you want?" Ramel's girlfriend asked, shaking.

"You know what I want. Y'all thought that shit was cool, setting my girl up to get raped and beat in the fucking bathroom of a club?" I asked.

"I didn't have shit to do with that! I jus—"

Whap!

I hit her again. I didn't have time for lies. I just wanted to see the bitch shake before I ended her life.

"Tell ya man here the truth, or I'll put a hole right between your eyes, hoe!"

Holding her head with blood falling down her face, she began to laugh.

"OK, fuck it! Yeah, we did it, so what? She had no business fucking my best friend's husband. You bitches got the game fucked up. You think we don't know shit and don't see the way you and her look at our men. I don't regret shit. Fuck you and her!" Ramel's girl-friend spat.

"Guess that's where you go wrong. Make sure the nigga you beefing over will do the same for you! Ummm, Ramel, I'm about to kill her ass now. Is that cool?" I questioned with a smirk on my face.

"Wait, Ramel, what's going on? After all I've done for you, this is how it ends!" she cried.

He nodded his head yes, and with that, I released two bullets to her head as she fell sideways. The sheet and bed frame were covered with stained blood and brain mass.

Ramel got out the bed and took the gun from me.

"Listen, it's time for you to go. Ditch the car at the chop shop I showed you, and when you get home, burn your clothes. I'll handle the rest. We gon' make this shit look like a robbery. Just head home and wait for my call tomorrow. I got you from here on out," Ramel spoke as I handed him the gun.

This shit was far from over. D-boy's wife was definitely going to get hers. I exited his girlfriend's house the same way I entered and went to the car. Pulling off and heading toward the chop shop, I was relieved it was over and was ready to get home. I grabbed my phone from the glove compartment. I'd left it powered off.

I dropped the car off ten minutes later and took the bus home. I still didn't have a single thought or emotion about what I had done. It was as if I was mastering the art of not feeling anything, and it was starting to scare me. I arrived home twenty minutes later. Getting off the bus, I took my hoodie off, exposing my tank top. I began walking from the bus stop to my house. Looking on the porch by the front door, I saw Manuel smoking a blunt.

Without saying one word, I walked up to the door. Sticking his hand out, he passed the blunt to me, and I took and few puffs and passed it back. No words were needed. My brother knew me like a book, and he also knew I wouldn't let this go. I also knew the reason he sat on the front porch smoking was to wait for my arrival back home. He smirked as I entered our home and went straight to the shower.

After taking a hot shower and washing my hands with bleach, I looked to see my clothes were gone. I smiled, knowing Manuel had taken care of them. I sat on my bed and closed my eyes as I recapped tonight's event.

Beep, beep.

I heard my cell phone go off, indicating I had a text message. I looked to see an unknown number pop up, and I read the message and smiled.

*Unknown: Goodnight, sweetie!

Ramel just couldn't wait until tomorrow.

6

I WOKE up early the next day and got ready for school. I knew today would be full of gossip about Ramel's girlfriend's death. This was gossip I needed to hear.

"Marcy, Milan, and Manuel, you guys come here for a second!" my mom yelled from downstairs.

We all came running in the order we were born; Manuel, me, and Milan.

Without a word, we all looked at our mom, who was dressed to kill for court with her coffee and briefcase in her hand.

"Wait, Marcy, I know you're not going to school looking like that. You need to go change into a dress, preferably," she said. Not in the mood to argue, I agreed. "Well, that's a first, but anyway, I was thinking since you guys' birthday is surely approaching, how would you like to have a party?" she asked.

"That would be nice, Mom," Milan answered first.

"I guess," Manuel added.

"Nope, I don't want a party. We don't have enough friends here to have a party. And I simply don't want one. What's the point? Just get me a car. They can have the party," I replied.

My mother's face displayed full disappointment, but I didn't care. I didn't want or need that kind of attention.

"That's fine, Marcy. You can exclude yourself from the party; that's totally fine! I'm done trying. I'm tired of your disrespect, so from here on out, do whatever you please," she replied back.

I went upstairs to change and headed to school. I didn't have time for her dramatics today. I had shit to do.

I walked into school thirty minutes later and went straight to the cafeteria for breakfast.

I saw everyone in the cafe sitting on the tables and hanging out before the bell rang for class. I spotted the crew that I knew had the latest gossip and sat within ear reach.

"No, she and Ramel were in bed, and somebody tried to rob them at her house," a girl said.

"Yes, and I heard the place was a complete mess! They either followed Ramel there or been watching them," another girl spoke.

"That's so sad. I know Ramel is torn up about this. They found him unconscious, but I plan to give him plenty of comfort."

"Bitch, Ramel, don't want your gap teeth ass! Plus, from what I hear, he has his eyes on a certain somebody," another girl spoke.

I listened closely to hear the name, but no one spoke it. They just changed the subject. I felt a little at ease that everyone was convinced that Ramel's girlfriend's death was due to a robbery. I stayed seated, listening to their dumb ass conversations until I figured it was a good time to leave. As soon as I stood up, the bell rang, and I suddenly had the urge to go to class.

I walked into class to see everyone there, including my brother sitting next to Rome. I found a seat on the other side of him. I sat and waited for class to start without speaking a word.

My phone vibrated, indicating that I had a text message

*Ramel: meet me at the bus stop in ten minutes

*@Ramel: On my way!

I raised my hand as I asked to use the bathroom right as class started.

Manuel and Rome both looked at me with confused looks on their faces. I shot Manuel a text, letting him know I was gone as I walked off campus.

Walking to the bus stop, I pulled down my rising, fitted, black spaghetti-strap dress that I wore with my black and white race runner Balenciaga shoes. I wore a jean jacket to make my outfit fit enough for the dress code, but walking off campus, I took my jacket off.

I approached the bus stop to see Ramel sitting in an all-white 2016 Audi. As he saw me approaching, he hopped out the car with his dreads pulled into a ponytail. He was dripped in all black with red Gucci Drivers and a belt to match. He also sported a bandage on the back of his head. I guessed he had to make the robbery look official.

"Oh my, don't you look handsome," I spoke as I approached him holding the passenger side door open for me.

"Thanks. I figured for our first official date, I would dress it up and make it real for you," he replied.

I continued to smile as I got into his car. I was more than confused. I thought we should be laying low, considering the fact that his girlfriend was dead. As he entered the car, we pulled off and began riding.

Breaking the silence, I started to speak. "Don't you think this may be a little too much? I mean, your girl isn't even in the ground yet, and you're riding around with me."

"Yes, and so? Trust me, we won't be anywhere around here. You'll learn that I don't give a fuck about anything people have to say about me," Ramel said as he turned the radio up and proceeded to ride.

I couldn't believe after all this shit, we were about to act as if it didn't happen. Maybe that needed to be my new concept for life. Quit worrying about the things I couldn't change and just keep pushing forward. That concept would sound so much better if I hadn't just killed someone yet again.

I laid my head back and listened to the music. We rode for an hour outside of the city limits to a place called Air. We pulled up, and I looked around, noticing the secluded area full of planes and land.

"What? You're about to kill me now?" I nervously asked.

"Shit, as gangster as your ass is, you might end up killing me." Ramel laughed.

"But not today. My man Bill up there owns this place and owes me a few favors, so today, I figured we'd do something I've always wanted to do. We are going to jump from an airplane," Ramel stated.

"I've done a lot of shit in my short years of living, but this cuts the cake. So basically, you want me to voluntarily kill myself?" I questioned.

"Shit, we gon' die together, but for some reason, your ass make me want to do shit I swore I'd never do in my life, so I figured we could do this shit together. Become fearless together and shit. Just bring your ass on unless you don't trust me."

I rolled my eyes as a smirk appeared across my lips. I opened my door, giving my already obvious answer. He returned my gesture with a perfect smile and exited the car as well. He walked over to me and grabbed my hand as we walked to greet Bill.

Whatever this was between us was moving fast as hell, and I didn't know what to think except to think about Royal. This felt all too familiar, and I didn't want it to stop.

"Wassup, Bill? This is Marcy," Ramel introduced.

"Hello, pretty lady. You guys ready for some fun?"

"Sure is," I replied.

"Well, let's go suit up."

Bill instructed us on what to do and how to properly strap our suits as we prepared to take off in the plane. I was scared as hell simply because heights were not my thing.

We sat on the plane as Bill started the engine and prepared for takeoff.

"You trust me?" Ramel asked out of the blue.

"Nigga, I barely know you, so for now, let's just say I'm learning you," I replied.

"Fair enough. I guess the next thing to do is enjoy the ride!" he exclaimed.

~

I crept inside my home at midnight on a school night. I checked my phone as I walked into my bedroom quietly. I set my things on my bed. As I prepped for a shower, I listened as my text message alarm went off. Grabbing my phone, I looked to see Ramel's name.

*Ramel: Goodnight beautiful, I had a great time and can't wait to see you again. A nigga really feeling you.

I smiled at his soft side. After an amazing day, I was feeling a lot better about Ramel.

*Me: meet me at the same spot tomorrow around the same time! Oh and I had a great day with you, thanks I needed that.

I powered my phone off. I needed to get some rest.

~

THE NEXT MORNING...

I awoke the next day tired as hell, but I also had Ramel on my mind. As much as I wanted to believe our situation was normal, it wasn't, and we were moving way too fast. The funny thing was the moment I started dealing with street niggas, my life had been anything but slow.

I hopped out of bed and powered my cell phone back on to see I had a few messages. I placed my phone down and proceeded to get ready. To avoid an argument of any kind, I pulled out my Maxi BCBG dress and sandals to match. I didn't have time to deal with my mother's smart remarks today. After I showered and fixed my hair, I sprayed my Juicy Couture perfume and headed out the door. Going to school was the last thing on my mind today.

I walked out the door to see my mother and sister in a deep conversation—so deep that they didn't notice my presence, so with that, I slid out the door and left. I walked up the road to the city bus stop. It was time to visit Khyrah since she was finally home. I walked onto the bus and took my seat. I laid my head back to find myself thinking about Ramel again.

After riding the bus to the Hills for what felt like forever, I exited and walked a block up the road to Khyrah's house. I felt an uneasy feeling in my stomach. No matter how hard I tried, I still felt like the world's most horrible friend ever. The entire situation was fucked up, but the fact that she didn't remember made it better.

Khyrah's mom, Keisha, was cool for the most part. She was raised in the streets, and in her heart, she knew some foul shit happened. Yet again, I had to tell her another lie in order to keep up with whatever any doctor may have told her about the mysterious person who dropped her off. I walked to the door and rang the doorbell. Ms. Keisha answered with a happy look on her face.

"Hello, Ms. Marcy. How nice of you to grace us with your presence finally!" she spoke as I walked inside her house in search of Khyrah.

"I'm just glad she's OK," I replied.

"Oh, your brother has been making sure of that, but she's in her room," she spoke as she walked off.

I walked to the back to Khyrah's room to find her sitting up on her bed, going through her phone. I took a moment to take in her physical features. She had lost a lot of weight, but she still looked like the Khyrah I knew.

"Hey," I said as I walked in cautiously.

"Wassup? About time you came to see me. I was about to start thinking you deserted me like D-boy," Khyrah said.

"I wouldn't dream of deserting you. I just hate hospitals. That's all."

"Yeah, your brother told me," she spat.

"So how are you feeling?" I inquired.

"Other than not remembering shit that happened, not hearing from you, and D-boy ignoring me, my mind has been going crazy. The only sane part is your brother. He's been helping and coming by every day."

"Yeah, I know," I replied, sitting next to her.

"Do you know what happened to me, Marcy? I mean, I'm just

clueless. My mom said it was a wreck, but something in me feels like there's more, and no matter how hard I try, I can't remember."

I looked into her eyes, blinking back the tears threatening to fall from my eyes.

"All I know is that you were in a wreck, but I'm glad you're OK. As far as D-boy, you deserve better, and you know it. When can you hang out again? You need to get out this house."

"You're right about that. I kinda have a date with your brother tonight, but I'm down to hang after that," she replied.

"Whenever you're ready, I'm down."

An awkward silence fell upon us before she spoke again. "You know I was pregnant by D-boy, and the moment I woke up and looked around, realizing I was in the hospital, I thought for a second that I had possibly had the baby or some shit."

I was shocked from the news she just spilled, and it made sense because she bled bad the night of her rape. Now I felt even better about killing Ramel's girlfriend.

"Oh my God, Khyrah, are you OK?"

"Oh yeah, I'm fine. I don't know what I would've done with a baby by a married man anyway. At least that's what I keep telling myself to help me move forward. Maybe it's good D-boy is ignoring me. Maybe his family is where he needs to be," she stated.

"You're very strong. I admire that in you, Khyrah," I added.

"So what's been up with you? Have you and Ramel finally decided to quit playing and take it there?" Khyrah asked. I looked at her for a second, realizing the fact that even after all she had been through, she could still remember the chemistry that was so evident between Ramel and me. At that moment, I knew I had to give it a try.

"I mean, we're cool."

"Yeah, for now. Trust me, he wants you, and honestly, there's nothing wrong with that. Take him from that evil bitch anyway. She can't hold his attention like you can anyway." I smiled at her bluntness but quickly remembered how Ramel's girlfriend was taking a dirt nap all because of me.

"We shall see. For now, let's catch up on some of this work," I said, grabbing her math book.

"Oh hell no, you're not helping me with my work. Your ass barely go to school. Shit, you're skipping school right now to be here with me!" she exclaimed.

"Then that should tell you how much I love you." I laughed as I grabbed a piece of paper and pencil.

7

ONE MONTH LATER...

EVERYTHING SEEMED to be back on track. It had only been a few weeks, but Khyrah was back at school and finally dating my brother. Ramel and I were somewhat dating; although nothing was official, it felt right. We kept it on the low. My sister was finally dating and holding her own secrets, which made me happy that her ass was out of my business. My mother was another story, but my life was finally on track. I was actually happy, and it was as if no one even remembered what happened to Ramel's last girlfriend. It was funny how gossip became a distant memory so quickly.

I walked into school with Khyrah and my brother, Manuel. Although things didn't work out with Rome and I, we all still hung together, but lately, he'd been missing in action since his new girlfriend was such a secret. I was just glad he finally had someone so it didn't feel awkward with my and his brother's situation.

Looking inside my bag, I saw I had a missed call. Grabbing my phone, I called Ramel back.

"Wassup, baby!" I sang into the phone the minute he answered.

"Shit, just missing you. Come meet me at the bus stop in a few minutes," Ramel added.

"I'm about to leave campus now," I replied, ending the call.

"I think I'm about to head out, guys. I thought about sticking it out until lunch, but I'll catch you guys later," I spoke as I watched Manuel and Khyrah head to class, and I walked off campus like any other day, eager to see Ramel.

Walking away from campus, I checked my appearance. My Armani tights and fitted shirt had my figure looking right with my black Nike Huaraches. I applied my Victoria Secret lip gloss and made sure my fire-red hair was in place around my bob. Satisfied with my appearance, I approached the city bus stop and took a seat. Looking through my phone, I received a text message from an unknown number.

*4045364404: Answer the phone

Before I could reply, my phone began to ring, displaying the unknown number. Not knowing what to think, I answered the call.

"Hello?"

"Well damn, shawty, I guess you forgot about a nigga," a male voice spoke on the other end. At that minute, my heart dropped to my feet.

"Royal?" I stuttered.

"Yes, ma'am. Damn, I miss you, shawty. How are you?" he inquired.

"I'm fine, Royal. How did you get my number? Are you calling from a cell phone in prison? Of course, I miss you! I just can't believe it's you," I said. After all this time, what I was forced to make a distant memory had resurfaced.

"Damn, baby, slow down." He laughed.

"Yes, this is my cell phone in prison. One of the guards hooked me up, but you know I can find you at any time, and I miss you like crazy. This shit been rough, and I know I put you through a lot of shit with your family. I'm sorry about that, Marcy. I just want to know how you been. How's the baby?"

I paused at that question. The day my mother forced me to have an abortion, Royal had been sentenced to prison time. Today was the first day I had spoken to him since the twelve months of his departure; although I was over it, hearing his concerns brought all those emotions I pushed away about the abortion back to the surface.

As I was about to answer, Ramel pulled up.

"Umm, Royal, I'm at school. Can you call me later sometime so we can talk?" I rushed.

"Oh shit, umm, yeah, shawty. I'll holla at you later. Aye, Marcy, I love you," Royal said.

"I love you too." I smiled as I ended the call. I headed to the passenger side of Ramel's Audi and hopped in.

My mood had drastically shifted, and I didn't know what to do.

"What's up, babe?" Ramel greeted as he kissed my cheek.

"Who got you on the phone smiling and shit when a nigga pulled up?" he joked.

"No one, just my dad," I replied.

"That's what's up. You hungry?" he questioned.

"Of course!"

"Good, because a nigga cooked at home. I'm kinda tired. You want to chill at my spot?" Ramel gestured.

"Ummm, that's cool." I laughed. This nigga thought he was slick.

We pulled up to the house, and I quickly jumped out and entered his home.

He walked in and went straight to his room. I entered the kitchen and fixed myself a plate of spaghetti. One thing I knew for sure was that Ramel could cook his ass off, and I loved it. Although we had been spending a lot of time together, most days we spent chilling and eating something he cooked.

Ramel returned, wearing a wife beater and Nike basketball shorts. I met him on the couch, sitting next to him while enjoying my food.

"That shit good, huh?" Ramel joked as I slurped down the noodles and meat.

I began laughing, not realizing how much I was enjoying the food. Putting the plate down, I finally looked at Ramel.

"You missed me, didn't you?" I asked.

"What makes you think that?" he shot back.

"Because around this time, you would be dealing with your businesses or handling your money at the trap houses, yet here we are in the morning on a Thursday. You cooked my favorite meal, and you're sitting still, just chilling. What's going on?" I scolded.

"A nigga just chilling today. Business is good, the trap houses are taken care of, and your fat ass is full. I'd say today was just a good ass day, and you're right. A nigga getting a little too used to you," he replied with a smile.

Without thinking, I covered his curved lips with a kiss. Normally, our kisses were short and sweet, but today I felt something different. A feeling grew into me that I hadn't felt since I laid eyes on Royal. Thinking of Royal, I attempted to break the kiss, but Ramel grabbed my body close to his and pulled me on top of him.

With his hands squeezing my ass, our tongues danced around in each other's mouths as we lay on the couch. My insides lit up with fire. I hadn't had sex in so long. I wanted Ramel in the worst way. I placed my free hand by the waistband of his shorts, attempting to free his manhood. The moment I came close, I felt a hand grab mine. Breaking away, Ramel sat up, causing me to change positions to the side of him.

"Marcy, hold up, not like this."

"What? Not like this? We were only about to have sex. What's the big deal? You tripping over your dead ex or some shit?" I spat, getting visibly pissed.

"First off, calm your hot ass down. If I would've had sex with you right now on my couch, then it would be just that sex. A nigga actually like your young ass, and I plan to give you more, but that's not until you turn eighteen."

I laughed. "Wait, what? Eighteen? Is that what this is about? My age? If you feel that way, then why you fucking with me!" I yelled.

"Those are a couple thing we're going to have to work on—your mouth and listening. I don't like to repeat myself, but when the time is right, it will happen. As for now, just focus on a nigga getting to know the real you. I'm not like them other niggas, beautiful. I plan to bring the best in you out for the world to see. All this mean and negative shit has to chill. It's unattractive, and I know there's another side. Look what you did for your girl Khyrah," Ramel said.

I sat in disbelief. No one had ever talked to me like that before. No one had even cared enough to pay attention to my flaws and help me correct them. On a daily basis, all I ever heard were the negative things about myself—never what or how to fix them. Royal became my crutch at an early age. He molded my mind and prepared me to fight the war of life by fighting, killing, and hustling. And after listening to Ramel, I saw he wanted none of that. He just wanted to get to know the real me behind the anger and bitterness.

After an awkward silence, I extended my hand. Looking down, Ramel twisted his face in confusion.

"Let's start over. Hello, my name is Marcy Gomez. Nice to meet you," I recited, smiling from ear to ear. He grabbed my hand and placed a soft, sweet kiss among my lips.

"So what we watching?" Ramel asked, changing the mood.

"Wait, what is your favorite movie?" I asked.

"I fuck with *Friday*; that shit with Craig and Smokey never gets old."

"What movie is that?" I questioned.

"What the fuck? Your ass don't know what the movie *Friday* is?" he joked.

"Don't blame me. Blame my want-to-be white mother and stuck-up father. We were never allowed to watch hood movies growing up," I informed Ramel.

Grabbing the remote, he typed in Friday, and the movie popped up on the screen. "After today, you'll be a *Friday* lover." Ramel pressed play and pulled me close as we began watching the movie.

Eight Hours Later...

I opened my eyes to my vibrating cell phone. I looked around to see Ramel sleeping next to me in his king-size bed. Taking it all in, I remembered falling asleep watching *Friday* a second time because it was funny as hell. I guess Ramel brought me to his bedroom and joined me to fall asleep. I unlocked my phone to see it was eight o'clock at night. My eyes grew big, and I knew my mother could possibly be looking for me. Soon after, text messages started rolling in left and right, but before I could check them, my phone rang again.

"Hello," I answered quickly, not looking at the name.

"Marcy Gomez, where the fuck are you!" my mother yelled, pissed due to the fact that she never used foul language.

"Calm down. I'm with a friend. I'll be home in a second," I calmly replied.

The line went silent, and soon after, I watched my phone light up, indicating that she had ended the call. It felt awkward due to the fact that my mother never used curse words or hung the phone up in my face, so I knew she was pissed.

"Ya mom mad, huh?" Ramel whispered. I didn't even notice that he was awake.

"Oh, umm, yeah, but she's OK. Could you take me home, though?"

"Of course. Let me get my keys. Meet me downstairs."

I allowed my feet to touch the plush carpet, and I exited the room and went down the stairs to find my shoes. I stood by the door, returning my overload of text messages. My mind was all over the place since Manuel texted saying some shit popped off at home. I began to think of Royal. Normally when I was in trouble, it was because of him. I hadn't even heard from him since the day he called me a month back, and I had an uneasy feeling about that.

"You ready, beautiful?" Ramel asked, breaking me out of my thoughts and causing me to smile.

I exited the house with him and jumped into his Ram truck, and just like that, we were off. The ride to my home was silent. My mind was so full of thoughts that I couldn't talk. Before long, we were pulling up to my home. The lights were on, and I knew something crazy was about to happen. I looked at Ramel as he pulled into the driveway.

"You need me to wait?" he asked.

"Oh, no, I'll be fine. Nothing I can't handle."

Leaning over, I placed a soft goodbye kiss to Ramel's lips as I exited the truck. Watching him pull off, I walked to the front door, pulling out my keys to open it. Unlocking the door, I stumbled upon a few suitcases and bags thinking nothing of it unless my mom was heading on a trip. I proceeded to my bedroom,

"I wouldn't take another step if I were you," I heard a voice say from the living room.

"Look, I know you're mad, but I was just kicking it with friends," I replied.

"Do I look like a fool to you, Marcy?" she slurred, sliding over a white piece of paper.

"Look, Mom, I can explain this shit. School just isn't for me, OK? I tried," I reasoned.

"Wrong answer, Marcy, but I refuse to fight with a child of mine who's practically been making adult decisions the moment she turned fifteen. Let me guess. You're skipping school again, coming home, and sneaking out the house because of a no-good ass thug again?" she questioned, standing up and facing me. By this time, Manuel and Milan were standing at the top of the stairs, watching the altercation.

"It's not like that, and you're so quick to talk down on them when, in reality, they're the only people that show me real love and attention!" I challenged back.

"Is that what you call it? Your father and I are not perfect, but the love we provide for you is more than real, Marcy. These street guys— the thugs you're so obsessed with—they use young girls like you. Real love wouldn't have you skipping school and ruining your future. Real love wouldn't put you in harm's way. Real love wouldn't damn near kill you. And real love wouldn't make you hate the few people that love you more than life. That money they supply you with comes with a price. That lifestyle comes with a price. Those 'I love you's' comes with a price! Look at Royal! You were pregnant by a thug that went to prison. If you would've had that baby, how would you survive, Marcy? Who would be here to help you then? If he didn't go to prison, how could he truly provide for you and your child? He has a record! Could he get a real job? Hell no! Not making the money he's used to seeing, guess what he goes back to! Hustling. Putting you and your child in harm's way! Then who would be there to pick up the pieces? Your father and his ditzy bitch or your mother, the one who's always been there to pick up the pieces for you!" she yelled as tears escaped her eyes.

"You don't pick up shit! You make it all worse! Did you ever stop to ask yourself how all the pieces you claim to pick up made me feel? Did you and Dad ever think to ask if I was OK after finding him fucking his secretary? Did it ever dawn on you that fucking a client, a well-known drug dealer who killed innocent people, my childhood best friend to be exact, would not bother me? Then to turn around and go through the courts to force me to kill the one thing I felt I needed more than it needed me—my child. Have you ever stopped to think of me? I'll answer that. No, you think of Milan..."

"That's not true," Milan interrupted.

"Shut the hell up. You're her golden child. The one that does no wrong," I directed toward Milan.

"Oh, she does wrong. Guess that's why she been hiding the fact that she's sleeping with my boy Rome, and she slipped up and got pregnant. I just want to know when we're y'all planning on telling us," Manuel interjected.

"It's not like that. Mom and I were just trying to make the best decision before I proceeded to tell you guys," Milan answered.

Shocked at Manuel's outburst, I took a second to process his words.

"Figure out what? So you're keeping it!" I yelled.

"Mom feels that it's best to not go through the abortion again after the depression you went through."

"It's not like that, Marcy. I just didn't want to kill another child," my mother added.

Tears began to escape my eyes. Realizing that every feeling that I'd felt about my mother up to this point was true. "It's always been clear that you were her favorite, and there's nowhere for me—hell, even Manuel—to fit in, and guessing by the luggage at the front door, I had an eviction notice already set up for tonight. So I'll say this. I wish you all the best, and if you didn't know it by now, I'm gone!" I yelled, unable to control the tears falling down my face.

"Marcy, it's not like that! We can work through this. Tell me what to do," my mom pleaded with tears falling.

"Kill yourself!" I replied, grabbing my bags and opening the door. I pulled my cell phone out of my Chanel bag, but the moment I looked up, I saw Ramel's truck sitting in the driveway. On cue, he exited the truck to help me with my bags.

Coming out the door, my mother proceeded to take my anger to another level.

"So this is the thug? Guess he promised you the world, and now you're ready to risk it all for him. Just like Royal. Where did I go wrong with you, Marcy? I just don't understand, but I do know leaving is not the option."

Ramel looked confused and offended but kept grabbing my bags and placing them in the trunk.

"Still finding fault in me, huh? Just know your perfect daughter and I are no different. She just happened to be pregnant by this thug's younger brother! Guess that makes him the hoodlum!" I laughed, heading to get into the truck.

"I'll never set foot back into your house again. Oh, and Mom... I hate you!" I yelled.

"Marcy, it's time to go," Ramel spoke as I entered the truck, and we pulled off.

As I wiped the last bit of tears threatening to fall, I turned toward Ramel. "So what now?" I asked.

"Well, until you and your mom get back on good terms or you apologize, I would like you to stay with me. You can have the guest room." Ramel smiled, lightening the mood.

"I think I can manage sharing a room with you," I replied, accepting his request to move in. I didn't know what to think. My life was on the fast track, and for the first time, I had no idea what to do.

8

"You going to answer the phone for your mom?" Ramel asked with his eyes closed. It had been a week since our altercation, and she'd called me every day since then.

Wiping the sleep from my eyes, I woke up after a long night of talking with Ramel. It was Monday and time to get ready for school. Ramel expressed how important finishing school was for me.

"You're too beautiful to be young and dumb. Finish school. That shit is important," Ramel stated last night. I smiled at the thought of his words. I walked into his walk-in closet and pulled down my Fashion Nova mid-waist jeans, my half Adidas sweatshirt, and my black and gold Adidas tennis shoes. I retired to the bathroom to do my hygiene routine and fix my hair. After spending damn near an hour getting ready, I exited the bathroom to find Ramel gone. I went into the hallway and bumped into Rome.

"Wassup," he spoke.

"Hey," I replied, which became the normal greeting since I moved in. He was barely here, and when he was, his room was the only place he acknowledged in this big ass house.

Walking down the stairs, I found Ramel in the kitchen, fully dressed and on the phone.

"Aye, Rome, come here!" Ramel shouted.

Running down the stairs with his backpack in hand, Rome appeared. I went and stood next to Ramel, planting a kiss on his lips.

"Rome, you and Marcy gonna have to take the Benz to school today; I got business to handle, and y'all need to be leaving now."

Rolling my eyes, I agreed to ride along with Rome. "That's fine, but I get to drive!" I yelled, grabbing the keys.

"Man, hell no! That's not fair," Rome added, running outside behind me.

I unlocked the doors and hopped in the driver's seat with Rome joining me in the passenger seat. As I backed out of the driveway, we were off to school. This would be my first day returning after leaving my mother's house, and I dreaded facing my sister. I communicated with Manuel on a daily basis.

"Marcy, I know this shit between us is weird for the simple fact of how shit started out with us. But going forward, it looks like we're going to have to break the ice and become cool. That shit with your sister just happened—just like you and my brother. Now that your sister is pregnant, and all this drama is going on, I don't need bad blood between you and me. A nigga already got enough shit to stress about. Plus, I can tell my brother likes you a lot, so I can't argue with that. So we are cool?" Rome blurted out.

I smiled at his attempt to smooth things over, and he was right. The moment I laid eyes on his brother, it was over for him and me. It was only right to become friends despite the bullshit, and he was definitely right about one thing. Less drama was surely needed.

"I agree, so yeah, we're definitely friends, lil' brah," I joked.

"Aye, chill on that shit. I'm older than you," he replied.

"But I'm dating your brother, so you know what that means? You have to answer me too." I laughed.

"Bullshit." He laughed.

After that, the mood lightened with us, and I knew that although my sister and I would never see eye to eye, she had someone in her life that would balance everything out.

We arrived at school both jamming off Lucci, a hot underground artist out of Atlanta. We spotted Manuel and Khyrah in the parking lot as we stepped out of the Benz.

"Wassup, sis," Mann greeted.

"Hey, girlie," Khyrah added.

From there, we all walked into school to start our day. I pulled out my phone to immediately text Ramel. As much as he wanted me to finish school, for some reason, I just didn't have it in me. The people I looked up to dropped out of school and still became rich. I wasn't a dumb girl, by far, but I just knew school wasn't for me.

I walked into Ms. Zag's class, quickly finding a spot toward the back of the class. Manuel joined me on the other side, and I saved a seat for Rome, who I knew went to check in with Milan.

I checked my phone to see that I had a text. Opening it, I saw that it was from the cell phone that Royal had in prison.

*4045364404: Wassup Marcy

*me: hello why haven't I heard from you?

*4045364404: I need to holla at you where you at? Can you talk?

*me: yes, I am in class about to head to the bathroom. call me in five minutes

I stood and took the bathroom pass, leaving my backpack behind to ensure my brother that I wasn't leaving school.

I walked into the hallway to see Rome and Milan kissing each other goodbye. Acting as if they didn't exist, I walked into the bathroom to await Royal's call. As if on cue, my iPhone began to vibrate.

"Hello," I answered.

"Damn, Marcy, I miss you. What's been going on?" he asked.

"Honestly, nothing, the usual," I vaguely replied.

"You know, it's funny that you used that word *honestly*. Don't bullshit me, Marcy. I know you like a book, and the biggest reason a nigga ain't been calling you has everything to do with our last conversation," Royal spat.

"It's not like th—" I attempted to interject.

"Naw, baby, let a nigga finish. The first and last time I called you, I asked you a question that you failed to answer. Then you made up a lie about school or some shit when we both know you hate school, and I highly doubt you were even present that day. Baby girl, a nigga know you, and when it comes to me, you never lied. You never rushed conversations, and you never failed to answer any question I asked. So a nigga came to the conclusion that you killed my seed and possibly got another nigga in your ear. So I gave you a little space, but after staring at this letter your mother took the precious time out of her day to write when I know she hates me lets a nigga know that everything I thought was right. So this nigga got you going crazy, huh?" Royal asked.

I closed my eyes, allowing the water built up inside to fall upon my cheeks. My emotions quickly became mixed with anger, fear, and sadness.

"Royal, just let me explain! It wasn't supposed to be like this!" I cried.

"I know, and I really blame myself for all this shit you going through, but to get involved with another nigga just like that has me wondering... was this shit even real to you? The baby situation, I get that. Your mom explained that shit. I can't even get mad. But you wilding out and leaving home to deal with another nigga? That shit got a nigga fucked up. Ya mom even asked me to talk some sense into you, but I'm not doing any of that shit. All I'mma say is I hope you're happy, and a nigga will be home sooner than you think."

And with that, the call ended before I could think, speak, or even try to fix this. My whole heart felt torn, and to know my mother caused another situation in my life to go sour made me want her dead.

Thinking quickly, I dialed Royal's cell phone only to get the voicemail. Thinking quickly, I texted Manuel to bring my things out of class. After getting his response of no, I went back in class and took my seat. My mind was on a million the entire class period, so I watched the clock, waiting for class to end.

The bell finally rang for us to head to second period. I jumped up and quickly walked to the door. I was on a mission and didn't need any distractions. I walked to the parking lot, taking the keys to the

Benz out of my backpack. Hopping in, I drove off of campus with one destination in mind.

Within thirty minutes, I pulled up to my mother's private criminal law practice and hopped out the car as fast as I could. Walking through the small door, I was greeted by her secretary Cassidy.

Not even giving her time to say a word, I walked past her, straight into my mother's office.

"Make them leave!" I yelled to my mother as her potential clients sat across from her with confused looks on their faces.

"Would you please excuse me while I speak with my daughter? I'll have my secretary contact you with our decision."

With that, her clients were up and out the door with Cassidy apologizing for my disruption.

"So you wrote a letter to Royal about what happened with us and that I'm living with Ramel?" I asked, visibly pissed.

"You left me no choice. I needed someone to talk some sense into you. I refuse to let you throw your life away for yet another thug who will eventually ruin you," she pleaded.

"You had no right to do that! And no one can ruin shit that you haven't already done! When will you get it that no one is to blame but yourself? I refuse to allow you to ruin Ramel and I the way you did Royal and I."

"Marcy, there's a lot you don't understand. Royal wasn't good for you. We had sent him to jail—" My mother immediately stopped talking after admitting that she had Royal sent to prison. Initially, he was caught with drugs, but the length of time he received didn't add up. One thing was obvious; my parents had a lot to do with his ten-year sentence.

Without thinking, I launched across her desk and attacked her. Knocking over chairs and paperwork off her desk, we began to fight. Falling to the floor, my fist connected with her face as she attempted to pull me off her.

"I hate you!" I yelled as I fell sideways, and she grabbed my free hand, finally restraining me due to the fact that she was stronger. I felt a pair of hands grab her and me.

"Don't ever speak to me again! I wish I wasn't your daughter!" I yelled, trying to charge at her again, but the pair of hands holding me back had a great hold on me.

My mother straightened her pantsuit without looking my way.

"Marcy, just go. You win. I'm done trying," my mother spoke, walking out of her office, leaving me to deal with my own fucked up emotions. I began to become calm and collect myself, realizing that I was left to fight alone.

Looking around, I decided to finally leave. I didn't know what I had just done, but I knew that I was finally free to live my life on my own terms.

I hopped in the Benz, took a few breaths, and closed my eyes. For the first time, I just began to cry. I cried loud and hard. Why was my life so hard at such a young age when life should really be at its peak for me? I cried even more for the fact I had killed two people already in my seventeen years of life.

At sixteen, I killed my first child from an abortion and lost the love of my life at the hands of my parents. I witnessed two people that I thought loved each other more than life cheat and hate each other in the same moment. Now my sister would get the pleasure of giving life and having her significant other right by her side—something that was taken from me. I swore my life could be a book. Now I was in yet another situation with a man that I prayed could turn my messy ass life around. As I broke down even more, my phone began to ring. Not looking at the screen, I attempted to decline, but I hit the answer button instead.

"Marcy!" I heard the caller yell, but I didn't have enough energy to answer.

"Where are you?" they yelled.

Noticing that it was Ramel's voice, I placed the phone to my ear and tried to talk, but only my cries could be heard through my phone.

"Send me your location, baby. I'm on my way," Ramel replied after hearing my cries. Ending the call, I shared my location with Ramel. I didn't understand for the life of me why I couldn't stop crying.

With my head bent on the steering wheel, I continued to let it out.

It felt like hours had passed when I felt the driver's door open, and Ramel pulled me into his arms.

Crying harder, I soaked his shirt with my tears.

"It's gonna be all good, shawty. Let that shit out," Ramel encouraged.

"Aye, brah, hop in the Benz and take it home for me," Ramel instructed his friend.

Grabbing my body, he picked me up and carried me to his truck. My eyes felt swollen, and the sunlight didn't help. Placing me inside his ram and making sure I was secure, he retired to the driver side and put the car in drive. Just like that, we were off and headed home. My emotions were all over the place, and I knew Ramel had to think I was a weak bitch.

After a few minutes, I was able to calm myself enough to stop the tears, but I still couldn't find the words to speak. Shortly after we pulled up to his home, he killed the engine and hurriedly came around the truck to open my door. Carefully, he grabbed my body and picked me up bridal style, carrying me into the house. Up the stairs and to his room that I now shared with him, he placed me on the bed as he went into the bathroom. I felt paralyzed. My world came crashing down, and I didn't know what to do next.

Within a few minutes, Ramel reappeared into the room and began undressing my body. I didn't have a clue what his plans were for the moment, but whatever it was, it wouldn't matter. I officially had zero fight left in me.

He started with my shoes and finished with my half sweatshirt. Sitting there completely naked, I looked around to Ramel pulling me into the bathroom. Snapping back into reality, I noticed a bubble bath ready in the jacuzzi-style tub. Without speaking, I helped myself into the warm water. I leaned back and laid my head on the back of the tub and closed my eyes.

"Take all the time you need, and if you need me, press that button on the speaker," Ramel whispered before he made his exit. I cracked a half smile, realizing that sometimes, a person's presence in your time of need speaks louder than words ever could.

9

"So I GUESS FINISHING school is not an option anymore?" Ramel rolled over and asked.

It had been two weeks since my encounter with my mother, and I had been too down to focus on anything.

Rolling back over to face him, I replied. "Honestly, school isn't for me. I've tried. Although I make good grades, I just feel that it's a waste of time. Ramel, listen, I plan to be successful and rich one day, and I know for a fact I don't need an education to get by. Besides, school is just a white man's game, and it's ran good."

Ramel burst into laughter as if I had just told the funniest joke ever.

"OK, T.I., but what do you plan on doing if school is out of the question?"

"I mean, I can sing or open a boutique. I'm very into fashion and beauty, so I've always planned on opening a beauty bar that supplies your beauty needs from makeup, hair, and even clothing. I want to sell high-end designer labels for affordable prices. I don't mean to be rambling on; I just don't get to speak on my dreams and ideas a lot since my parents didn't feel my dreams were sensible."

"Don't stop. I think that shit sexy. I want you to accomplish all that and more, and your man's definitely going to make sure it happens for you," Ramel replied as I smiled, excited that he was on board.

"I guess in the meantime, I can get down with you," I blurted out the blue.

Ramel twisted his face in confusion.

"Listen, baby, the money I make from counting at the trap houses is cool, but with the extra time on my hands, I think I should step it up a notch," I added.

"Step it up in what way?"

"I mean, I know you have plenty of money, but there's something about being able to work and make my own funds. Plus, I can be of any help. After all that you've done for me, I'm down for whatever," I said, scooting closer to him. Ramel lay quietly as if he were in deep thought. He looked me up and down before kissing my lips.

"Say no more," Ramel replied as he sat up to take a leak. I was more than thankful for his gratitude. I knew that I would be stepping into a lot. Some would say I was crazy, and others would root for a down ass chick like myself. But at this point, I had nothing to lose and everything to gain.

"Get dressed," he commanded.

I sat up and proceeded to do as I was told. I walked into the closet and pulled out my black knee-length bodysuit with my army-print commander jacket and black and red Fendi fun-flair slip-on trainers. I walked into the bathroom to see Ramel's shirtless body in the mirror as he brushed his teeth. I stood in awe of him. Ramel's muscular body and toned legs made you want to suck the soul out of his body, and the fact that he wouldn't have sex with me until I turned eighteen killed me.

"Like what you see?" He turned around and smirked.

Without answering, I walked to the separate sink and began to brush my teeth. It took no more than thirty minutes to get ready as I combed through my pretty girl, twenty-eight-inch ponytail.

I followed Ramel to the car. As we prepped to leave the house, I had a feeling that after today, a lot of things were about to change.

We hopped into his Audi and pulled off. Ramel had been awkwardly silent since earlier, and I didn't know what to think.

"You know this shit so crazy to me. All the women I've dealt with on a personal level always wanted a nigga to take care of them and change their lifestyle. But you be wanting to get your hands dirty with a nigga. Why is that?" Ramel blurted out.

"That's simple. Because I'm not a needy chick, and I feel like if you're in it, then we're in it together."

"I swear, your last nigga groomed the hell out of you. I've never seen such a thoroughbred to be so fucking young. This shit be blowing a nigga mind," he stressed.

"Thanks for the compliment, but going forward, it's about us. Forget the past, and let's build our future and possibly run it up," I said.

"That's that shit I'm talking about. Aye, roll this up," Ramel said, handing me a little box.

Grabbing the box, I opened it up. Grabbing the gold rolling paper, I broke the weed down and proceeded to roll his blunt. I rarely displayed this side of myself, but smoking weed was what I used to cope with the unexpected.

After two blunts and an hour ride, we finally got off the highway and turned down a long dirt road. I looked around in confusion. Where were we? What was going on? But I knew not to ask any questions. As much as I didn't want to trust him in the beginning, Ramel had done a great job of making me feel secure in whatever we were doing.

Watching the tall and short trees fade away, we finally reached a big field that was covered in grass and a warehouse that looked abandoned to the naked eye. Riding around to the back, we parked where the car was out of view. Killing the ignition, Ramel opened his door and walked around to assist me with mine. Grabbing my hand, Ramel led me to the door that opened from the inside, indicating that someone knew we were there the moment we pulled up. I looked around to see the place surrounded by cameras. This shit looked nothing like your normal trap house.

Walking behind Ramel as he firmly gripped my hand, I could tell he was second guessing whatever was about to go on.

"Wassup, Ramiel," a man with glasses greeted, followed behind about five more greetings.

"Wassup, fellas—oh, and lady," Ramel responded, looking at everyone and the gay-looking girl in the back by a computer.

"Why he called you Ramiel?" I whispered.

"Because that's my real name. You know niggas can't pronounce shit right, so I just adopted the name Ramel," he replied.

"Fellas, this is my girl, Marcia. She cool," Ramel spoke, giving them a false name.

"Well, I'm John John, and this is the crew. I'm pretty sure your man has hipped you to what goes on here since you're the first person he's ever brought here," John John recited, looking at Ramel.

Looking confused, Ramel took my hand and showed me around.

"This is the crew, and this is the building where all the magic happens. Like I told you before, I do fraud, but just on another level. And it's because of my guys that I'm able to run a tight ship. We do everything from credit cards, making fake checks, making fake IDs, and selling drugs and pills. We pretty much do it all and run it through an underground website. We get orders and fill them, charging whatever our hearts desire. We get new identities, new social security numbers. I mean, you name it, and it's all at your disposal," Ramel expressed.

"Now the next question is, are you ready for all of this? Counting money in a trap doesn't have shit to do with this," Ramel assured.

Taking a moment to take this whole scenario in, I knew the risk would be a lot, but hey, Ramel had done more than enough up to this point.

"Whatever you need, baby, I got you," I replied, kissing his lips.

"Well, there you have it, fellas and lady. Welcome our new team member, Marcia. Right now, you'll just piggyback off of what John John needs help with. You can report here three times a week, and the other two, count at the trap until you get comfortable enough to do your own thing," he assured.

I smiled, feeling excited. Ramel really put his trust into me by bringing me to this spot. Shit was moving so fast, but one thing I couldn't deny was my love for fast money and how I allowed it to take over my life.

I grabbed Ramel's hand, and we exited the warehouse and headed back to the vehicle. Walking to the passenger side, he opened the door for me. I was starting to get used to the gentlemanly gestures and thinking that Royal and Ramel were so different yet also the same. He jogged to the other side, and we were off to the next destination.

"You hungry?" he asked.

"Of course," I replied.

An hour later, we pulled up to a cafe that served breakfast all day along with lunch. The place was packed full of workers on lunch break. Parking and walking around to open my door, Ramel grabbed my hand and led me into the cafe. The line to be seated was long, but the food smelled too good to leave.

"You alright?" Ramel whispered, squeezing my hand a little tighter.

"I'm fine, just hungry," I replied as he leaned in and kissed me on the cheek. I closed my eyes, enjoying his soft lips on my skin. As he released, I opened my eyes to be greeted by my mother holding her takeout bag. *What a fucking coincidence,* I thought. I surely wasn't ready to face her this soon. Ramel grabbed my hand a little tighter to ensure me everything would be OK. Before I could even think or muster up words to speak, she paused and looked at us for what felt like an eternity before she turned away and walked off without a word spoken.

I guess we both felt the same. I didn't have the energy to fight with her, and at this point, it was best to act as if we did not exist to each other.

"You OK, baby? We can leave," Ramel whispered again.

Resting my head on his shoulder, I didn't speak. I just gripped his hand tighter and walked forward as we were called to be seated.

10

"No, Khyrah, life is actually looking pretty good. Plus, my birthday is in four days, soooo," I replied, handing her the $5,000 that I had saved up. I didn't believe in banks saving money, and I needed my own put-away stash. Khyrah helped with storing my savings at her house.

"So it's Christmas next week as well. Has your brother mentioned anything about my gift?" Khyrah sneakily asked. I rolled my eyes before answering her. She was terrible at surprises. Before I could speak, her phone began to ring.

"I swear, your phone rings more than mine. Damn, my brother that sprung?" I laughed. Noticing that I was laughing alone, I saw an awkward look on her face. "Umm, am I missing something? Was that not my brother?" I questioned.

"Marcy, that was D-boy, and before you protest, let me explain. After I woke up from the coma, I didn't hear from him for months until one day, he popped up to my house. Now he's calling nonstop. So before your brother would notice anything, I finally decided to meet up with him to talk. We talked about that night. After confessing that I didn't remember anything, he switched to expressing himself, telling me how much he loved me and missed what we had, how he's sorry for not coming around sooner. He just didn't want to see me in a fucked up state of mind. Him and his wife are getting a divorce because he wants to be with me. Marcy, he said so much that night that I honestly don't know what to think. To make matters worse, he kissed me, and I didn't stop him. I know you must think I'm the most horrible person in the world, and I really care about your brother but—"

"Khyrah, if there's a but in your sentence, then it's already done. Honestly, I'm not here to judge you, because I've been there before. But as Manuel's sister, I will say he likes you a lot, and you owe him that much too. At least tell him how you feel," I reassured her.

"That's why you're my girl. I'm just so lost and confused. I love your brother, but I'm still in love with D-boy, and this is all so fucked up," Khyrah expressed, putting her head down into her hands.

I rubbed her back, wanting to slap the shit out of her memory loss ass. This bitch had some nerve to try my brother for that fuck nigga, and to top it off, I had yet to catch his wife. But when it came to matters of the heart, I didn't indulge, because you couldn't help who you loved.

Little did she know, my brother was in love with her. Had it not been for her, he would've dropped out of school with me. The little shit he did at the trap did not compare to the shit he did in Atlanta. My brother used to get in trouble for all kinds of shit—robbing, running the streets, selling drugs, and beating niggas' asses around the way. Manuel had calmed down a lot and was even taking sports more seriously. I was honestly very proud of him.

Releasing my hand, thinking of how far my brother had come made me a little upset with her. I wasn't perfect, but my brother stood by her side through the lowest point in her life. He nursed her back to health and helped her with remembering shit. I decided it was time for me to leave before I said or did something I didn't mean. The Lord knew I loved Khyrah, but when it came to D-boy, no one stood a chance.

I grabbed my things after expressing that I had to meet Ramel. I called Manuel after leaving her house. Yeah, I was torn between a friendship and blood, but one thing I didn't play about was my brother, so you're damn right I was about to tell him.

After four rings, he finally picked up.

"Where are you? Can you meet me at my spot?" I asked without saying hello.

"Yeah, after I grab Khyrah. I'll swing through. Everything alright?" he replied.

"Yeah, I just need to talk to you without Khyrah!" I exclaimed.

"Aight, I'll swing through in ten minutes," he said.

I ended the call, hopping into Ramel's Audi that I seem to drive all the time anyway. I hit Ramel's name, giving him a call.

"Hey, baby, what's good?" he spoke into his iPhone 6 Plus.

"Nothing, what are you doing? I miss you," I replied.

"Wrapping some shit up right now. I'll be home in a second," Ramel added.

I ended the call and headed home. I began reflecting on the past few months. Life was pretty good. I was making money with my man, and he treated me like a queen; although sex wasn't on the menu, in four days, that would all change. I was happy and gaining weight, and my family didn't bother me one bit. I would be lying if I said that I didn't think of my mother and sister. I talked to my father occasionally, but it was always quick and to the point.

I thought about Royal often. I knew he hated me, and I didn't blame him. At times, I felt as if I owed him my life, but at this moment, I couldn't give him what I didn't even own. Now that I was out on my own, regardless of how he feels about me, I planned to make sure he was straight on all levels, especially money. That's why I saved more than I spent. The money stashed at Khyrah's house was more than a savings for me; it was for Royal as well.

Trapped in my thoughts, I pulled up at home, noticing an all-white 2015 BMW Beamer in the driveway. The car looked nice and fit for a female. I remembered telling my mother that I wanted this car for my birthday.

Knowing that Ramel wasn't home, I searched for Rome. "Rome, whose car is that outside!" I yelled into the living room. I took my shoes off at the door and walked toward him. Walking into the living room, I saw Rome with my sister, Milan, sitting next to him. Completely taken aback, I twisted my face.

"Oh, wassup, Marcy? Didn't think you would be home so soon," Rome expressed as I looked her up and down.

"But that's your sister, I mean, Milan's new car. We were hoping that you guys can possibly talk," Rome blurted out.

"Your infamous mother strikes again. Damn, I now y'all loving the fact that I'm not there anymore!" I yelled.

Milan stood to her feet, exposing her little belly. As cute as her baby bump looked, it still didn't take away the pain of having my own torn away from me.

"I told you this wouldn't work, Rome," Milan expressed, preparing to leave. I guess my silence told it all.

"Ladies, my brother and I care about you ladies a lot. And we can't have the women we love fighting, especially when a baby is in the mix," Rome spoke.

"Rome, that's where you went wrong. This is some shit that can't be fixed, and I would appreciate if you and your brother stay the fuck out of it!" I yelled, walking up to the master bedroom.

Laying on the bed, I closed my eyes, pushing all my thoughts to the back of my brain.

I forgot that Manuel was on his way until my room door opened minutes later.

"Get your lazy ass up!" Manuel yelled, grabbing a pillow, hitting me with it. My mood instantly changed, knowing that I had someone who had my back no matter what—my brother.

"Nigga, I'm up, just calming down. Your boy Rome is trying to play God and make Milan and I make up." I laughed.

"Yeah, I told that nigga to stay out of it. You're too stubborn for that. But what's up?" Manuel replied.

"Oh, I just wanted to know if you were down for a party for our birthday this Saturday," I lied. I had every intention to tell Manuel about Khyrah. But after my encounter with Milan, I didn't need my twin brother in a fucked up mood like myself.

"Man, you're lying. I know you didn't call a nigga way over here for that. Besides, ain't Ramel planning you a party anyway?" he added, not realizing that he had just spilled the beans about my surprise party.

I smiled, excited about his outburst

"Man, Marcy! Don't say shit! A nigga didn't know it was a surprise, obviously," Manuel bargained.

"Well, today is your lucky day. Your secret is safe with me. Now go get your lady." I laughed, pushing him out of my room.

I could admit it felt weird. Some days, I felt as if Ramel and I were moving too fast, and other days, I felt as if we were right on track, filling up the missing pieces in both of our lives.

Since I didn't have much to do for the day, I lay back and decided to make a few videos on Snapchat. Ramel entered the room as I lay there, taking pictures.

"What the fuck you doing? I hope you posing like that and sending the pictures to me and only me," Ramel said in with a slight attitude.

"Of course. You and snapchat." I laughed.

"I don't think you understand what I'm saying. Posting all them sexy pictures and shit on the internet won't work for me, Marcy. You showing niggas what's mine, and that shit not ladylike for a girl with a man!" Ramel yelled.

"First off, nigga, lower your tone. All you had to say was don't post sexy pictures online, but since you come in here with an attitude, here it is. I don't see anything wrong with posting pictures of my body or anything else as long as I'm not fully naked. You are making a big deal out of nothing, and I'm not taking the pictures down," I challenged back.

"Marcy, I'm going to ask you one more time to delete them pictures, or I will have your whole account deleted," Ramel stated calmly as he stood next to the bed, looking as if he could kill me.

"Ramel, do what the fuck you want to do! You're acting childish and jealous over stupid ass Snapchat! Your ass stay gone all day! I leave, handle business, and come back to an empty house anyway, so the one day you come home early, you want to trip about Snapchat? I'm not about to do this with you today!" I yelled, again pissed off. Up to this point, we pretty much had a schedule, and we definitely didn't argue over petty shit like this. Actually, this was our first argument since I moved in a few months ago.

To keep things from escalating, I stood to my feet and began to walk out the room. Grabbing my arm, Ramel grabbed my phone and threw it against the wall. I snatched my arm back, looking at him as if he just lost his mind.

"So you just break my shit like that!" I yelled, trying to push him with all the strength I could muster up. Grabbing my arms with force, he threw me on the bed, and before I could fight back, he fell on top of me, crashing his lips into mine. As much as I wanted to push him off me, I knew the sexual tension between us was at an all-time high, and I wanted him in the worse way. It had been over a year since I last felt a man I love inside of me.

As he rubbed his hands up and down my body, I wrapped my hands around his neck, sticking my tongue down his throat. Grabbing my tank top, he pulled it over my head, exposing my small, bare breast. As he took the left breast into his mouth, I grabbed his dreads as he sucked like a newborn baby. Ramel's lips were soft and wet just how I liked them.

Sex was an art to me, and the messier it became, the better the chance you had of creating a masterpiece that couldn't be duplicated. Roughly turning me on my stomach, Ramel pulled my tights down, and I lay there, naked. He took his left hand to spread my butt cheeks and began to lick away at my ass. With his right hand, he found my clitoris and began to massage it in a circular motion. I began to grind my hips as he licked and fingered away at my insides.

"Fuckkkk, it feels so good, baby, shittttt." I moaned, stuffing my head into the pillow.

Quickening his pace, he flipped me back over, devouring my sweet spot. He flicked his tongue over my clitoris while sucking. After each lick, he flicked. He then used his fingers to massage my clitoris again as he fucked me with his tongue, sticking it inside my strawberry hole, licking around and coming back out for more. This shit was driving me crazy. His tongue was definitely a tornado tearing up my pussy.

"Oh my God! That shit feel sooo goood, daddyyyy!" I yelled, feeling my body about to tighten and release the best part of me.

As I was nearing my orgasm, Ramel abruptly stopped. Sitting up with his mouth covered in wetness, he smiled.

Opening my eyes, I realized what had happened. "Why the fuck you stopped, nigga?" I was pissed.

He laughed and stood to his feet and retired to the bathroom. Still naked and horny as fuck, I followed him.

"So you just gon' do me like that, Ramel? You're really going to do me like that!" I yelled, walking into the bathroom as well.

"I didn't do shit, baby. I'm just chilling," he replied, pulling his pants down in front of me. I watched his rock-hard dick shoot piss into the toilet.

"You're an idiot," I replied, rolling my eyes, visibly pissed.

I walked back into the room, heading to my closet. I grabbed my Armani workout tights and shirt and retired into the guest bathroom. Since he wanted to play stupid ass games, then I had one better. I hurriedly went into the bathroom and turned on the shower, locking the door. After getting the water as hot as I liked it, I placed my bare body inside.

Instantly grabbing the soap to lather my body, I began to rub my pussy gently because it was still tender from the bullshit Ramel had just pulled. Playing with my rag in between wiping, my body temperature began to get hot again. Dropping the wash rag, I quickly inserted two fingers into my warm spot to finish off the feeling Ramel created. I began to think of the ways he could make my body feel with his manhood inside of me.

"Yes, Ramel, right there," I moaned, envisioning him taking over my body instead of my fingers. I arched my back and rotated my hips as I began to think about the time Royal and I made love on the roof of the house my mother and father once shared. The way his manhood filled my body with so much pleasure made me feel as if I could never come for another man that way.

Before I knew it, mixed with water, my cum fell down my legs and into the shower drain. Breathing heavily and feeling rejuvenated, I picked up my wash rag and begin to finish washing my body. I couldn't believe how I went from fantasizing about Ramel and switching to thinking about the way Royal used to fuck the life out of me. I knew I needed some dick fast before I fucked a complete stranger. Laughing at my thoughts, I finally turned the water off and proceeded to exit the shower.

"That's the sexiest shit I think I've ever seen," Ramel admitted as I exited the shower. Embarrassed and still obviously pissed, I grabbed my towel and moved past him. I couldn't believe this nigga just watched me masturbate.

"Well, I had to finish what your wack ass started." I sneered.

"This shit would've gone smoothly if you would have just done what I said and deleted your Snapchat account," he admitted.

"So you doing all of that because of petty ass Snapchat? You need to grow the fuck up, Ramel!" I yelled, wiping the water from my body. Acting as if he wasn't there, I went into the master bedroom to finish getting dressed. After completing my hygiene routine, I walked back into the house to see that Ramel had left. I also noticed that Milan and Rome were gone as well. Looking around, I noticed one thing— without them and Khyrah, I really had zero friends. I decided that not having friends would change after today. I grabbed the keys to the Audi and left. I knew exactly where to go this time of day.

Thirty minutes later, I pulled up to the hood that held D-boy and Ramel's trap house that I worked at first. Getting out of the car, I could see the hood was packed and full of thugs and the women who loved them. I parked the Audi a couple of houses down from the trap and exited the car. Seeing the usual hoodlums hanging around, I began speaking to the ones I knew from being at the trap numerous times.

I walked toward the trap house before I walked around the hood in search for Alexandra, a white bitch that was more hood than any full black girl I knew. I fucked with her when I would come to work, but since I'd been doing other things, I hadn't kicked it with her lately.

Walking up to the trap, I noticed Khyrah's car parked a few houses down. I rolled my eyes, wondering where the hell my brother was. A few hours earlier, she was just telling me about D-boy and was now right over here in public like old times.

"Damn, bitch, long time!" I heard someone yell. Turning around, I saw Alexandra, whose nickname was Allie.

"I came here looking for your extra ghetto ass. Hey, bitch," I returned, hugging her.

"What's new?" I asked

"Same old shit. It's crazy you're popping up here. I got some shit to tell you," she said.

"Wassup?" I inquired.

"Walk with me to my apartment right quick," she answered, so I followed her to the next block where her apartment sat on the corner.

Walking in, I fell in love with her black and red decorated home. From the outside, her place looked ran down. "So what's up?" I asked, cutting to the chase.

"It's some new hoes from Georgia that just moved this way and been living in the hood. Two twin sisters with their mom, and word on the street is the slim-thick, brown-skinned one, Kiona, got her eyes set on your man, Ramel," Allie explained. "Supposedly, he got her working with him, cashing fraudulent checks and shit. And I know this because her twin sister, Tiona, be kicking it with my home-girl Laniqua, and she told me," Allie added.

Taking it all in, I knew better than to show my true feelings in front of irrelevant people, so I tried to play it cool.

"Is that right? Well, which house she stays in?" I inquired.

"They live three houses up from me."

Without saying a word, I walked to the front door.

"Aye, Marcy, what are you about to do?" she questioned.

"I'm about to handle this shit," I replied, opening the door and walking out.

"Well, bitch, count me in," Allie said, following right behind me. Side by side, we walked as Alexandra directed me to the twins' home.

"The off-blue house right there," Allie spoke as we approached the house. Looking around as if she didn't know what to think, I left Allie standing in the yard as I approached the front door.

Pulling the screen porch door open, I proceeded to knock.

"Who knocking on my damn door!" an older woman yelled.

"Yes, I'm looking for Kiona," I spoke sweetly into the door.

"Kiona, get the damn door!" the lady yelled, still not opening it.

The fact that I had to wait for the hoe to open the door made my nerves go through the roof. The door finally opened, and a pretty, long-haired, tall girl with slanted eyes answered the door. Seeing my face, she stood quiet for a second as if she were fond of me.

"Kiona, right?" I asked to be sure.

"Yes, how can I help you?" she shot back.

"All I need to know is one thing. Are you fucking with my man, Ramel?"

"Your man? Sweetie, you might want to ask him, and I really don't appreciate you coming to my home with—"

Whap!

That was all you heard as I slapped the shit out of her. I then pulled her out her doorway and off the porch. With her hair in my right hand, we fell to the ground, and I was now on top of her, punching her with my free hand. She scratched at my face, attempting to get me off her. She finally grabbed my hair, pulling me off her as I threw blows to her face.

She began throwing blows back, but I had the advantage on her, and I knew the chances of her whooping my ass were slim. They could thank my boxing classes for that. I threw an uppercut that drew blood while on the ground. Before I could throw another one, I was lifted in the air and pulled away.

"It ain't over, bitch!" Kiona yelled, spitting blood.

"Fuck you, dumb hoe! It's whatever every time I see you!" I yelled back.

"Ramel, get your bitch! I told you about dealing with them young and dumb hoes!" Kiona yelled again.

Finally looking around, attempting to calm down, I noticed the crowd standing around as Ramel pulled me toward his truck.

"What the fuck you out here doing!" Ramel yelled, visibly pissed.

"No, the question is what the fuck are you doing? You really trying me with these hood rat ass hoes, Ramel? You know I don't play, or maybe you forgot," I replied as the onlookers watched.

"You really tripping, Marcy, and embarrassing yourself. I thought you knew me better than that. Man, get the fuck out my way," Ramel added as he tried to walk away.

"Fuck you, Ramel!" I yelled, completely embarrassed. Was I really tripping? Could this whole thing be a lie? I knew I probably handled it wrong, but I was dick deprived and falling in love with him. Keeping the little bit of dignity I had left, I walked to his car. I drove and left the hood.

11

FOUR DAYS LATER...

"I KNOW, Khyrah. I fucked up. And to make matters worse, it's my birthday, and I still haven't heard from him," I spilled, checking my phone again. It had been three days since I spoke with Ramel or even been home. To make matters worse, I hadn't heard from him, and it was like he didn't even care.

"It's going to be OK, Marcy. At least you're not battling two relationships because you're too much of a coward to be honest. It's your birthday, and since your brother is missing in action, how about we have a girls' day," Khyrah added.

I rolled my eyes at her remark. I hated that I had to depend on her for support. Yeah, I had money, and I could be staying in a hotel, but I needed moral support as well, and other than Khyrah, I barely had friends.

"Well, I might as well get out of the house. You only turn eighteen once, right?" I stood to my feet and grabbed my bag. I had brought a badass mid-thigh Alexander McQueen dress. But due to my crappy mood and change of plans, I grabbed my long, black maxi dress that hugged every curve and held a high thigh split on my right leg. I slid on my Tory Burch sandals and retired to the bathroom to fix my pre-wanded red and black Ombre extensions.

"Well, don't you look cute," Khyrah complimented me.

"Thanks. I'll be ready in a few minutes after I apply my makeup," I replied, looking her over. Khyrah sported her Fashion Nova thigh dress and thigh-high boots with her blonde bob slayed to perfection.

After an hour, we were finally dressed and ready to leave. It was approaching 5:00 p.m., and I was hungry as hell. I still had Ramel's Audi, which I definitely planned on driving today.

"Before we head anywhere, let's get something to eat," I demanded.

"Cool, and after that, I want to check out this new bar they built in town. It's like a sports bar. Maybe that'll be fun to party with the white people on South Beach. I think it's called Fame," Khyrah recommended.

"I'm down for whatever takes my mind off of Ramel."

Driving for twenty minutes in traffic, we pulled up to Soul Sista soul-food restaurant. As usual, it was full of people. I parked and exited the car with my girl on my heels. Walking to the front of the line, skipping everyone, I pulled out a hundred-dollar bill as the host grabbed our menus and seated us. One thing I learned from my mother and Royal was that money talked, and that's why I loved it. Looking back at all the hateful stares and pissed off people, I laughed.

The restaurant was full of black people. One thing I learned about living in Miami was that the niggas sported gold teeth with thick dreadlocks. And the women all had enhanced bodies and lace fronts. This concoction alone made you the shit in Miami. Once we were seated, I knew exactly what I wanted to eat.

"Is it me, or are all these niggas staring at us?" Khyrah asked nervously.

"It's definitely not you. Don't look, but here they come," I instructed as two men approached our table. One, of course, sported the thick dreads, while the other who looked my way sported a low cut with a grown man's beard. His low eyes and butter pecan skin caused me to stare more than I should have.

"Hello, ladies. I'm Cheddar, and this my boy—"

"Sampson," the low-cut one interrupted before his homeboy told us another ridiculous nickname like his. "Would you ladies mind if we joined you? Everything on us, of course," Sampson offered.

"Ummmm, sure," I replied. It was my birthday, and what I really wanted wasn't happening, so fuck it. Rolling her eyes, Khyrah agreed as well, and the men joined us for dinner.

After our orders were taken, Sampson began to speak.

"So, beautiful, what's your name?"

"That's not important. You could be a stalker," I replied.

"Trust me. I'm the last nigga trying to stalk you, but I will say if I have to earn the right to know your name, then I'm with that," he said as I displayed all thirty-two of my teeth.

Two hours later, we all were so wrapped up in our conversations that we didn't realize the time.

"I hate to ruin such good vibes, but we have plans and need to go," Khyrah interrupted.

"We definitely don't want to hold you beautiful ladies up, so here's my number. Use it whenever ya nigga fuck up again." With that, Sampson grabbed my phone and inserted his number.

I smiled, and we parted ways. His conversation alone was refreshing; although I was honest about my relationship, he didn't pressure me. That alone made me respect and gain curiosity about Mr. Sampson.

Getting in the car, Khyrah and I headed to Fame, the bar that she was so eager to try out.

Typing in the address on my phone, we headed fifteen minutes down the road. Thinking about Ramel and how much I missed him, I began to get out of the mood to party and decided to finally head home and apologize to my man.

"Don't get mad, but I think I want to head home and spend the rest of my birthday making up with my man," I spoke as Khyrah typed away on her phone.

"Oh, hell no! It's your birthday! You can't do that, Marcy!" Khyrah yelled.

"Why the hell not? I'm not feeling going to a bar that we probably can't get into, and if we can, we definitely can't drink. So what's the point? Plus, I miss Ramel, Khyrah. I need to make up with my baby," I confessed.

"OK, look, let's go and peep the scene. If it's lame, we can leave, and you can finally get out of my bed and take your ass home to your *man*."

Rolling my eyes, I agreed simply because we were five minutes away.

As we pulled up, the parking lot was full of cars. As we pulled up to the valet parking, the building looked as if no one was inside from the outside. Looking around, I realized how quiet the inside was as we walked to the front door. The valet driver opened the doors to the bar as we walked in. It was pitch-black dark inside the building. I immediately turned around, scared as shit. I refused to be set up or die this easily. Grabbing my clutch, I removed my small pistol I had purchased a few weeks ago as all the lights shut on.

"Surprise!" I heard many different voices yell as the DJ began playing 2 Chainz.

"Oh shit! She got a gun!" someone yelled as a few others jumped and screamed.

"Whoa, baby, let me get that," Ramel said, grabbing the gun from my hand as I felt embarrassed. I looked around, finally smiling, lightening the mood. I instantly realized I was set up, and Khyrah was in on it.

"Damn, the birthday girl packing. Happy Birthday, Marcy! Round of shots for everyone on the boss man Ramel!" the DJ shouted.

Hugging my brother and wishing him a happy birthday as well, I looked around and noticed my homeboys from the trap and their women. I noticed a few people from school that I was cool with when I attended and a lot of other people from around the way. Grabbing my hand, Ramel led me by the DJ booth, which held a VIP section.

"Damn, you looking good, baby. Can a nigga get a kiss?" he asked.

"You made me go through all this just for a surprise party?" I questioned.

"Damn, so you mad?"

"Hell no," I replied, placing my arms around his neck, placing the sloppiest kiss I could muster up to his lips. I knew we had a bunch of onlookers, but I did not give a fuck. I missed my man. Grabbing my ass, he now had me horny and ready to leave just that quick.

"Let me stop before I fuck the shit out of you right now," Ramel whispered in my ear.

"Shots?" the bottle girl asked.

One by one, she handed shots of Patrón to Rome, Ramel, my brother, who was hugged up with Khyrah, and myself.

"Keep them coming!" shouted Manuel.

Before I knew it, I had taken five shots back to back, and I wanted my man right now.

The DJ decided to change the tempo and played Bryson Tiller's "Exchange."

"*This what happens when I think about you,*" I sang into Ramel's ear as I grinded my body onto his. Feeling his rock-hard manhood, my juices began to soak my G-string. As the liquor began to take control, I grabbed Ramel's hand, leading him out of the section. Looking around the bar, I noticed a door ajar close by the bathroom area. Walking to the door and pushing it open, I turned the light on to see a desk and a couch.

"Shit, I think this is the owner's office, baby," I spoke.

"So? Who gives a fuck," Ramel replied, cutting the light off and locking the door. Grabbing my waist, he lifted me onto the desk and kissed my lips with so much passion that I couldn't keep up. With one hand, he went up my thigh and ripped my G-string from my body. Pulling my dress up over my head, he aggressively sucked my titties. The effects of the liquor had us both wanting sex rough and hard. Spreading my legs, he dug his face into my sweet spot, sucking my juices with every lick. Arching my back, I began to ride his face as my head began to spin.

"Yes, suck that pussy, baby!" I yelled as he sucked my clitoris as if it were his last meal.

Replacing his tongue with his fingers, he kissed me deeply, and with one swift movement, he inserted his manhood deep within my cave, taking my breath away. He moved slowly in and out of me.

It had been a while since I had sex, and although there was pain, the pleasure quickly took over.

"Damn, this pussy so tight. Fuck, you gon' make a nigga bust quick." Ramel moaned.

"Yes, cum with me, daddy! I want you to come inside me!" I yelled.

Grabbing my waist, Ramel quickened his pace. I tightened my pussy muscles with each stroke.

After tightening them for the third time, Ramel released all of his babies inside of me. If I weren't on birth control, I knew I would probably be pregnant.

"Fuck, that was the best pussy a nigga ever had. Damn, bae, how you tighten your pussy on my dick like that?" he asked as he helped me off the desk.

"Just a little trick I learned."

"That shit felt good as hell." He laughed, pulling his Balmain jeans up.

"Let's get back to the party before they come looking for us," I demanded as I put my dress back on.

Finally ready, we both walked back into the party as if nothing had happened. He grabbed my hand and led me back to the section.

"I need more shots!" Khyrah yelled.

"I got you, babe," Manuel replied, leaving the section to order more liquor.

As he left, I scoped the crowd to see everyone having a great time.

"Thanks again, baby. This party meant a lot—" My sweet compliment to my man was short lived when I noticed D-boy walk into our section.

"Wassup, baby," he addressed Khyrah, kissing her on the lips.

"I think you need to leave!" I yelled.

"Bae, chill out. I got this," Ramel assured.

"Aye, D-boy, I think it's best you leave, and I'mma holla at you later," Ramel stated.

"Damn, my nigga, it's like that? It's cool. Khyrah, let's go," he demanded, grabbing her hand.

"What the fuck going on?" my brother, Manuel, asked, setting the new bottle of Patrón on the table.

"Nigga, what it look like? I'm taking my lady home," D-boy challenged.

"Your lady, huh? Is it true you back fucking with this lame ass nigga?" Manuel asked.

"I'm sorry. It wasn't supposed to happen like this," Khyrah pleaded.

"Yeah, now run alon—" D-boy attempted to say right before my brother landed a right punch to his face. Without a thought, I jumped over Ramel and threw another punch as my brother and I went to work on D-boy. I felt a pair of hands grab me, pulling me out the bar along with my brother and everyone in the section.

Pushed into the parking lot, I was pissed, but I was more concerned about my brother. It looked as if the whole bar was now standing outside, and with this crowd, I couldn't see my brother.

"Baby, calm the hell down. You tripping," Ramel spoke, pulling me toward his car.

"Wait, where's my brother? I need to make sure he's OK!" I yelled.

"I'll check. You just get in the car, NOW!" he demanded, but before I could move a muscle, I heard two gunshots and tires screech as they left the scene. My heart dropped to my feet as Ramel and I took off running to see who was shot.

Pushing through the crowd, I looked to see a body lying on the ground. Getting closer, looking at the familiar frame, I instantly dropped to my knees in fear.

"Oh my God, Manuel!" I yelled, grabbing his barely breathing body. I held onto his body, cradling him.

"Someone call the fucking police!" I yelled with tears falling down my face.

"Manuel, please hold on. I'm right here. I got you. Please fight for me. We got shit to do, brah!" I pleaded as everyone watched. I saw Ramel on his phone, calling 9-1-1.

"I-I love y-you," my brother attempted to say, holding onto his last bit of breath in his body.

"I love you more, Mann. Don't speak; don't say anything. Just fight, please fight! I can't do this without you, Mann," I cried as his life slipped away.

"My nigga, you gotta hold on," Rome spoke, kneeling down next to me with fear and sadness written all over his face.

It was all a blur after that moment. All I remembered was the ambulance pulling up and the workers pulling him from my arms. I felt as if my life had left my body, and all I could do was stare. Ramel grabbed me up off the ground and carried me to the car.

"Rome, meet me at the hospital!" Ramel yelled as we pulled off.

12

SITTING in the hospital waiting room, I tried my best to pull it together as Ramel held me in his arms. So far, Rome, Ramel, and I were the only ones in the waiting room.

That was short lived when I heard footsteps running down the hallway. Without looking up, I knew it was my mother and sister.

"Where is my son? What happened!" my mother yelled, directing her rage toward Rome.

"Look, all I know is one minute he and Marcy were fighting a dude in the club. We all were thrown out, and after that, we heard gunshots," Rome spilled.

"The infamous Marcy strikes again. My son is laying up in here fighting for his life because of you," my mother said, now looking toward me as if she could kill me.

"Me? Oh, right, I guess it is easy to blame me, right? I swear I hate the ground you walk on. Don't say shit to me!" I yelled.

"And I'm to the point where that's perfectly fine. Just know that if my son dies, his blood is on your hands," she replied.

Done listening to her, I stood to my feet and walked to the vending machine. I cried, thinking of my brother and how I couldn't live without the one person that I knew loved the real me. I fell beside the vending machine, unable to stand due to the pain and tears staining my face. Before I completely hit the ground, I felt a pair of hands grab me and hold me.

Not even looking up, I broke down. Everything I held inside came to surface.

"He's going to be OK, Marcy. I just know it," I heard Milan say.

Looking up, I pulled away from her and just looked. We were all so different yet all the same. Carried in the same womb, we walked, talked, and grew together. I knew if I lost Manuel, Milan would be all I had left. I also knew that as mad as I was with her, none of this was her fault; and if that had been her lying in the hospital bed, I would feel the same as I did about Mann. As I grabbed her into a tight embrace and forgot that she was pregnant, she began to break down and cry. I knew my sister missed me. Regardless of the things we went through, we had each other's backs, and she and Manuel would always be my first and only real best friends.

"I'm so sorry," she cried. "This is all my fault. I didn't mean for this to happen, Marcy, and you guys are suffering because of me."

"It's not your fault, Milan. You're only doing what you were taught to do. I'm done blaming you for something you had no control over. I love you, and you're the only sister I have," I responded, feeling her hard, round belly against mine. I closed my eyes, attempting to make peace with the only real thing that separated me from my sister—her pregnancy.

"Hey, the doctors want to speak with you all at once," Rome spoke, walking up to us with a slight smile. I knew he was happy that we finally made up. I grabbed her hand, and we walked back to the waiting area where the doctor and nurses waited.

When we walked up, they began talking to my mother. "Your son suffered gunshot wounds to the chest, and one grazed the left side of his head. He lost a lot of blood, but through that, we were able to stabilize him. During surgery, he suffered a seizure and is in a comatose state at the moment," the doctor stated.

"What does that mean? You can't wake him up!" Milan shouted.

"Waking up solely depends on your brother. I'll be honest, our main focus is monitoring him through the night and hoping that any long-term permanent damage hasn't been done due to his seizure," he added.

"Can I see him?" my mother asked with tears falling down her face.

"At this moment, I would say no. We need him to gain strength and nothing to make his levels increase. Go home, get some rest, and we will call you if anything changes," the doctor informed before walking off.

Not even looking my way, she grabbed her things to leave.

"Let's go, Milan!" she yelled.

Looking at me with sadness in her eyes, Milan hugged me and left.

"Baby, I'm not leaving! I'll sleep in the waiting room until I can see my brother. After that, I'll call you to come get me," I spoke, looking at Ramel, who had an expression on his face that I couldn't read.

"You sure?" he questioned.

"Yes, now get some rest, and I'll call you when I'm ready," I replied. Grabbing my face, Ramel kissed my lips before leaving.

"Aye, Marcy, I love you," Ramel said, turning around. I smiled. I had been waiting for those words since I moved in with him, and although it wasn't the right time, I loved him back, and that's what mattered.

"I love you too, Ramel," I answered as I took a seat to begin the waiting game.

"I'mma chill here with you, Marcy," Rome added. I knew he was sad about his boy being laid up in the hospital.

Looking at my phone, I saw Khyrah's number appear. I quickly ignored the call. If she'd done what I told her from the beginning, we wouldn't be in this situation. A piece of me regretted not telling my brother when I intended to. All of this was so fucked up.

"Hello, are you Marcy? I'm Detective Rodger. I would like to go over what happened to your brother if you don't mind," a tall, white man dressed in a suit said as he stood in front of me. Against my better judgment, I decided to tell him what I knew, which was us getting kicked out the club then hearing gunshots.

EIGHT HOURS LATER...

I was awakened by Rome handing me a coffee. I had no idea what time it was, but I knew that by now, we could possibly see my brother.

"It's 9:00 a.m. The doctor said we could go back and see him two at a time, so after you fully wake up, we can head back," Rome instructed.

I was too excited to sit and drink coffee, knowing that I could see my brother now. Preparing myself to see him and talk to him without hearing his voice or seeing his eyes made me do something I hadn't done in a long time. I began to pray. I prayed for his strength, I prayed for his health, and I even prayed for myself and my sister.

"Lord, I'm sorry," were the last words I said in my prayer as I stood to my feet to check in for visiting. I walked to the front counter and asked to visit Manuel Gomez.

"Are you his brother and sister?" the receptionist asked, looking at Rome and me.

"Yes," I replied, knowing that only immediate family could visit.

"Can I have your names?" she asked.

"Marcy Gomez and Rome Brown," I answered.

Looking over her papers, her expression changed. "Umm, Rome Brown is cleared to visit, but I have strict instructions from Manuel's mother that Marcy Gomez is not allowed to visit," the receptionist stated.

"There must be some mistake! I've been here all night. I'm his sister! I was the one with him when he was shot!" I yelled.

"I understand that, but due to strict orders, I'm going to have to ask you to leave," she replied.

I looked at Rome with tears in my eyes, and he shook his head.

"Tell him I love him, please," I said with my voice cracking from the pain.

"I got you. It's gonna be OK," he assured.

I grabbed my phone and called Ramel. It was time to go home and handle the real situation at hand. I waited outside the hospital, fuming mad. My mother just kept throwing punches, and if she weren't my mother, she would be six feet under right now.

"Marcy, is he OK?" Khyrah approached me from the parking lot as I waited for Ramel.

"Why does it matter to you? Bitch, you left him, and you have some nerve showing your face here today!" I yelled, obviously taking my anger out on her now.

"I know, and I'm sorry. I didn't mean for this to happen. I just need to know if he's OK," she pleaded.

"Khyrah, I'm going to tell you once more. You need to leave because as far as my brother is concerned, he's dead to you."

"Don't say that! You and I both know he loves me and wants me right there with him! And I love him too, Marcy," she pleaded.

"You're right; he definitely loves you. That's why when D-boy's wife set you up to be raped and beaten inside a club, Manuel and I were the ones to help you. That's why Manuel visited you every day, nursed you back to health, and even stayed in school—because he loves you. Do you know who the fuck my brother was before we moved here, and he met you? He didn't give a fuck about bitches, education or anything. That nigga damn sure would have never caught him slipping like that after the club. My brother turned soft and even became somewhat of a good boy because his stupid ass fell for a weak, dumb bitch like you! Now get the fuck out my face and stay the fuck away from my brother, or so help me God, I will kill you!" I spat with nothing but venom dripping from my voice.

I didn't care about her feelings. I didn't care about her well-being. All I knew was that if she didn't leave within the next minute, only God himself would keep me from jumping on her ass and beating her to death.

The look on her face said something that I couldn't explain—as if she felt hurt, betrayed, and sad all at the same time. Without one word, she walked away toward her car, which was the best decision she had made in a long time.

Looking at my phone, I saw a text message from my sister, Milan.

*Milan: Meet me later, you can use my ID to get back and see Manuel and again I'm sorry Marcy

I smiled as I agreed and thanked her as well. Some may say that when all hell broke loose, if you would just pay attention, blessings also surfaced at the same time. But at this point in my life God, blessings, church, etcetera seemed so far away from my thought process. My father always taught me to *"Orar,"* which meant pray in Spanish when things would get hard or I would fail a test in school. My first time praying in years was last night, and still, my faith wavered, and I felt as if only I could truly fix this.

13

"I KNOW, Ramel. It's been a week. And I know that's your boy, but I'm also your girl, so take it as you want, but whether you help me or not this time, when I see him, he's dead," I said, sitting on our king-size bed. I knew he was stressed, having to choose between a long-term friendship and his girlfriend, but I didn't give a damn. He sat across from me, rubbing his chin hair in deep thought.

"Let me ask you something... When I helped you kill my ex-girl-friend, did it ever cross your mind to think, why did that occur? Although from the day I met you, I knew you were different, but the fact remained that I didn't know you. Why would I let a girl that I just met—someone who just moved here—why would I allow you to just come around and kill one person that has been in my life for years?" he asked.

"I wondered that a lot, Ramel. Why did you think trusting you has been so hard, but I knew I would find out soon," I replied.

"She wasn't trustworthy, and she was fucking D-boy as well. So make no mistake, I want him dead as much as you do. But sometimes, revenge takes time, or in other cases, they dig their own hole and fall into it. D-boy makes me a lot of money, and other than my businesses and the fraud shit I do, a big profit of my money comes from drugs.

My supplier is always on point, and D-boy makes sure I don't touch shit but my money."

"But at this rate, you don't think his snake ass will fuck you over with the drugs and the money? Look what he's done so far. You don't think something worse will happen?" I asked.

"It definitely will, but by then, he'll be dead. I need you to keep your eye on the prize. No one has consistent work on hand available to them like me. The shit is always pure, and the prices are better than any nigga in the city. The best part is that no one knows who my connect is. The point I'm trying to make is that I need you to trust me like I trust you. I know you went through a lot with your last nigga, and he taught you how to survive in the streets. But let me teach you how to survive in and out the streets. Can a nigga do that?" He laughed, making light of the situation. "Plus, you never make the right decision when your emotions are all over the place," he added.

"OK, Ramel! I hear you! Just keep me as far away from him as possible, please!" I yelled, knowing that if I saw him or his wife, they were dead on sight.

"That's my girl. Now can daddy get some head?" he asked. I knew he was feigning since the night of my birthday party, but my mind had been so wrapped up in killing D-boy, ignoring Khyrah's calls, and checking on my brother that I barely talked to my man anymore. The even crazier part was the fact that my brand-new all-red 2016 Mercedes-Benz, SL-Class Convertible was sitting in the driveway, waiting to be taken for a spin.

Thinking back to the day Royal and I got into our first argument, his words rang in my head as I scooted closer to Ramel. "If you want to keep your man, never let him leave the house with a hard dick." I laughed to myself as I released his manhood from his Ethika briefs and began deep throating right in the middle of our bed. I went down so far on his shaft that you would've thought I could swallow it whole. Once I came up, I spat on the tip and began to massage it in with my right hand while I sucked the tip and sides.

"Damn, you the shitttt." Ramel moaned as I went harder, jacking him off while sucking the life out of his now soaking wet shaft. "That's right. Make that shit nasty. Oh, fuckkkkk."

I smiled as I continued. His words and pleasing moans made me want to suck the life out of him. With his long arms, he gripped the back of my hair tightly, pushing my head further down. Without warning, Ramel released his liquid inside my mouth. Sucking like a newborn baby hungry for milk, I swallowed all of his babies before I came up for air.

Leaning back on the bed, Ramel was out of breath and tired. I stood to my feet to brush my teeth. Giving head was something I knew I was the shit at, but it was always a must that I brushed my teeth right after.

As I grabbed the Colgate to place on my toothbrush, my phone began to ring. Not bothering to look, I answered immediately.

"Hello," I spoke as I began brushing my teeth.

"Marcy, don't speak. Just please listen. I'm just trying to understand and make sense of what's going on."

"Make sense of what? Are you deaf? I already told you what's up," I mumbled before I spat out my tooth paste and proceeded.

"I know, and I'm sorry. I just don't know, and I'm lost, and I blame myself for what happened to your brother," she cried, and from the sound of her voice, I could tell that she had been crying for days. As much as I wanted to have an honest conversation and tell her it's going to be OK, I just couldn't, knowing my brother was suffering, and there was nothing we could do.

"The only way I would accept that wack ass apology is if it were you laid up in the hospital fighting for your life and not my brother. Until that can happen, don't fucking call my phone again. You are dead to me and my brother!" I yelled, ending the call. Finally being able to rinse my mouth out, I finished with my teeth and got dressed. Ramel was spread out on the bed, fast asleep.

I placed on my mid-waist jeans and half-shirt hoodie. Grabbing my Mercedes keys, I exited the house. I rolled my eyes, as my phone began to ring again. This time, I answered in a hurry.

"Hola, Papi," I greeted my father.

"Hola, *hija,*" he responded.

"How are you? When are you coming?" I dived right in with the questions.

"Actually, I've been here since last night. I just left the hospital with your *hermano*. We need to talk, Marcy," he added.

"I know. Can you meet me in an hour at a diner on South Beach called Caliente?" I asked.

"See you soon," he replied as he ended the call.

I loved my father. Despite his imperfections, he was always so cool, calm, and collected. He was very wise and spoke with plenty of sense—that was unless you pissed him off. I always knew it was in my blood to be a hustler. My Spanish side, which came from my father, came from a long line of them. The Gomez Cartel didn't play. They supplied many states with drugs as they rested their Cartel on the outskirts of Columbia.

My grandfather, Sir Gomez, was a vicious man and a man of his word, which was the reason we never met him. I knew of my father's family, but who I didn't know or ever met was any of my relatives. The day my father chose to marry a black woman was the day his father and family disowned him.

My mother was studying in Colombia for a year and met my father. They fell in love, and the rest was history. I'd begged to know the whole story because in my heart, I knew there was more to tell, but my parents refused to speak on it. I knew my father still had ties, and if there was ever any danger, all he had to do was make one phone call, but after not speaking to his family for over eighteen years, I knew it would never happen.

With my thoughts running wild, I pulled up to the diner. A few minutes early, I spotted my father sitting on the outside patio, waiting patiently. I hopped out my car, excited and sad to see my father. I walked up to the patio, and he stood to his feet without a smile but with a look of concern and defeat on his face.

As I took a seat, he began to speak. "What is going on?" he asked in his thick, Spanish accent.

"I know what it looks like, and I've got it covered," I replied.

"Well, it doesn't seem like it. I put you in charge for a reason, and you've failed me," he replied, and my heart sank to my feet.

"I know," was all I could say.

"You're not like your brother and sister, Marcy; you're stronger, wiser, and quicker. What your brother tried to be, you already are. Why must he be mixed in your street foolishness time and time again? You're just like my father!" he yelled.

My father was the one person I spoke to with respect, but today was not the day for insults.

"Street foolishness? Was it street foolishness when I damn near killed for you? When Royal and I kidnapped a witness for you to win a case? Was it all street foolishness to you then? News flash, *Papi*, Manuel was in the street life long before I even indulged in it, and he was damn good at it. He messed up this time because he attempted to do right in life and fell for the wrong girl. What happened to him was a love affair gone wrong, but I can assure you it will be handled. Oh, and please don't compare me to any of your family members that hate us," I whispered as I stared him in the eyes.

"I'm sure it will, and I didn't come to bring insults like your *Madre*. I just want my children to live and be happy. He's my only son for God's sake! I will never be the same if I lose him. What do you need from me to make sure this happens and goes away?" he asked.

"I'll be in touch," I responded, standing to leave.

"Sit down!" he yelled, and I rolled my eyes as I took a seat. "Now who is this love interest that has you leaving home and quitting school? Is he like Decari?" he said, referring to Royal by his real name.

"No, *Papa*, he's nothing like Royal. I care for him very much, and he treats me like a queen," I replied.

"And you're sure about him?" he asked.

"Yes, sir."

"OK, well I need to meet him before I leave Miami in a few days."

"That can be arranged. Well, I have to go, *Papa*. I'll catch you whenever you're ready to meet up. I love you," I hurriedly said as I stood to hug him goodbye. What I thought would be a thirty-minute lunch lasted an hour, and I didn't even eat shit.

"I like your new car!" I heard him yell as I waved goodbye.

Grabbing my Gucci shades out of my purse, I left. My father not only left a bad taste in my mouth, but his words brought back more memories of Royal that I tried to forget. In Atlanta, my father was a top criminal justice lawyer who had a great reputation for winning cases. That was until he was faced with his biggest challenge—winning a case against his ex-wife. My mother. She tore his ass up in court, and my father began to feel the pressure. Since he knew of Royal's involvement in the streets, he reached out and paid him and me to get rid of the witness.

Snapping back into reality, I realized that if I made it out alive, my life could be a movie.

With my ringing phone snapping me back to reality and displaying Khyrah's number again, against my better judgement, I picked it up.

"I promise I'm changing my number after today!" I yelled into the phone, riding down Collins.

"Marcy, just wait. I know where D-boy is, and I owe it to you to find him. I'm going to text you the address. Head there as soon as you get it. I don't know how long he will be there alone," she whispered, sounding a little shaken.

Not trusting her, I told her to send it before ending the call. I received the message immediately and headed there. Checking my glove compartment, I made sure my gun was there. I also called Rome to meet me there. I knew Ramel would kill me, but the only other person who wanted D-boy dead as much as me was Rome.

14

LYING BACK with my head pressed against the seats of the limo, I felt as if I were living a dream. Dressed in all-black Givenchy, I looked around to see a family with sadness, fear, hurt, and confusion written all over their faces. Ramel grabbed my hand tightly as the only twin I had left functioning on her own, Milan, rubbed my shoulder. With all of us hurting from our recent loss, I never thought it would come to death.

I looked over at Rome, and he caught my gaze and turned to look out the window. I knew this was a lot to deal with within a few weeks. What was supposed to be one of the best birthdays, my and my twin's experience left us with a pain that would forever stay. When we pulled up to the church, the doors opened as all of us exited the limos. I looked to my left to see my mother with tears in her eyes, giving support to others. Everyone began to line up as the family walked in to view the body while the friends waited.

My heart broke into a million pieces because this death, I knew deep down inside, was my fault. They say God makes no mistakes, but this time, I found that hard to believe. As the line began to move closer, my mind traveled back to the day that brought us here.

"Rome, I'm right around the corner. I rode around the large storage unit

three times. I don't see any cars or anything. And I don't see any cameras around this raggedy area either," I spoke into my phone.

"I'm about to pull up. Just follow me, and we can go inside and check it out. Whether she lying or not, I can't let that nigga get away with what he did to my boy," he assured.

Against my better judgement, I stopped the car and waited for Rome. He pulled up in no time, and we made our way to the storage unit up the road.

Getting out of the car, we both grabbed our weapons.

"Put these on," Rome said, handing me some gloves.

"Whatever happens, tell your sister I love her," Rome stated.

"And tell your brother I love him," I replied as we both smiled.

With Rome going first, we opened the unlocked door with our weapons drawn. The place was dark with one light shining on a chair in the middle of the floor. Walking closer, I saw Khyrah sitting in the chair with a gun hanging from her hand by her side.

Confused, I spoke first. "Khyrah, what the fuck is going on?" I asked with my gun still pulled.

Noticing I was there, she sat up and pointed the gun in her hand to her temple.

"Whoa, Khyrah, what the fuck you doing? Put that shit down!" Rome exclaimed.

"I can't do this anymore. I'm not strong enough to live this life. Look what I've done to you, Marcy, and worse, look what I did to your brother. This is all my fault! I don't deserve to live!" Khyrah cried.

"Wait, I know I said some fucked up shit out of anger, but this wasn't what I meant when I said leave me alone. You can't do this. I know it all seems fucked up, but my brother loves you, and he's going to pull through. We're the Gomez family; we don't die. Just put the gun down, and we can talk about all of this," I said, stepping closer.

"Don't take another step, or I'll pull the trigger," she replied, clocking the gun back.

Trying to think quickly, I motioned for Rome to step toward the back of her.

"Marcy, you hate me, and your brother hates me. Rome, I know you hate me. Your mom will hate me when she finds out the truth. Everyone will hate me. But don't worry. I'm going to fix this. You should've left me to die the night I was raped. But I fixed it. This storage is in D-boy's wife's name, and this gun is also registered in her name, so my death will be at the hands of her. Just tell my mother I love her. Tell your brother he was always the better man, and when he finds someone to really love him, I'll be smiling from up above. You were a great friend, Marcy, and for the record, I never lost my memory. I knew this day would come the night you killed Ramel's girlfriend for me. I was never in love with D-boy or your brother... I was in love with you," Khyrah spoke.

With that last statement, I was taken off guard, and before I could yell for Rome to tackle her to the ground, a bright light flashed, and the gun went off. Brains and blood covered the floor as her body fell to the ground. Rome was stuck with his gun at his side while I looked on in confusion. I had so many unanswered questions that would now be forever sealed. Rome, snapping back to reality, grabbed my arm and pulled me toward the door to leave.

Running outside, I fell and began to cry hysterically. I didn't know why or what had just happened. All I knew was that my best friend had confessed her love for me before taking her own life.

"Marcy, you too gangster to be acting like a dumb white girl right now. Get the fuck up and get out of here before we end up in jail for this shit," Rome whispered so no one would hear us.

Jumping up, still crying, I ran to my car with my gun still in hand. I placed it in my trunk and put the safety back on. I hopped in my car and pulled off, heading home with Rome right behind me. I didn't know how I was able to drive home. I walked into the house with darkness surrounding me, but my mind couldn't even register what was going on at the moment. I walked into the room to see Ramel getting dressed. I passed him without saying one word and went into the bathroom. Opening the shower door, I turned the hot water on and stepped into the shower fully dressed. Dropping to the shower floor, I stared into space as the hot water covered my body and began to soak my jeans and shirt. Thinking back, I didn't even realize that I still had my gloves on as well.

"Marcy, are you OK?" Ramel asked behind the shower door. Unable to speak, I remained quiet.

Opening the door, I felt the cold air seep in and take over the hot water heat. With his clothes still on, he dropped to his knees and began taking off my clothes. He started with my hoodie, throwing the wet clothing onto the bathroom floor. Then he unbuttoned my jeans, sliding them down my wet body.

I remained in a state of shock the whole time. Out of all of the dead bodies I'd seen and the couple I was responsible for, this one, I just couldn't believe happened. And although I didn't pull the trigger, I was the one to blame for the death of my best friend. Now fully naked, Ramel began to remove his clothes as well. With our bodies standing as if we were one, Ramel grabbed the soap and a rag off the rod and began to wash me.

"I know you in a state of shock, but you're going to have to tell me what happened, Marcy, so I can help you. Tell me what happened, baby, so I can help you deal with this shit," Ramel pleaded.

As much as I wanted to reply, I was mute, and my mind was traveling far away from my body.

"Khyrah is dead," I spoke, not knowing where those words came from.

Walking closer to the casket, I couldn't even muster up the tears to cry. I felt as if I were all cried out. I watched as my mother held and comforted Khyrah's mother as she broke down at the casket.

Not being able to take anymore, I released Ramel's hand and ran out of the church. Finding the limo, I opened the door and took a seat inside. Placing my head on the window, the tears I thought left came back and flooded my face.

"I'm so sorry, Khyrah," I whispered to myself.

The only grateful part was the anonymous tip about Khyrah's body being in the storage unit and D-boy's wife not having a solid alibi. She was now under investigation for Khyrah's murderer and would be awaiting trial soon. D-boy was nowhere to be found, and after all this shit, that was in his best interest.

If Ramel needed anyone to take D-boy's spot, I thought it was the perfect time to put my street skills back in the game or allow me the ability to find someone who could. Scamming was easy and made me plenty of money, but the shit was too much work, too much computer shit, too much covering your ass, and too many hit-or-miss situations.

I closed my eyes. My head was hurting, and I needed to get away. What I really needed was for my brother to wake up and be OK. I needed the other piece of me to be out here keeping me sane and telling me whether I was making the right decision or not. I felt empty right now, and through it all, Ramel had been nothing but a great support system, but I knew he was tired of the constant drama.

With my mind drifting to sleep, I felt a pair of hands grab me and pull me into an embrace.

"I think we need a vacation. How about we leave town tonight? Too much shit been happening way too fast. We need some time to ourselves," he spoke.

"I agree," I replied, falling asleep in his arms.

MIDNIGHT...

Grabbing my luggage, Ramel escorted us to the first-class terminal. I still had yet to find out where we were going, but at this point, I did not care. I tried to block out all my thoughts of the past few weeks as we walked toward the terminal. Before I headed out of town, I stopped by the hospital, still acting as I were my sister to see my brother and keep him up to date with the current events. The only thing I would wait to share was the fact that Khyrah was gone forever.

"Baby, the focus for this trip is for you to relax and enjoy yourself. I feel bad that you're going through all this shit. So if I can help you in any way, allow me to do that," Ramel stated, knocking me out my train of thought. Taking a deep breath and then releasing it, I agreed to enjoy a peaceful time with just us two. Handing the tickets to the lady, we boarded the flight.

"Have a great time in Colombia," she recited.

I looked at Ramel, and he began to explain immediately.

"Oh, I figured since this is a part of your heritage, and you've never been here, you could experience your first time here with me since I've never been here either," he admitted. I knew better than to believe that shit. Ramel had business to handle here and felt bad leaving me behind.

"I would rather be here with you than anywhere else," I replied. Ramel didn't know my family's history. All he knew was that I was half Colombian and black and that I didn't speak with my Colombian family at all. Taking a seat on the plane, I became a little nervous. Vacationing in Colombia meant I could come in contact with family and not even know it. I didn't even know how my grandfather looked, but I assumed like my father.

"You're alright?" Ramel checked.

"Umm, yes, I'm cool. Just thinking to myself," I replied, taking a seat.

"Thinking what?" he inquired.

"About us. I really appreciate your patience with me, and since the day we met, it's been nothing but non-stop drama. I'm surprised you haven't been thinking about leaving me yet. Everything has just happened so fast. I know I question you all the time, but some shit just seems too good to be true after all I've been through," I expressed.

"That, I can understand, but you have to realize you're not the only one who's been through shit and had it hard. Just because I don't broadcast it doesn't mean problems don't exist for me. Marcy, I want you to understand something. I didn't fall in love with your surroundings. I fell in love with you. My mother always told me if they make your heart skip a beat with their presence alone, then you might need to take a second look at them. I question a lot of shit, but how I feel is never a question. A nigga had the chance to become the man in my city at a young age, but them groupies and dick pullers never knew the real me or even cared to know. All they wanted to know was what a nigga like me could supply them with. But with you, it's like when you look at me, you stare straight through to my soul. That's why I quit playing the cat and mouse game and came at you hard," Ramel said.

I smiled at his honesty, but there was one thing I needed to know for sure.

"Did you fuck that girl I jumped on in the projects?" I questioned.

Staring straight into my eyes, Ramel blinked twice. "I did not fuck her. I'm a man, so I'm going to say this the right way. The bitch did give me head, but it wasn't until after you whooped her ass and left for a few days. I know I fucked up, and that's not what you want to hear, but that shit just happened. I haven't spoken to the bitch since then, and I don't plan too, because I love you, Marcy."

I rolled my eyes. A piece of me was pissed because the day I spent sulking and being sad over him, he was out getting his dick wet. I could respect him for his honesty on the matter, and I refused to allow this bitch to mess up my vacation. So for now, I'd just push his buttons to see how much he really cared.

"Glad you could be honest about it. So you mean to tell me while I was out sad and tripping over you, your ass was enjoying head from a hood bitch? You know what? Don't worry. When we get back home, I'll pack my things and leave," I replied, smiling on the inside because the look on his face was priceless.

"Marcy, you not going no-fucking-where unless it's in a body bag. Let's get this straight because I could have lied to your ass about that wack ass head that hoe gave me. But I didn't. I told you the truth, and now we're here. Don't let that hoe ruin our trip. Plus, we got too much ahead of us. I want you to push all that shit with Khyrah, that hood bitch, D-boy, etcetera out your mind," he replied. His ass didn't know what to say after I told him I would leave, because that foolishness he just allowed to leave his mouth was beyond hilarious. Ramel would definitely pay for his little slip up, but leaving my man was never a thought in my mind. But his little angry outburst was kind of cute.

Throwing the towel in, I leaned forward and kissed Ramel's lips as he smiled. Grabbing his hand, I relaxed my head against the plush seats as I prepared my mind for this eleven-hour flight. Closing my eyes, I reached in my bag to pop a pill that helped relax my mind on many occasions.

COLOMBIA...

I was awakened by the sound of the flight attendant welcoming us to Colombia. She began to speak of the tourist attractions that we could check out during our stay here.

Standing to his feet, Ramel grabbed my hand, pulling me up to stand beside him. I guess he wanted to be one of the first ones off the plane. I kept up with his quick pace, and we stepped off the plane, making our exit. We didn't have to check baggage claim, because the little carry-on bag I had was all I brought. He didn't want us to bring any real luggage since we would be shopping anyway.

Walking toward the double doors that led to the outside, I saw someone holding a sign that said the Browns. I attempted to take in everything I was seeing at the moment, but since he was moving so fast, the scenery at the moment was short lived. Quickly hopping in the car, I realized it was a limo that would carry us to the *Casa* resort we would be staying at.

"Why are you moving so fast?" I questioned.

"Because I'm horny as hell, and we have dinner plans with a couple of friends later," he answered.

"You're just full of so many surprises, aren't you?" I asked sarcastically.

"Not really. I just have to run some things by an old friend who happens to live here," he admitted.

"That Louis Vuitton Bamboo purse I showed you the other day... I want the black and the red one," I responded, obviously annoyed. Those purses together were an easy six grand. He agreed to buying me one and told me I would have to buy the other with my own money. I guessed he was eating those words now.

"I'll take you to get them tomorrow." He laughed.

I didn't know how to take Ramel at times. I was used to knowing what I was getting myself into from the beginning with a man. But with Ramel, shit seemed like a mystery most of the time, which was another reason I stayed with him. The fear of not knowing kept my curious ass on my feet with him.

Sitting in the limo, he grabbed me close to him, kissing on my face and body.

"Baby, just chill until we get to the resort," I demanded.

"You know how long a nigga had to wait to get this pussy? Don't trip now. Blame that wet ass shit between your legs." He laughed.

Grabbing me to straddle him, he motioned for me to release his manhood from his Versace briefs. Grabbing my tights, he pulled them off. Sitting exposed, I quickly covered his Johnson with my juices.

"Damn, this shit so wet, baby, fuckkkk!" he yelled. "I knew you wanted this dick," he spoke, grabbing my waist, pushing deeper inside as I rode his shaft for dear life.

I rolled my hips in a circular motion before I began to bounce my ass up and down his shaft. I began to get into the groove once his moans became louder. But that shit was short lived because before I knew it, Ramel had filled my insides with his love.

Getting off him, I looked at his ass breathing hard as if he had just run a damn marathon.

"Damn, that was fast," I admitted.

"I know. I couldn't hold that shit in. Don't worry. I'll tear your ass up later," he replied, buckling his Balmain jeans.

Putting back on my tights, I couldn't do anything but smile. That was our second time having full-blown sex since my birthday night, and I needed a nut more than his ass did.

As we arrived at the resort, it was like a place straight out of a magazine. There were tropical trees everywhere, and the pool led into the ocean. The room we were escorted to was a mini home built out of straw, clay, and bamboo. From the outside, it looked raggedy, but the moment we stepped inside, we saw the place was installed with marble floors and countertops.

There were smart TVs everywhere from the living room to the kitchen, which had stainless steel appliances. The kitchen also had a tray full of fruit and finger sandwiches. We began to walk around, down the hallway that led to the bedroom.

The bedroom was equipped with a queen-size canopy bed and plush white covers and pillows. There were rose petals spread around the covers that read 'welcome.' Looking around some more, I walked into the bathroom that held a jacuzzi-style tub and a shower adjacent from it with a detachable shower head. The bathroom mirror took over half the wall in the bathroom with lights that decorated it.

I was in pure heaven. Ramel had outdone himself. He knew exactly what I needed. Before I knew it, I had undressed myself and pulled my hair up. Reaching for the shower door, I looked around for the handle to turn the hot water on, but there wasn't any. Standing naked and cold, I spoke out loud.

"Where's the hot water!" I shouted to no one in particular. But to my surprise, the hot water came on. I guess it worked by voice command. Opening the roll of soap, I grabbed a sponge cloth off the door and began to lather my rag as the hot water soaked my body.

I wasn't surprised when I felt Ramel step into the shower and take the rag from my hand. He began by slowly washing my back softly. He was really acting like Prince Charming. I knew he had a sweet side, but lately, he'd been working overtime. I knew he was just trying to get me to feel better, but I didn't want a pity party because I was sad.

"You don't have to be so nice just because I'm sad and going through a lot," I spoke as he washed down my legs. "Ramel, I know you hear me talking to you!" I yelled, but still, I got no response.

"Here you go, questioning me again. All you have to do is let a nigga know if he wasting his time. All this second-guessing is getting annoying. A nigga tired of explaining himself to you. I don't know what you're used to, but if it's too much to handle to the point you keep questioning me, then go be with the last nigga that treated your ass like street royalty," he replied before exiting the shower.

I felt like a ton of bricks had fallen on me. I didn't expect him to react like that. I knew Ramel was a good dude, and I did have a habit of comparing him and Royal. The way Royal treated me, I thought it was like a man should treat his woman. Although I killed with Royal, set niggas up so he could make money, and even kicked a few bitches ass about him, I felt like no one loved me the way he did.

True enough, we had our problems. We fought on some occasions, but we loved even harder. It was just so different with Ramel. He was interested in pleasing me, making sure I was happy, and making smart moves. With Royal, I broke my neck to make him happy and to prove to him that I could handle his lifestyle. Things were changing, and it had me second-guessing if I deserved someone like Ramel.

Finishing my shower, I decided to allow him some time to himself as I lay across the bed completely naked. Resting my eyes for a second, I ended up dozing off into a deep slumber.

~

THREE HOURS LATER...

"Marcy, get up and get dressed. We have a dinner date tonight, and I need you to get right!" Ramel shouted from the bathroom.

Opening my eyes, I looked around the moonlit room. Sitting up, I stood to my feet with the towel still wrapped around me. Looking at the time, I noticed it was seven in the evening.

"How can I get dressed if I didn't bring any clothes?" I asked, walking in the bathroom to see Ramel brushing his teeth. Without a word, he pointed behind him to a hanger that held a mid-thigh, red, tube dress and Louboutin, So Kate nude pumps to match, and a red and nude clutch. He must have gone shopping while I was asleep, and the saleswoman helped him pick this out.

Grabbing my carry-on bag, I placed my makeup on the counter, and I prepped to apply.

Looking over at Ramel, I could still tell he had an attitude that I knew I had to fix. "You mad at me?" I blurted out.

"Naw," he replied.

"Well, why yo—" I began saying as he walked out of the bathroom

as if I weren't speaking to him. "So you're going to act like an asshole!"
I yelled to his back as he ignored me.

"I swear this nigga can really strike a nerve," I said to myself.

After finishing my makeup, I spruced up my thirty-inch, jet-black
Mink Brazilian hair. After brushing my teeth and applying lotion, I
finally squeezed into my new dress. Ramel definitely outdid himself
with this dress. It hugged every curve; even my little breasts sat just
right. I put on my shoes and grabbed my clutch.

Admiring myself in the mirror, I looked damn good, and I knew if
his ass continued to be mad after seeing me in this dress, then I
would have to work overtime to fix this. Spraying on my perfume, I
was finally ready to take my position beside my man. Walking into
the living room, I noticed Ramel sitting on the couch in an all-black
velvet Armani suit with black Drivers to match.

He stood to his feet after noticing me. He looked me up and down
as if I were a snack. I smiled as he turned away and headed toward
the door. Guessing that was my cue to follow, I walked to the limo
and opened my own door to get in. Ramel sat with his head facing
the other direction as we pulled off. At this point, I couldn't allow our
trip to be like this, but I hated being the bigger person.

"Ramel, can you please stop being mad at me?" I asked sweetly.

"That depends. Are you going to stop acting like a little girl?" he
replied.

"Really? So you think just because I have trust issues, I'm acting
like a little girl? You know what, nigga? Fuck it. You can't blame me
for the shit that I been through. You knew what this consisted of from
the beginning, so if you can't take it, then fuck it!" I yelled, pissed at
his response.

"That's cool with me. Fuck it then. You making me pay for
another nigga mistakes, so you think that shit is not supposed to
piss me off, Marcy. We have been doing this trust issue dance for
damn near five months now. I don't know what the fuck you want
from me, but either you learn to trust a nigga, or you can step
because this shit is really a turn off," he spoke, looking dead into my
eyes.

"How the fuck you say that when you just had a whole bitch sucking your dick!" I challenged.

"And why the fuck did that happen? Your insecure, trust issues having ass allowed a hood hoe who has been wanting this dick since high school fill your head up with lies. So instead of talking to a nigga, you assumed and made a fool of yourself."

"Oh, you're really taking it there tonight, aren't you? Regardless of how I reacted, you had no business allowing that hoe any access to what's mine whether we going through a rough patch or not. That's signs of a weak ass fuck nigga," I challenged.

Taking a few moments to laugh, Ramel's anger was visible. "One thing I won't tolerate is being called out of my name. Maybe you should try sucking my dick as viciously as you just spit them words out your mouth. Let me let you in on a little secret," Ramel stated, moving closer as I jumped back. "Oh, don't worry. I'm not gonna put my hands on you. If I have to whoop your ass for you to act right, then I damn sure don't need you. So no need to run from me," he said, noticing my body jump when he moved.

"Just back the fuck up and leave me alone. I'm done with this," I replied, turning away.

"You got a lot to learn," Ramel stated as he reached over me and opened the door. I didn't notice that the car had come to a complete stop.

"Get the fuck out," he instructed as he exited the vehicle as well. He walked around the car, taking the lead as I followed behind. We walked into the restaurant, and there was a live band playing, with many tables scattered everywhere. The place was dim lit and smelled delicious. Still pissed, I remained quiet as Ramel talked to a hostess.

"He's waiting for you," she replied. Ramel turned and grabbed my hand.

"All I need you to do is act right for the night. Whatever happened in the limo, we will talk about later," he assured, telling me to fake as if we were the best couple in the world at the moment when, in reality, I wanted to shank his ass right then and there.

Rolling my eyes, I grabbed his hand as we followed the server to the top floor that overlooked the many tables and entertainment below. Arriving at our expected table, my eyes scanned the table. I noticed two black girls and one older Colombian man that sported black and gray hair. His features were very handsome as he stood in his long-sleeve Versace button-up, slacks, and loafers that caught my eyes.

"Hola, Ramel. Long time, my friend," he greeted.

"Likewise, *Papi*," Ramel returned as they embraced in a hug.

"This is my girlfriend, Marcy," he introduced. I stepped from behind Ramel to be in full view as the man he referred to as *Papi* reached out to grab my hand. Holding it for a second, he kissed it and offered us a seat.

The two black women stared.

"Oh, where are my manners? This is Kimberly and Jasmine, my wife and girlfriend," *Papi* expressed.

"Hello," they both greeted. They looked to be not much older than myself.

"Let me get a round of drinks for the ladies!" *Papi* shouted as the hostess rushed off to put the order in.

"So, my friend, what brings you here?" *Papi* asked Ramel.

"Business as usual. D-boy is out. Some shit popped off, and he's missing, so we need to take another route," Ramel stated, getting straight to the point.

"That seems to be a serious problem," *Papi* replied.

"I know, and I wouldn't have come to you, but I'm out of options at this point. The money we will lose from D-boy's area will be a major loss, and I know how you feel about that."

"Indeed, you do, and you also know that once all debts are paid, that will be the day you can live freely. Now, I agreed to this, even allowing your workers to deal my drugs, respecting the fact that your father didn't want you to touch any drugs, but this seems like you will have to get your hands dirty this time, Ramel," *Papi* suggested. Ramel immediately shook his head in defeat.

"It's bad enough my father died in your debt of three million. I've paid you one; just give me some time. I'll figure this out," Ramel replied, defeated as I got an earful. I grabbed his hand, reassuring him it would all be OK. I knew how much it meant to Ramel to keep his promise to his late father. But when you couldn't beat them, you joined them until you found a way.

"We got this," I whispered low enough for only Ramel to hear. He sat up, and I knew my words had made him feel a little better. It was the truth. I had my man's back no matter what.

"Well, while your figuring things out, I guess you will be taking over D-boy's area until further notice. And since I like you, young man, I'll send my nephew, Jose, over to watch over things for you. Should you have any problems, he will be at your use," *Papi* added.

Ramel sat firmly, agreeing, but in his mind, the world was over. The moment the waitress came back with the drinks, he downed two immediately.

"Now let's party!" *Papi* yelled, standing to his feet, grabbing his women to join. I looked over at Ramel, who was taking another shot. I grabbed one to join him before standing to my feet and joining the fun. I pulled him up and began dancing on him as his liquor took effect in his body.

"*Tú hablas español?*" *Papi* leaned in and asked me as we all danced.

"*Hablo un poco de español*" I replied, letting him know I spoke a little Spanish.

"What are you mixed with?" he asked, reverting back to English.

"Colombian and Black," I replied.

"I thought so. What's your name?" he inquired in his thick accent.

"Marcy," I replied, giving him my real name for the simple fact that he could find out my whole family history if he wanted to.

"Last name," he said.

"Gomez," I replied.

"Marcy Gomez, do you know your *familia* from here?" he questioned, which began to make me uncomfortable.

"No, I've never met them," I admitted.

"You should ask your father about your *familia*. I know a lot of Gomezes from this area. If you're a part of their *familia,* then you should definitely find out," he replied, grabbing a drink and pulling his women closer.

Ramel was now feeling good and obviously ready for some pussy with the way he grabbed me close. As I stared at *Papi,* it dawned on me that I never told him whether my mother or father was Columbian. All I admitted to was being mixed.

The night winded down, and although my mind was in many different places, it was time to go. I exchanged numbers with *Papi's* wife and girlfriend. They turned out to be cool.

"Ramel, my friend, I hope to see you before you depart back home. Matter of fact, I like your woman. You guys stop by *mi casa* on your way out for breakfast," *Papi* invited.

"We leave in two days. We will definitely stop by," Ramel agreed, knowing better than to decline his invitation.

After giving everyone hugs, we were back in the limo, headed to our villa. Ramel was fucked up, but he was doing a great job of keeping his composure. I sat back, feeling bad about our argument earlier. Being younger, it was hard not to show my true age at times. But I also knew this was one argument that could've been avoided, and after everything I'd been going through lately, I needed peace in some area of my life.

"I'm sorry," I blurted out, breaking the silence.

"I'm sorry too. A nigga didn't mean that shit. I just want this shit to last, and I need to make sure your head is in this as well. A lot of shit is about to change, and I just need to make sure you rocking with a nigga," he replied.

"I got your back, boy," I answered, kissing his lips, and just like that, we were making love as if it were our first time.

15

"A NIGGA AIN'T NEVER RODE horses," Ramel said as we finished riding along the beach. Grabbing my hand, he pulled me into the water.

"Baby, I can't swim!" I yelled as we went further into the salt water.

Stopping before we went too far, Ramel looked into my eyes.

"This is where I leave you. If you trust me or willing to allow yourself to trust me, then going deep into this water means you know I won't let anything happen to you. If you don't trust me, then I'll leave you here, and you can get back to shore and go about your business."

Looking into his brown eyes, I scanned his long dreads that were halfway wet. His muscles glistened from the water and sun reflecting off his skin. I knew this was yet another test because we couldn't have a relationship without trust. And after everything this far, I thought I was finally ready to trust Ramel. Grabbing his hand, I wrapped my arms around his neck and my legs around his waist.

Smiling from ear to ear, Ramel continued to go deeper in the water. Still able to stand in the water, Ramel stopped again. I was still holding on to him, knowing that I couldn't reach the bottom anymore since I was shorter than him.

"Let go. I'm about to teach you how to swim."

"Umm, no, I'm good."

"Just give me your hand. Just like this. I promise I'll never let anything happen to you that I wouldn't let happen to me first. Now lean back into my hands," he directed.

I turned around and lay on my back with his hands underneath me. I was scared as hell, as the water began to gather around my face.

"It's OK, baby. Just breathe. Now slowly move your arms and kick your legs. Then we going to turn around and do it on your stomach," he said. We stayed practicing this position for thirty minutes until I was finally able to float and hold myself up in the water.

"Look at you, gorgeous. You think you're a pro now, huh?" he said, laughing as I lay on my back. With his hand under my bottom, Ramel tugged at my bikini bottoms, pulling them off. "Hold yourself up. I got you," he said, still holding on, spreading my legs apart. As he pulled my exposed pussy closer to his face, I grabbed my bikini bottoms out of his hand.

With my legs sitting on his shoulders, I sat up as he buried his face into my sweet spot. He wasted no time parting my pussy lips and replacing his fingers with his tongue. I moved my hips as I gripped his head as his tongue went up and down my clit. With his left hand holding my ass in position on his face, he used his free hand to finger my warm, pink insides. With every lick, suck, and finger stick, my body jerked with pleasure and excitement.

Maybe it was the rush of fucking in the middle of the ocean, knowing someone could see us, or maybe it was the satisfaction of experiencing sexual pleasure in a crazy place with someone I not only loved but trusted as well.

Whatever it was, for the first time in my life, I released the best part of me onto my man's face that flowed freely away in the water. My body felt like it wasn't inside me anymore as if I had just given all of me to his tongue.

"Shit, I love you, Ramel!" I shouted as he released my leg, and I slid down his body. I held my arms around his waist, too weak and scared to move anymore. Grabbing my hands, he took my bikini bottoms and slid them back on my body.

"Aye, Marcy," he said as he pulled me around to his back. "I love you too," he said as we made our way back to shore.

We walked on the shore as he made sure I could stand up straight. Grabbing my bag, I reached inside and handed him his jewelry and phone.

"We can walk back to our villa. It's not far. I'mma need you to pack everything up. We actually going to lunch with *Papi* in a couple of hours. He having some type of party and want us to swing through, but I don't plan to stay long," Ramel revealed.

"Oh, OK. Baby, can I ask you something? How long have you been dealing with *Papi*? And do you know his real name?" I inquired.

"Naw, I don't know his real name, but I've been dealing with him for a few years now. He actually good people. He's been like a father figure since my parents died. It's just when it comes to business, that's one area he doesn't fuck around with. My father owed him a lot of money when he died, and to keep him from taking over my family's businesses and losing everything, I made him a deal he couldn't refuse, and he took the amount owed down to three million. That's why I do fraud, supply the hood with drugs, and run my family business. After this debt is paid, we can live our lives as we choose; and if I make it out, I plan to get as far away from this lifestyle as I can," he confessed. I always thought his lifestyle was a choice, but to know he did this to protect his family made me love him even more.

"Baby, don't worry. We are in this together. We are going to figure out how to make this money together. And when this is all over, we can move away, get married, make babies, and live happily ever after," I replied, feeling like a kid in a candy store, floating on a cloud.

"I definitely plan to do all of that and more, but it's bad enough I've let you in this far. I can't bring you in on this. It's too dangerous. Promise me you will just have my back and understand that shit is about to change," Ramel pleaded.

"But baby, I can help you. I kno—"

"I don't want to hear shit about what another nigga taught you or had you out here doing. I know in the beginning before we started dating, I had you out here working, but now you're mine. No nigga that claim he loves you will put you in harm's way over any money. That's little boy shit. Like I stated before, just have a nigga back. Figure out what business you want to open up, cook, clean, fuck me on the regular, and don't stress. And I'll do my best to keep you happy." Those words that just left his mouth pissed me off but also turned me the fuck on. We walked closer to our villa, and I was ready for a hot shower. There was no need to speak any words. It was evident that I had to take a back seat and be his woman, not a rider.

I walked into our home for one more day and retired to the bedroom shower. Ramel went into the living room on his phone. I grabbed my phone to text my sister, Milan, checking in on our brother and Rome. Assuring me that everyone was OK, she sent me a picture of her at our house, wearing my new Burberry bikini. I was more than sure she and Rome had been living it up since we'd been gone. I smiled at her little round belly before texting her to take my shit off.

Grabbing my towel, I untied my hair and went into the shower to wash whatever the ocean water left off my body.

Taking what felt like a thirty-minute shower, I felt refreshed and ready for the day. Deciding not to wear any makeup, I dried off and applied lotion all over my body. With my towel wrapped around my body, I went in search of Ramel.

Walking into the living room, I found him on the couch, asleep. Watching his chest move up and down, I couldn't believe that I was actually falling for someone else other than Royal. Everything about Ramel screamed real man, and the more time I spent with him, the more I realized that the love I felt for him was different than any I ever felt.

Dropping to my knees, I decided to wake him up with a mouthful of pleasure. Pulling his pants down, releasing his manhood, I grabbed his piece and placed my mouth all the way to the end of his shaft as I began sucking. After two licks, he grabbed my head, pushing it further down.

"Hell no, nigga! You need to take a shower; your shit taste like salt!" I yelled, referring to the ocean water we had just came out of.

"Duh, from the beach water. Your shit tasted salty too, but I dealt with that shit to please you," Ramel returned as he got up to go take a shower.

"Wash, or I throw up on your dick. You choose!" I yelled at his back as he went to wash his body. I thought about joining him but decided against it since we had plans.

I went into the bathroom to finish getting ready. Within minutes, I was dressed in an olive-green half shirt and matching wide-legged pants. I threw my hair into a high ponytail and put on some gold hoop earrings.

Waiting for Ramel, I walked outside to enjoy the scenery.

"You ready, beautiful?" I heard a voice ask as I looked around. Wrapping his arms around my waist, he kissed my neck. I wrapped my arms around his neck and kissed his lips. "We have to go, baby," he spoke grabbing my hand and pulling me toward the car that was waiting for us. I looked him up and down as the diamonds on his Rolex danced from the sunlight. His dreads were neatly twisted to perfection, and he was dressed in Givenchy Moto jogger pants with a red and white Givenchy shirt to match.

"You look great, baby," I complimented as we headed toward *Papi's* estate.

The ride seemed as if it took forever. I dozed off a few times and decided to give Ramel head to help the time pass. Right as he burst in my mouth, I sat up to swallow his kids. As we pulled up to the gate of the estate, I sat in awe as the gate opened, and we pulled up to the biggest mansion I had ever seen in person. There were men standing around, holding rifle scopes, nine millimeters, and shotguns. This place looked like it came straight out of a magazine. The house was gold and white with Versace symbols and print all around the outside. The ground walking up to the door was done in marble with gold and black Versace print.

Papi greeted us at the door in his Versace robe and slippers. I laughed at his young swag although he was old enough to be someone's grandfather. Stepping out the car, I followed Ramel's lead as we walked inside *Papi's* home. He greeted me with a kiss to the cheek.

"Welcome to *mi casa!*" he yelled in his thick accent. Looking around, I saw women in bathing suits running around. I noticed older and younger men and women. I even saw children running around. The house had an indoor pool where children and women were jumping in, enjoying themselves.

"You guys hungry? I figured since you guys are used to eating a certain way, we would do barbeque on top of the rice, beans, empanadas, and pastelitos de carne. Whatever you don't see, my chef can make," he offered. I was in shock. My father made many Spanish dishes, and once the divorce happened, I hadn't had any since then. My mouth watered for everything, and I instantly became excited. I looked around. This looked like a real family; the countless laughs, affection, and love shown made me yearn for a real family again. Clutching Ramel's hand tightly, I hoped one day we could share this kind of love with our own family.

"Come take a walk with me. Let me show you my *familia,*" *Papi* instructed us but looked directly at me. Following his lead, we walked down a long hallway where family photos were displayed everywhere.

"You see, this here is my late wife, Rosa. A beauty, she was, and very special to me. She gave me three sons and wanted a daughter so bad, but that never happened," *Papi* explained, looking at the photo. She was beautiful.

Walking further down, we were shown pictures of his mother, father, sisters, and cousins.

"Here are my boys. Jose, my youngest, Geraldo, my middle child, and that last one right there is my oldest," he spoke as he took a step back for us to look.

I walked closer and looked over all the handsome teenage boys in the pictures and stopped when I reached his last son. As I looked up, there were guns pointed toward my and Ramel's head while *Papi* met my glaze.

"Now I want the truth. How long have you known?" he questioned as we stood frozen like deer caught in headlights. I was sure by now Ramel was confused, but after looking at that picture, I knew exactly what his words meant.

"Would it matter if I told the truth right now or not? It wouldn't change the truthful fact that I just realized who you were after seeing my father in the pictures of your sons."

"Wait, *Papa,* this is Manuel's daughter?" one of the gunmen asked.

"Hold your pistol up, Jose. She and her little boyfriend think they can play me," he instructed.

"I think she's telling the truth, Papa," his other son Geraldo inserted.

"Kill them!" *Papi* yelled as he turned to walk away.

"Wait, wait! I have no reason to lie! I've only been dating Ramel for a few months. I had no idea who you were or even that you were still alive. I thought you hated us and would kill us if you ever met my twins and me because my father married my mother—a black woman—and escaped your empire," I surrendered.

My grandfather, *Papi,* burst into laughter along with everyone else.

"Is that what your *Papa* told you? He could always come up with good lie. Maybe that's why he became a lawyer. Come and sit with me in my office. We need to talk. Your uncles, Jose and Geraldo, will escort you there," he said as he proceeded to walk away. Ramel never flinched or acted out of character. In a weird way, he acted as if he accepted his fate even if it were because of me.

I took a seat in the plush black chairs that sat in front of *Papi's* black hardwood desk. His office was huge and held bookshelves with books filled up to the ceiling.

"Now how is my son Manuel?" *Papi* questioned.

"He's fine. My mother and him have divorced, and he's dating a white woman," I admitted.

"You spoke of twin siblings, so there are three of you? I know you're the oldest, and the twins are younger than you, correct?" he inquired.

"Oh, no! I'm the oldest by five minutes. We are triplets. I'm Marcy, my brother Manuel Jr., and my sister Milan."

After that statement, he twisted his face in confusion and shook his head.

"Tell me more about yourself," he added.

I looked at Ramel, who shook his head for me to continue with the truth.

"There's not much to say. I'm the problem child, so I get in trouble often. My mother and I don't get along. In fact, I don't live with her at all. I push the limits and live my life. I also make my own money and have found a way to do that since I was old enough to walk. There's not much to me. I don't trust easily, and some might say I'm a firecracker," I said, looking into his eyes.

"Just like me, and as far as your mother, she's always been that way. Don't let her get to you. But I will say your story seems to be missing a couple of pieces, but I'll allow your father and mother to reveal that truth," he replied. "I never thought I would see this day," he spoke, pulling a picture out of his drawer and handing it to me.

I looked at the picture, and it was a photo of me as a baby.

"Why am I the only one you have a picture of in your desk?" I asked. Shrugging his shoulders, he stood to his feet.

"Come. Let's meet your *familia*," he spoke as we stood and followed his lead. My mind was in overdrive, but I definitely had plans of asking my mother and father the truth about their relationship with my grandfather.

We ate, danced, and talked all night. I met aunts, uncles, cousins, etcetera. I was overjoyed and felt at home. I felt complete. I noticed Ramel sitting back, watching as I danced with my little cousins and tried different foods with my aunts. Something was telling me that this family loved my father, and the reason he kept us away was a lot deeper than the wack ass lie he told.

The night began to peek through the sky, and Ramel and I had a flight to catch back home, so it was time to wrap this reunion up.

"I'm having the time of my life, baby," I said, hugging Ramel as we looked around for *Papi*.

"I know, and I'm happy for you. Let's find *Papi* and get out of here," he replied.

"I'll take you to him," Jose spoke from behind us.

We both followed him down a long hallway that led into the ground under the house. The deeper we walked, the worse the smell became. I knew many smells, and the one for death, I was very familiar with. Walking toward an open steel door, we walked into a room that resembled a vault. I looked around, and there were men standing around, two men strapped to chairs. My grandfather stood in the middle, speaking Spanish as the bloody men begged for their lives.

"Nice of you to join us. These two are your cousins Amiro and Lesido. This is what happens when you steal from the *familia* and mess with the enemy. Any last words, you dick lechon?" he spat.

They both cried out in pain and prayers. As gruesome as this scene was, I found excitement in their begging at the hands of my family. That kind of power made my blood rise with excitement and a sense of respect.

"I have a better idea. Hand them your guns," *Papi* instructed two of his gunmen, pointing at Ramel and me. Taking the gun from their hands, I pointed it straight toward the head of one of the men strapped to the chair. Ramel held his gun, waiting for instructions.

"Seems like you've done this before, but I don't think you have it in you to kill this man. He has a whole family. His wife has cancer, and if he dies, his children will be foster kids. You sure you have it in you to make this kill? Who knows? I'm an old man; I could be wrong," he egged on, but I knew what he was doing—calling my bluff.

Without a thought I let off two rounds into the forehead of the man sitting in the chair. I heard two more shots behind mine, indicating that Ramel also killed the other man. Blood and brains filled the room as the men began cleaning up our mess. My grandfather looked on with a look of shock and admiration in his eyes.

"Welcome to your real *familia*," he spoke, grabbing the gun from my hand. Although I'd killed before, something about this felt different as if I had sold my soul. We all turned to make an exit out of the vault.

"Get them cleaned up, and see that they make it home our way and with the drugs," *Papi* demanded.

I looked at Ramel, knowing we were both thinking the same thing. Regardless of what he said earlier, we were in this together— ride or die.

16

A MONTH LATER...

"WHO THE FUCK keep calling your phone private, Marcy!" Ramel yelled, grabbing my phone.

"I don't know! I keep telling you that!" I replied.

"Hello, who the fuck is this!" he yelled into my phone as the caller hung up.

"Change your number," he said as he exited out the house to start his day. Since coming back from Colombia a month ago, our lives have been busy. He slept all day and stayed out all night while I took care of home, counted countless amounts of money daily and focused on getting my GED. I was honestly bored and itching for action, but Ramel refused to accept my assistance. So to pass the time, I hooked back up with his crew that did fraud and got my hands dirty two days out of the week without him knowing.

Making sure he was gone, I ran into my closet and opened my Gucci shoe box to retrieve my brown paper bag. Opening the bag, I pulled the box out of it and went into our bathroom to take the test. Opening the box, I pulled it out, already knowing what to do.

Pulling down my shorts, I peed on the stick enough to get the answer I had been dreading for the two weeks ago when I missed my period.

Placing the test on the counter, I wiped myself and went into the bedroom to wait. The sad reality was that other than my overly pregnant sister, I had no one to share this news with. Manuel was still in a coma but making progress, and my best friend was dead. I guess it was time to connect with my friends from Atlanta soon. With my thoughts running wild, I stood to my feet to check what I already knew.

Watching the two lines appear on the stick, I was definitely pregnant, and I knew it happened in Colombia.

I was very excited, nervous, and not ready for a baby. I knew I wanted a family with my man, but the timing was definitely off, so for now, I planned to keep this a secret.

Grabbing my oversized Gucci bag and shades, I made my way out of the house to visit my brother, Manuel. Although the news I just received had my emotions everywhere, something had me feeling nervous and scared all of a sudden, and it wasn't from my recent news. Cranking up my car, I looked around to make sure I was safe and made my exit out of our driveway. It took me twenty minutes to make it to the hospital. Checking my bag, I looked to make sure I had Milan's identification card. I stepped out the Audi, looking like a bag of money with my light-blue Fashion Nova jeans, royal-blue, thigh-high boots, and light-blue, off-the-shoulders jean jacket shirt. My hair was in a frontal bob wig with a Victoria's Secret love scent all over my body.

Walking into the hospital, I showed the ID and walked toward my brother's room. I was relieved that no one was in there at the moment. Placing my bag on the sofa, I pulled the doctors chair close to his bed and just watched him breathe. Lord knew I missed the hell out of my brother. It was going on two months that he'd been here, and the only progress he made was moving his legs and arms here and there.

"Mann, I need you to wake up. It's been too long, and I need you right now. Things are crazy. I don't even know where to start. I will say I took a trip to Colombia, and I met our grandfather. He was actually cool. Whatever Mom and Dad has been feeding us has been lies.

Something else went on, and I plan to find out. Milan is huge, and in two months, we will have a niece. We are back talking and closer than we've ever been. That's as good as it's going to get, though, because your mother is dead to me.

"Since meeting grandfather, who happened to be Ramel's plug, business has been booming. Even Rome is making money now. That fuck nigga D-boy went missing after what he did to you, but it's only a matter of time before I catch him one day. Shit feels empty without you. I miss you, and I need you. Guess what? I found out I'm pregnant today, and the only person I wanted to tell was you. I don't know if I'm keeping it or not. Ramel doesn't know.

"I'm just lost. You know it's hard for me to play an in-house girl-friend role. Ramel won't include me in any business except counting money at home. I don't even know where his new trap houses are—well, that's what he thinks. I keep tabs on all that shit, though. All he's doing is driving me to find my own way to hustle.

"You know some women own businesses, go to college, and build brands, but truthfully speaking, that's not me. I love the hustle, I love to grind and get my hands dirty just to run up a check. That's why I'm connected with Ramel friends that do fraud, and I know it's wrong, going behind his back, but I can't help it," I admitted, breathing heavily from spilling my heart out to my brother, and even though there wasn't a response, knowing that he heard me made my life feel that much lighter.

Resting my head on his bed, I sat quietly until my phone indicated I had a message.

*John John: I need you to pick up something today, can you make it?

*me: I'll be there in a few!

I kissed my brother's forehead as he slept. Grabbing my bag to exit the hospital, I quickly found my car. Jumping in, I made my way to the meet-up spot.

Placing my Pandora on Kodak radio, I prepared to vibe out and enjoy my lengthy ride. I texted Ramel, telling him that I was having lunch with Milan. Resting my head against the seat, I enjoyed my ride.

Watching the trees and empty road ahead of me, my mind wandered on the many areas of my life. I thought about the child Royal and I made and how that child would be today if it were alive. I took my eyes off the road as my phone began to ring, displaying a private call again. Who the fuck could be calling me private? Since last week, the calls had been coming at least three times a day, and it was making Ramel's mood shitty toward me. Ignoring the call, I tried to relax again.

Forty-five minutes later, I was pulling up to the warehouse that Ramel once brought me to. Stepping out the car, I walked in to meet up with John John. I walked in, and everyone seemed to be busy, making money as usual.

"About time you show up," John John joked.

"Nigga, shut up. What do you need? And how much am I making off of this?" I questioned.

"I need you to take this black book to my girl Suzie. It has names, socials, and addresses. Also, this check needs to be cashed. Suzie will meet you, and she will cash the check since she has an identification card with this person's name on it," John John stated.

"Wait, you want me to transport this shit? What if I get caught? Ramel will kill me and you for that matter. You know he doesn't play about riding with that shit," I revealed.

"I know, but you are my only option. They don't drive or have licenses. They all practically live here. And the runner we had quit. Look, I'll double the pay, so $10,000 to make the run. You got this," John John instilled.

Grabbing the book from his hand and the check, I agreed, knowing it was wrong, and I could be in big trouble. But $10,000 for a quick drop off? I couldn't refuse that. Throwing the book in my trunk and placing the check in my purse, I got into my car as quick as I came.

I drove off, and my mind was on edge. I was scared and nervous and couldn't believe I was doing this, and to make matters worse, I knew Ramel would break up with me for this. I turned up my music and tried to think positive so nothing would deter me from completing this mission.

After riding for thirty minutes and seeing signs that I was almost to the road that would lead me back to the city, I began to relax. Out of the blue, my phone began to ring, making me jump and swerve on the road. Looking down, trying to straighten my wheel and gain control, I saw it was the damn private caller calling again. Finally, on the right side of the road, I gripped the steering wheel, attempting to calm down. That was short lived because soon after, I saw red and blue lights flash in the mirrors of my car.

"Fuck!" I yelled out, loud pulling over. I instantly began to sweat and become scared as hell. I felt nervous and like I could shit on myself right then and there. Watching the female officer exit her car, I knew I had to act normal.

"Afternoon, ma'am. Is there any reason you were swerving back there?" she asked.

"Umm, no, I just dropped a piece of candy I was eating and tried to pick it up," I lied.

Staring at me for a moment as if she were trying to figure out if I lied, she spoke. "I see. Well, you look sick. Can you hand me your license and registration please?" she asked. Without a word, I reached in my purse as the contents fell on my lap and onto the floor, including the check. She looked at my license and then down at the check before she walked off to her car.

Texting Milan in case I didn't make it out of this situation a free woman, I texted her the county and to bail me out without telling Ramel. Placing my phone down, I knew I was up shit's creek when another police car pulled up.

"Ma'am, I'm going to have to ask you to step out of the car. We need to check your drugs and alcohol level."

Knowing my rights but not being the one to argue since I knew I was riding dirty, I obliged and stepped out of the car. As she proceeded to check me, the male officer began to search my car.

"Ummm, sir, with all due respect, you cannot search my car without probable cause!" I yelled.

"I'm going to need you to quiet down and wait right here," the lady officer said as she cuffed my hands and placed me in the back of the car. For fifteen minutes, I sat in that cramped-up seat, scared for my life. This shit was not worth it.

"Well, Miss Marcy Gomez, it looks like your going with us," the officer spoke outside the window as she held up the black book and the check. I knew I was beyond fucked, but I had to hold it together. Just like that, we were off to the county jail for booking, and this was something I never dreamed of in a million years.

After two hours of questioning and my refusing to talk, they marked me guilty and charged me with grand theft of over $10,000 for the check and identity theft. Within two more hours, I was booked and sent to the waiting cell, awaiting first appearance to receive a bond in the morning. I knew I would get it since this was my first offense.

I wanted to cry because I knew Ramel would kill me. I wanted to kill myself for this shit. I knew I didn't have to do this to myself; my nigga made plenty of money. But I couldn't depend on that. I watched my mother work hard each day to make her own money, and when she and my father divorced, she earned his money plus her own. My mother was definitely one paid bitch, and that alone made me still love her somewhat.

"You look too pretty to be in here," a dark-skinned girl said, walking up to me.

"Likewise," I replied, admiring her beauty. She resembled a tall, dark Juju off *Love & Hip Hop*. She was thick and gorgeous.

"What are you in for?" she asked, sitting next to me.

"Fuck shit that I didn't have to do. What about you?" I asked.

"Riding for the wrong nigga," she replied.

"I definitely know what that's about. I'm Marcy," I introduced myself.

"Hey, I'm Naomi," she replied.

With that, she and I had a conversation all night until it was time for her first appearance. We both received bonds. Mine was for $40,000 and hers was for $50,000.

Seeing Milan's big ass at first appearance made me smile. I knew I would be out in a couple of hours, and I planned on helping Naomi get out as well since her nigga left her to take the fall with his drugs.

Two Hours Later...

"Gomez, you're free to go!" a guard yelled. Gathering myself, I stood to my feet to leave.

"Don't worry. You'll be out of here in a few hours as well. Use that number I gave you," I said to Naomi. As we parted ways to check out, I grabbed my jewelry and purse. I was glad to see Milan's face.

"Wait, Marcy, there something I have to tell you," she admitted.

"Can it wait until we get into the car? I'm dirty, tired, and ready to get home," I replied, walking out the door on her in search for the car. Once I found the car, and I speed walked to the door. I was surprised as hell to see Ramel sitting in the driver's seat, looking straight ahead.

"Don't say shit; just get your ass in this car," he demanded. I looked back to see Milan mouthing sorry, and she got into the car behind us.

I sat in the passenger seat, not knowing what to expect. I just planned to play it cool to see where his head was at.

"Ramel, I'm sorry. I know I fucked up, but please don't be mad at me," I spoke, breaking the silence, but instead of replying, he remained quiet. I leaned back into my seat, grabbing my dead phone and closing my eyes. If he wasn't going to talk, I wasn't going to make him.

The thirty-minute ride home felt like forever with the silence. His ass wouldn't even let me turn on some music. Missing the exit to our house, I looked at Ramel sideways, but he still refused to say a word. We got off on the next exit, which took us to South Beach. Riding down the strip, I wondered where the hell we were going. Before I decided to speak, we pulled up to the Fontainebleau hotel. Pulling by the front door, Ramel finally spoke.

"Get out," he said.

"Wait, what are you doing?" I asked with tears in my eyes.

"This room is paid up for a month. Since it's obvious that you still refuse to trust me, I'mma let you be by yourself since it's clear that's the only person you can depend on anyway. Now get the fuck out," he demanded.

"Ramel, that's not true. Don't do this. I'm sorry. We can work this out. I won't do none of that shit again. I do trust you, please," I begged.

"Marcy, after all the shit, you, of all people, know what I'm dealing with now, and you pull this shit. I have no more words. Get the fuck out my car, get your shit out my trunk, and call me when you grow the fuck up!" he yelled this time, which made me jump. I felt as if my world had just fallen apart. I was in full-blown tears that wouldn't stop falling. He slid me a key with the room number written on it as I opened the door. There was nothing I could do or say. I knew his mind was made up, and I had done the ultimate fuck up.

Grabbing my things out the trunk, I realized he didn't even leave me my car. I stood and watched with tears still falling as he pulled off and left. I didn't care who saw me or how foolish I looked. It was that moment that I realized that I loved Ramel more than I'd ever loved any man. My heart had broken into a million pieces.

17

THREE WEEKS LATER...

"YOU HAVE REACHED THE VOICEMAIL OF—" was all I heard before I hung up the phone. I wasn't eating, sleeping, or even thinking straight. Milan made me eat when she would visit since she knew I was pregnant and losing weight by the day. But I didn't care about that. I just wanted my man back. I needed Ramel more than I needed to breathe.

My phone started ringing out of nowhere. I jumped, praying it was him, and sadly, it was another damn private call.

"Who the fuck is this? Quit calling my phone if you're going to be a coward and not say shit!" I yelled, about to hang up.

"Marcy, wait," I heard someone say and I pulled the phone closer to my ear.

"I need to see you," I heard the voice clearly. My heart began to beat fast. I didn't know what to say or think.

"Royal, you know I can't come see. You and my mother made sure of that," I replied.

"Marcy, I'm out. I got released. I don't know how or why, but I'm home, and I need to see you. I'm in Miami. Where are you?" he whispered.

"Oh my God, where are you? I'm coming to you. Now give me

your location!" I yelled, looking in the mirror and fixing my hair. I couldn't believe my ears. I didn't know what to think. My heart was skipping beats. I couldn't believe this at all.

"I'm about to send it over. I'm down here on the strip by the Versace mansion. I'll wait. How long will you be?" he questioned. Looking down at my phone, I told him thirty minutes as I rushed to take a shower and get ready. Glad that I wasn't showing, I put on some jeans and a half shirt and my Tory Burch sandals. I was nervous and excited.

How the fuck did Royal get out of prison, and what was going on? Was I being set up? Was Ramel testing me? Was this a joke? I planned to find out. I allowed my natural curls to flow freely. Rushing out my room, I booked an Uber and hurried down the hallway to the elevator. I felt like my life was moving at a pace I couldn't control. Still not being able to get Ramel off my mind, I dialed Rome as I waited for the Uber to pull up.

"Wassup, sis?" he answered on the third ring.

"Rome, what am I supposed to do?" I blurted out, tired of trying. "I can't eat, sleep, think, or even breathe without your brother. I know I fucked up, but what do I have to do to get him to believe me?"

"Honestly, sis, that nigga tripping too. If he not home, sleeping, he in the streets, giving niggas his ass to kiss. He is always in a bad mood lately and even tried me the other day about some money. I don't even know what to say anymore, but y'all need to work this shit out because it's fucking up business," he admitted.

"That's just it. How do I do that? He won't answer my calls or text me back. I'm stressed. I know my child is feeling all of this," I slipped before I knew it.

"Wait, you're pregnant too? No fucking way. This shit must be a twin thing." Rome laughed.

"That shit is not funny, and your brother doesn't know, and I would like to keep it that way. A baby is supposed to bring joy and happiness. Shit is not supposed to be like this," I admitted.

"Yes, I understand. I'll be glad when your sister drops our load. I won't say shit, but I will have a talk with him. He done taught you a lesson long enough." Rome laughed, but I didn't find shit funny.

I hopped into my Uber as I ended the call with Rome. I texted Milan that Royal was out and in Miami. I knew she would have a lot of questions, but right now I didn't need the headache.

Pulling up to the street the Versace Mansion was on, I hopped out the car and walked the rest of the way. I didn't know how to address Royal, and all this shit was weird, but I definitely needed to see him right now.

Walking closer, I saw Royal standing there with his low-cut waves swimming around his head. He looked down at his phone, sporting Gucci frames with diesel fitted jeans, a Burberry Polo, and Burberry Loafers.

As I stood a foot away from him, he finally looked up and spotted me. It was as if time stood still, and no one walked this earth but us two. Royal was a lot of things to me, but one thing I could never forget was the fact that he was my best friend before anything. Without thinking, my feet left the ground in a full-fledged run toward him.

As his arms spread open, I flew unto his body as we embraced as long-lost friends. This moment, I'd dreamed about since the day he was taken from me had come to past. But sadly, it would not be the return he was hoping for. Breaking away from his embrace, I stared at him.

"Damn, you look beautiful," he spoke, breaking the silence.

"You look great yourself," I replied.

"I'mma cut straight to it. I'm back, baby, and I want to marry you," he admitted, wasting no time. I guess reading the expression on my face, he continued. "Look, I know you with that clown ass nigga, but you know how we roll. And daddy's back, so how do you want to handle this? You can break it off, or we can dead the nigga," he replied, and I knew he meant every word.

"Wait, Royal, it's not that easy, and I see you're just jumping right into things. Before we talk about all of that, I need to know how you got out of prison. Something is not adding up. You had a lot of years left."

"Damn, you wanted a nigga to rot? Why does it matter? A nigga is free and ready to love on you," he said, kissing my lips. "Plus, we need to get back to Atlanta. I got some shit lined up, and I need you in on this shit. A nigga need to get back on top, and I can't do this shit without you."

"Rame—shit! I mean Royal, I'm not doing that shit anymore," I tried to cover up the fact that I just called him Ramel.

"Marcy, I'm not even going to address that flaw shit you just said. I see the nigga got your head gone. Damn, I never thought I'd see the day that the girl I raised, taught, and molded would give her heart to the next nigga. I can't even hate on that shit, because I love you too much, and if that makes you happy, then so be it. I actually thought I would come home to marry you and raise our child, but I see you had other plans," he spoke.

"It's not my fault. My mother made me get an abortion, just like she had you sent away," I returned as he looked my body up and down.

"And I guess you gon' have this nigga baby next, huh?" he spoke.

"It wasn't planned," I admitted.

"Wait, so you're pregnant now?" he asked. I knew he was speaking in future terms when he asked that question, but I was tired of running from the truth.

"I can't lie to you, Royal."

"This shit is beyond hilarious. You just like the rest of these bitches... Have a nice life!" he yelled as he walked off.

"Royal, wait! Please don't do this!" I yelled as he ignored me. With tears streaming down my face, I booked an Uber to pick me up. I was sure many people were looking, but I didn't give a fuck. What surprised me is the fact that Royal didn't haul off and hit me right then and there. He was never good with his emotions.

As my Uber pulled up, I got into the car and pulled away. I wiped my tears because although I was sad, I couldn't help that I was in love with another man. And I wasn't about to apologize for that.

Hearing my phone ring, I looked to see Milan calling. I answered on the first ring, needing to hear her voice.

"He's awake," she whispered into the phone, referring to our brother. Without a reply, I hung up the phone and directed the driver in the direction of the hospital. Although I couldn't see him right away, I planned to sit in the waiting room until my mother and Milan left.

I reached the hospital in no time, which didn't matter, because that was the same moment my mother was walking through the door. We both locked eyes as I spoke first.

"You know, I wondered what I would say when I saw you after coming back home from Colombia. But words couldn't express how I feel right now. I know something is up with you, my father, and my grandfather, and I plan to find out," I blurted out, and she looked shocked.

"You met your grandfather?" she questioned with a look of confusion on her face.

"Yep," I replied quickly as I walked away to head toward the waiting room. I looked back to see her stuck in her tracks, which let me know there was definitely more to the story. Going to the third floor, I took a seat and looked through my phone. My mother walked past me to the check-in desk and walked back to my brother. I was kinda sad that this awesome moment would have to be shared separately.

"Ma'am, you can come on back," someone said, standing in front of me.

I looked up to see the receptionist. I stood to my feet and followed her back to my brother's room and walked inside. My mother and sister were crowding around Manuel as he sat up in the bed. With tears in my eyes, I walked over and hugged him. He hugged me back and didn't let go. Breaking the embrace, I began talking to him.

"Welcome back," I spoke.

"He's going to have to gain his strength back for walking and talking. So for now, all we're getting is a nice smile," Milan admitted.

Manuel's big smile spread across his face gracefully. For a second, standing around, talking, and laughing felt like old times except my mother was sitting on the couch in her own world. I guess what I said struck a nerve; she'd been quiet the entire visit.

An hour later, the doctor came in to check his vitals.

"We don't want to overstimulate him, so how about we wrap this visit up? One of you can stay overnight with him, but the rest of you can return tomorrow."

"I'll stay," my mother said.

Manuel shook his head no and pointed at me.

"You want Marcy to stay?" my mother asked, looking at him with shock written all over her face.

He nodded his head

"Well, OK, baby. Get some rest, and I'll be back tomorrow," she spoke, not being the one for confrontation.

Her, Milan, and the doctor made their exit as Manuel looked directly at me.

"What, nigga? Why are you looking like that?" I asked, taking a seat.

"You," he whispered.

"I knew you could talk. Why weren't you saying shit?" I inquired.

"Because I was waiting to talk to you. What's going on? All that shit you came here and said had a nigga fighting to wake up," he replied.

"What the hell? Did you hear me? That's crazy! I didn't think you would remember."

"Oh, I did, and I'm back, so what's up."

"Where do I start... Ramel is pissed at me. The day I left you, I got arrested for fraud. So not only am I staying at a hotel, Royal ass is out. I don't know how, but he's wanting me to go back to Atlanta and set some niggas up, but Manuel, I'm done with that life. I just want Ramel to forgive me so we can work things out and raise our child," I stressed.

"Damn, this shit is crazy. Not only are you pregnant, but you're in love with a nigga that ain't Royal too. I never thought I'd see the day. Damn, I need to shake back and get right. That nigga Royal not gonna let you go that easily, so watch yourself, sis," he spoke, concerned and sad that he would have to learn how to walk and move again through rehab.

"Don't worry. You know I got me. But there's something else I need to tell you... Khyrah's gone," I admitted.

"Yeah, I know," he replied, looking down.

"I tried to help her... Wait, how do you know?" I asked, realizing what he said.

"She told when she came to visit. I tried so hard to fight and come back to help her, but I couldn't. But a nigga don't want to talk about that. I want to see what's up with Grandfather," he replied.

"See what's up how?" I questioned.

"Marcy, it's no secret that school is over for me. The nigga don't have to know me or like me. I just need some work to make some money."

"Well, Ramel has the shit here already. Why not just deal with him?" I asked.

"Marcy, you sound stupid. How does that look? The grandson of a Cartel leader selling shit for one of the plug's flunkies." He laughed.

"Don't call my man a flunky, but I understand. Do what you need to do. I'll hit him up as soon as you're ready, and you can meet his crazy ass." I laughed, thinking of his old, young-acting ass.

"I'll be ready sooner than you think."

"But for real, Marcy, look out for yourself. Don't trust nobody, and eat some fucking food. You look sick," he joked, but I didn't find the humor in that, especially being pregnant.

"I guess I'll get something to eat and head back to my hotel unless you want me to stay," I offered.

"No, I need some rest and time to think. Head out and come back in the morning."

"OK, love you," I replied, kissing his cheek and heading out the hospital room.

I was happy as hell to have a piece of my heart back. After all the bullshit I'd been through, having him wake up instilled a little piece of hope in me that my life would get better.

Walking down the hallway, toward the exit doors, I saw Rome and Ramel walking toward the doors to enter the hospital.

Approaching them, I spoke first. "Wassup, Rome," I said as he hugged me. He replied and asked about Manuel.

"How's he acting? Does he remember anything?"

"He's the same, and he remembers everything, but just take it slow with him. I'm sure he's waiting for you to get there. I'll be back tomorrow," I replied, dismissing them as Ramel just stood there as if I didn't exist. That alone made me feel as if I didn't want to exist at that moment. Before I burst into tears, I hurried off without one word to him.

"Aye, Marcy, let me holla at you," I heard the words I'd been waiting to hear for damn near a month. Holding back my tears that threatened to fall, I stopped.

"For what it's worth, I want to give you these," he said, handing me the car keys to the car he bought me. "I'm not the type of nigga to take shit back even if we are broken up. You can go to the house and get it while we're here. And anything in the house you may need, go ahead and get it. There's a key under the plant by the door. That's if you want to."

My heart fell to the floor, and I had no one to blame but myself. With the keys in my hand and not enough courage to speak any words, I turned away and walked to the corner.

"That's it? You can't even tell a nigga bye? No hug or anything!" he yelled at my back as I continued to walk away. I would love to hug him, kiss him, and tell him how much I miss him, but in reality, it was over. And that was something that I couldn't face right now in his presence.

18

THREE DAYS LATER...

WASHING MY FACE, I made up my mind. I was heading out to get a lawyer for my case. The police officers didn't even read me my Miranda rights upon my arrest. I also didn't consent to a search either. After that, I planned to find a place to stay and work on making better decisions. I wanted to get my GED and open a clothing boutique since I loved fashion. Maybe I could start singing again. All I knew was the life I planned with Ramel didn't seem so promising anymore. I needed to plan for our child, and when the time came, I'd allow him to take his position as his or her father. But right now, until my heart could take it, I'd rather he not know.

Grabbing my clutch and phone, I checked the mirror, making sure my Gucci sneakers matched my special-made one-piece I made with the Gucci stripes down the side. Having too much time on my hands had me experimenting and trying new things. I even sewed my baby a headband.

I rubbed my little stomach, ready for my day to start. I had money saved, so finding a nice spot wasn't an issue, but that money would never last without income coming in. I knew I could call my grandfather for help, but I didn't want his help, and I didn't need him knowing that Ramel and I were having problems. He needed to know that his money was being made without any problems. One thing I did plan on doing was visiting my father really soon to find out the truth about my Colombian family.

Walking to valet to get my car, I heard my phone beep, indicating I had a text message.

Opening my phone, I saw it was Royal.

*Royal: I don't like the way things ended with us a few days ago. You know we better than that, and if your happy then I'm good.

*Me: I'm glad to know you feel this way, I never meant to hurt you and I hope we can be friends.

*Royal: Hell yeah, I got too much love for you not to be my homie. But I'm heading out tonight, so how about we meet up for dinner for a last goodbye?

*Me: Of course. Is 8 tonight a good time?

*Royal: I'll holla at you then, oh and Happy Valentine's day!

I pulled up my calendar, looking at the date. I didn't even pay attention to holidays anymore after the incident on December 10th with my brother. Although today was considered 'love day,' things were finally looking up, and I guess not having anyone to share this day with made me forget this holiday as well. Getting into my convertible Mercedes, I placed my Gucci shades on my eyes and enjoyed the hot Miami sun as I started 'love day.'

7:00 p.m.

I placed my one-piece red bodysuit on. The pant legs were wide, but the material hugged my body just right. I let my natural curls flow freely and stepped into my Giuseppe heels. I was simple but cute. I was definitely not the same girl he left prison with. Even my dress code changed. I was becoming a woman. I honestly didn't feel up to meeting Royal. I wanted to stay in bed and go over the condos I looked at today. Pulling out my phone to text Milan that I was meeting Royal, I also shot him a text that I was ready and to send his location. Within a minute, he sent it, and I was out of my hotel room and on my way to meet him.

Placing his location in my GPS, I was out the hotel and in my car, heading to him. I hoped this meeting would be short and sweet, and I hoped that he would find whatever he was looking for in life. My mind was still in disbelief. At one point, this man was my life. He had my whole mind, body, and soul wrapped around his finger. A piece of me wanted to keep in touch because I still cared for him, but I was completely in love with Ramel.

I looked at my GPS and was twenty-five minutes away from him, so I turned on Drake and vibed out.

Before I knew it, I was pulling up to an empty store parking lot. There were a few cars there but mainly him and me. To be honest, I didn't recognize where I was at the moment either, which meant we were saying goodbye, and this wouldn't take long. Parking my car, I texted him and waited.

I heard knocks on my window that caused me to jump.

"Get out," he instructed.

Opening the door, I got out of the car. "What the hell is this place?" I questioned.

"Some storefront by the bus stop over there," he replied.

"Oh, you're catching the bus home?" I asked.

"Yeah, you know a nigga just got out. I gotta get right, but it look like this nigga got you riding good. Convertible, huh? You just keep throwing this nigga up in my face." He sneered.

"Wait, what? I would never," I tried to say, but it was evident Royal had other plans, and never in a million years did I think it would come to this.

"Give me the keys," he demanded.

Not wanting confrontation with him, I handed the keys over.

"Your mom was right. This nigga got you gone," he said, looking in the car.

"So let me guess, she's the reason you're out?"

"Right, and the fact that you aborted my seed... Did you think I would leave this bitch with you still carrying his baby!" he yelled, visibly pissed.

"Don't do this, Royal. I'm sorry. If you need money, I can help you. Just please don't do anything stupid," I pleaded, cursing myself for leaving my gun in my room.

Without one word, Royal punched me in the face, and I fell. With blood covering my hands, I jumped up and swung back.

"Stupid ass nigga!" I yelled as he grabbed the back of my head, pushing me to the ground and crashing his foot into my body. I heard something crack as I lay on the ground, trying to pull myself together. Feeling the bottom of his shoe crash into my stomach brought instant pain and tears.

"Fuck you and this baby!" he yelled in anger. I screamed with each kick and punch. Feeling bones crack, I balled up in the fetal position, holding my stomach as sharp pains took over. With the amount of pain he caused, I couldn't fight back even if I wanted too. My face felt swollen as my eyes shut. My breathing slowed down, and I lay on the ground as his Timberlands continued to bruise me. Royal whooped my ass so bad that I could no longer feel his licks. My body went numb as my lower abdomen shocked my body back into recognition with pain.

"Hey, what are you doing? Stop that!" I heard a voice yell in the distance as Royal ran and jumped in my car. Hearing my tires screech, I knew he was gone. But I also knew that my unborn child was also gone. Not even able to cry, I lay there, ready to accept whatever came my way—especially death.

"Oh my God, baby, call the police! She's hurt badly!" a lady yelled as her man followed her directions.

"Ma'am, hang on. Help is on the way. It's going to be OK," she assured. "Can you tell me your name?"

"K... arma," I replied. I knew the shit I did would eventually catch up to me one day. I just didn't expect it to happen this early and at the hands of Royal. Not even able to open my eyes due to the pain surrounding them, I fell into a deep sleep of unconsciousness.

...

"Get the vitals! She's a young female beaten badly! Ma'am, can you tell me your name!" I heard someone yell as a thousand hands pulled on me. I attempted to wake up but fell back asleep. I was moving in and out of consciousness, trying to hold on, but the unbearable pain kept knocking me back into unconsciousness.

"Marcy Gomez," I whispered as the nurse checked my faint pulse.

"Who did this to you?" she asked.

I closed my eyes again, and this time, I couldn't wake up.

What I assumed to be hours later, I opened my eyes to a room full of people. My mother, father, Milan, Rome, Ramel, and Manuel. My brother was in a wheelchair. All of their faces sported worried looks as if they didn't know that I would wake up.

"Oh, thank God she's awake!" Milan yelled.

"Marcy, you had us all worried. Thank God you're OK," my mother said, sitting next to me. I looked at her, attempting to speak, but my mouth was too sore to move it. I scrunched my face to show my displeasure for her presence.

"*Hola*, baby girl, how are you feeling?" my father questioned. I rolled my eyes as the dumb questions kept coming. Looking down, I saw my right leg in a cast. My left hand was also wrapped up, and a brace was wrapped around my back and ribs. Pain shot through my body as I tried to move.

"This shit hurt," I mumbled, knowing they wouldn't understand me. Realizing and remembering what happened, I rubbed my free hand over my stomach, hoping my baby survived. I locked eyes with Ramel as he looked at me with a hard stare.

Motioning for them to hand me the dry erase board, I wrote a message that I hoped they all would understand. *Everyone get the hell out*

They all looked, and some laughed.

"Yes, I think it's best we do not have so many family members in here. One of you can stay, but how about the rest of you come back tomorrow?" the doctor spoke, walking into the room and reading my message. I laughed to myself.

"Since I'm her mother, I'll stay," my mother said, trying to make herself more important than my dad.

Not in this lifetime

Everyone laughed again.

"I'll stay," Ramel blurted out. Everyone agreed and gathered their things to go.

"I love you," Milan said as she kissed me goodbye.

"Marcy, I love you," my mother repeated as she attempted to kiss my cheek, and I turned my face away. She was putting on a united front for my father, but when this was over, I planned to pay her a little visit.

Standing in the doorway, she watched as I kissed my father back as he said his goodbyes, along with Rome and Manuel. Once everyone was gone, the doctor proceeded to speak.

"So, Ms. Gomez, you are one lucky woman. You've been in a medically induced coma for two days. As you can see, you suffered a broken ankle, sprained wrist, fractured jaw, and three cracked ribs. Some of the swelling on you face has gone down; your left black eye will heal just fine. And we were able to place your nose back into place. You have a long road to recovery, but you will recover back to your normal self, and that's what matters the most. I would like to ask you, did you know you were with child at the time of your attack?"

Looking at Ramel, I turned away, nodding my head yes.

"Well, the child didn't make it through, and a nice woman actually witnessed you being attacked. I'm sure the officers will be by here for questioning soon, so get some rest, and if you need me, just press that button, and my nurses will assist you," the doctor spoke before writing down my vitals and leaving out the room.

"How long have you known?"

Knew what?

"Marcy don't play dumb," he replied.

I was two days away from being two months

"And this is the perfect example as to why we're not together now. You don't even trust me enough to tell me you're pregnant with my child. Or the fact that this Royal nigga pop back up in your life out the blue with no explanation, and you were going to see him. I swear you be blowing a nigga mind, and you want me to trust you? This shit is so bogus, and even after all this, a nigga still love your ass and miss the shit out of you," Ramel expressed.

I wanted to cry, but I couldn't. All I could do was write that I was sorry.

"Marcy, do you know what that baby would have meant to a nigga? You are the first girl to ever get pregnant by me. For a second, a nigga thought he couldn't have kids, and all this time, you living in a hotel, stressed the fuck out and pregnant. I can't even blame you, though, because I handled you like a child. Maybe that's why you kept shit from me and acted like that. Instead of being your man, I acted like I was your dad, and that shit wasn't right. So we're both to blame for this shit. But that's all about to change.

"Getting that call that you were hurt and might not make it had a nigga wanting to go with you. At that moment, I realized I couldn't imagine my life without you. And as crazy as these six months have been, this is the most I've ever loved a girl other than my mother. I guess all I'm saying is that I want you to come home. I want us to work on another baby. I want us to build our future together, and I also want you to be my wife, Marcy Gomez," Ramel stated, pulling a box out of his pocket and placing it on top of my stomach. He popped open the top to reveal an Annello by Kobelli two-carat TDW four-teen-karat white-gold square-frame engagement ring.

I was overwhelmed with emotions. I looked at Ramel in disbelief. I also blinked my eyes a few times to make sure that I wasn't dream-ing. Raising my left hand but remembering it was bandaged, I held my right hand out for now as he placed the huge nugget on my ring finger until I could switch the hand. Admiring the diamonds dancing, I knew I had met the man for me at the young age of eighteen. Ramel changed my life for the better.

"When the officers come in here to question you, don't say shit. Now, all I need to know is where that nigga Royal at. I need his spots in Atlanta, his family members' names. I want everything on this nigga, and I need it ASAP," he demanded.

I understand and I will give you all of that as soon as I'm better. This is one job I refuse to let you do without me. Oh, and he took my car

Looking at me up and down, he smiled.

"Just get some rest, baby. I'll take care of everything. I will say you mess with some ole crab ass niggas. That pussy ass nigga took your car and beat your ass because you in love with a real nigga. You need to thank God you met me. I don't know where the hell this crash dummy would have led your ass." Ramel laughed, but I didn't find that shit funny. I didn't know any better, and there was a time when I worshipped the ground he walked on. I knew my trials and tribulations with love came from not getting it at home, and I was too far gone to ever look back.

You know my mother was the reason Royal was released from prison. She's the one that put him there and the one who had him released. So in a way, I feel as if she did this to me as well

"That shit with your mother, you gon' have to fix it or let it go. Nobody's mother is perfect, and what you think she may be doing to hurt you, she may just be feeling as if she's helping you. Either way it goes, y'all need to work it out," he advised.

I didn't want to work anything out until she was ready to express the whole truth. Maybe being a mother wasn't in the plans for me. My second pregnancy gone, just like that. The fact that Ramel was here to cope with the loss made me feel a little better, but a part of me felt torn and scared to produce another child.

I'm going to rest, I love you

Placing the board down, I closed my eyes. This was enough for one day. The only good thing to come from all of this was the fact that I would soon be Mrs. Brown. A smile crept upon my face as I lay there, attempting to fall asleep.

"Umm, baby!" Ramel yelled, waking me up out of my sleep. "Your sister is in labor."

That was the second-best news I'd received all day, but my heart wouldn't allow me to spread joy, knowing my child didn't make it. Looking at Ramel, I closed my eyes as a tear slid down my cheek.

19

TWO MONTHS LATER...

"So INFORMING me that you were hurt and almost dead isn't important?" my grandfather questioned.

"I know, *Papa*, but I didn't want to worry you. Everything is handled," I assured him, standing up from my sewing area Ramel made in our room. I had pieces all over the room, and when I was ready, I planned on showing my talents to the world. I had everything planned out, but for now, I made pieces for Milan and myself.

"Like hell it is. I will see you soon," he said in a stern tone as he ended the call.

"Baby, why would you tell him that?" I asked, looking at Ramel's dumb ass.

"There was nothing to tell. He already knew the truth; I just confirmed the rest with him," Ramel admitted as he rubbed my ankle. Getting back to normal was harder than I thought, but he was there every step of the way, even putting up with my crazy ass mood swings from the medicine I was on. Although things were back to normal, the scar under my eye would be a permanent reminder of what I thought love was.

"You know, business is actually going great. But I need you to watch yourself when I'm not around. D-boy is back in town and moving weight on the east side of town."

"What? And you're allowing this to happen? I don't get it. Why are you not having this man killed by now? And the fact that Royal is still walking around as if he didn't almost kill me. Baby, I trust you—don't get me wrong—but your version of revenge is going to kill both of us before it's over. I don't get it. You can have these niggas whacked at any time, yet you choose to wait a year," I said, trying to knock some sense into his head.

"You worry too much, baby. That's my job. Just don't go out without the proper help. I got niggas on call for you and Milan at this point."

"Yes, sir, daddy," I replied as he kissed my lips. Before I knew it, the kissing became deeper as he pulled me on top of him. Gently rubbing my breasts, he took one in his mouth as my boy shorts began to get soaked with wetness. Tugging at my underwear, I stopped his hand.

"Baby, we can't do this," I expressed. As his kisses stopped, he took a long, hard look at me before agreeing. Since the incident and even being cleared by the doctor to start regular daily activities, I still couldn't bring myself to have sex with Ramel. He tried often, and I stopped every advance. The hardest part was telling him that I was scared to have sex because of the fear of getting pregnant and losing another baby. So to save face, I used my healing as a way to avoid sex, but I knew that wouldn't last for too much longer.

Whaaa! Whaaaa! was the next thing we heard on the baby monitor.

I was saved by my niece, Rylee. Ramel and I were playing babysitters while her parents went out on a date night. Since giving birth, Milan and the baby moved in with Ramel and me to be closer to Rome and get help with the baby. I was sure my mother was having a fit, but she made sure she sees her every day.

Jumping up in panic mode, Ramel went to retrieve our niece. She was beautiful and brought so much joy to our lives. I couldn't believe something so little could bring so much joy although she was spoiled as hell.

"Give her to me," I replied, grabbing her heated bottle off of the dresser.

The moment he put her in my arms, the crying stopped, and she was trying to hold her little head up to look at us.

"I'll give you six months. Then you're definitely having one of these," Ramel joked. I ignored him by playing with her.

"You actually look good holding the baby. What would you name our baby?" he inquired. I rolled my eyes, having enough of this baby talk. I popped the bottle in her mouth to help her go back to sleep. Visibly ignoring him this time, I held Rylee close to my chest, humming as she rocked back to sleep.

After her warm bottle and burping, my beautiful niece was back to sleep. I stood to my feet and walked her to her room, placing her in the crib.

Returning to our room, I noticed Ramel getting dressed.

"Where are you going?" I inquired. I waited for a few seconds, but he didn't respond. "Ramel, I know you hear me talking to you!" I screamed.

"And I know you heard me talking to you. Now, like a man, I'mma say I have some shit to go handle. Now, as my woman, you need to tell me why you cuffing that lil' pussy and avoiding the conversation about babies," he replied as I heard the front door beep, indicating that Milan and Rome where home.

Taking a leap and trying to do better, I decided to tell the truth.

"I'm scared, Ramel. I don't want to have sex because I'm scared of getting pregnant. I was pregnant by Royal before, and my mother made me abort it. So being pregnant this time was like my second chance to do it all over again. Losing our baby shattered my heart, and I feel like I'm cursed. I don't want to do this right now. My heart can't take losing another child, baby. And I'm sorry." I cried, thinking of the heartache. Pulling me into a hug, he kneeled in front of me.

"Baby, listen. I want you to understand that putting that ring on your finger means that I love you. You are my main concern. Do a nigga want kids? Hell yeah, but that's only to see our love multiply. Whether you give me children or not, loving you will always be my main concern. Don't stress yourself about that shit, and when it's meant to be, it's gonna happen. And a little Razelle will be running around here sooner than you think," he assured me, smiling, showing all thirty-two of his perfectly white teeth.

"I love you, boy, but I don't know about naming our child Razelle. How do you know our future baby will be a girl?" I asked.

"Because a nigga know. But I love you more, girl!" he answered back as he kissed my lips. It was the little shit like this that had me falling deeper in love with my man.

"You want to ride with me?" he asked, and of course, I hopped my ass up to join him. I had been dying to see how he was running his operation now that he was back in the streets.

I threw on an all-black velvet jumpsuit and my BCBG sneakers.

Running into Milan in the kitchen, I explained to her about her spoiled child's last diaper change and bottle feeding before I followed Ramel out the house and to his truck. I made sure my pistol was in my purse. I kept it close to my side everywhere I went now.

Pulling off from the house, we went to one of his new trap houses on the eastside. Pulling up, I laughed due to the fact that I knew nothing of this place, and he opened it up to embark on the territory D-boy thought he had. I guess my baby had a plan after all, and he would get his revenge soon and very soon.

Hopping out the car, we entered the wooden house to see the normal shit—young niggas playing the game, one in the kitchen, and two in the back, counting money.

"How it's looking?" Ramel asked, approaching Chris in the kitchen.

"Shit looking great. Definitely better than that wack shit they been selling over here. We definitely about to piss some people off with this one," he replied, pulling his nine-millimeter out of the kitchen cabinet.

"Long as y'all niggas stay strapped and ready. I pulled y'all over here because I knew if no one else can, y'all can handle whatever comes this way. Stay ready and holla if you need me," Ramel instructed as he slapped hands with Chris. Going to the back, he grabbed a duffle bag of money, and we headed out of the house.

I looked around, on alert, making sure we were in the clear. Hurrying to the truck, we got in and pulled off.

"You hungry?"

"Hell yeah," I replied as his gas light came on.

"You want to get gas first or food?" he asked.

"It's whatever you want to do," I replied.

Pulling into the gas station seven minutes later, I opened my door to go pay for the gas.

"Hey, Marcy!" I heard someone at the pump behind us yell. Turning around, I saw it was Michelle, a girl from school that would give me her notes when I would miss days. I walked up to hug her, and we began conversing.

"I'll go in and pay since you're talking!" Ramel yelled, stepping out of the truck.

"Get me some of those ring gummy bears!" I yelled, referring to the gummies they made out of a big circle with a hole in the middle.

"So you're looking great and still hanging in there with Ramel, I see," she said.

"Of course. That's my baby." I blushed.

"Yeah, given his reputation and the fact that your still around means he must really love you." It was obvious she was being nosy, but I loved nosy bitches. As she continued to talk, I noticed a red Kia Optima that pulled in after us and sat a pump over. They had been there as long as we had and still hadn't gotten out of the car to pump gas. With the windows being too dark to see through, I began to wonder.

"So how's your fine ass brother? I heard he was shot, but he's OK, right?" she inquired.

"Yeah, he's fine," I mumbled as I noticed another car pull up beside the car sitting at the pump. It looked as if they threw something in the driver side window and rode off.

Ramel was now walking out of the store with my candy, oblivious to what was going on. As my world went in slow motion at that moment, I clutched the one thing I promised to never leave without. Ramel reached the gas pump as he unscrewed the cap. The car pulled up close to us, and someone hopped out with a gun drawn. Without a thought, I pushed Michelle to the ground as I dropped my purse, revealing my small pistol.

As he crept up on Ramel, I stood behind him. As quick as he jumped out the car was as quick as his life ended.

Pow! Pow! Pow! I fired one shot to the back of his head and was confused at the other two shots I heard. Looking around, I spotted Ramel standing at the pump with his weapon drawn as well. Looking back, I heard the tires screech from the red car as they escaped, leaving their dead homeboy.

Michelle was screaming for dear life. I walked over and helped her up as she stood, shaken by the dead body in front of her.

"Michelle, I need you to listen to me. Please calm down. I know this looks crazy, but I need you to keep this between us."

Grabbing my purse off the ground, I reached inside and pulled out $500 I kept on me at all times.

"There is more where that came from, just trust me. Here's my number. I have to go, but call me, and I'll give you five grand. Just keep quiet," I ordered as I rushed to the truck, praying she would follow my directions.

Jumping in the truck, Ramel sat, ready to leave the scene.

"Baby, you're not going to get the surveillance footage?" I questioned him as he sped down the highway.

"No need. I watched them clowns follow us from the moment we left the trap. That's why I went to that gas station. I do business with the owner. When you were going in to pay, I planned to get out and let them niggas think they had the perfect shot. But when you started talking, I went in and watched the surveillance footage in the back. I seen the car pull up and dump a gun in the driver side of the red car. That's why I came back outside," he replied.

"Well, if you knew all this, then why did you leave me out there alone?" I asked, flabbergasted.

"You were never alone. What you did not pay attention to was the lil' niggas standing at the stop sign. You had more than enough backup. The fucked up part about it was the nigga we just killed was D-boy's little cousin Speed. That's why I'm stressing to you that you have to watch your back at all times. But it didn't matter. You were on point to whack that nigga before I could fire a shot," he said, shocked.

"I know. Who's your bitch?" I laughed.

"You are. That shit kind of got a nigga dick hard. You gangsta as fuck, baby," he admitted, grabbing his dick as he slowed down, doing the speed limit.

Opening the candy that I told him to bring me out of the store, I placed one of the rings in my mouth. As the sweetness took over and created juices in my mouth, I reached over and moved his hand. I pulled his Nike sweats down enough to release his rock-hard dick. Without a thought as the candy created more saliva, I placed my mouth down his shaft as he drove.

With my tongue and the candy ring in my mouth, I slid it down his manhood as if it were a condom. The candy split as I slid it as far as it could go without tearing apart. I tightened my jaws as I swallowed his Johnson with each lick and suck.

"Oh shit. Eat that dick, babyyyyy." He moaned as my spit dripped down his dick. Feeling his manhood touched my esophagus, I was enjoying this more than he was. Feeling the truck swerve a little, I popped up.

"You better drive this damn truck, or I'mma stop sucking," I demanded.

"Shit, my bad, baby," he replied, grabbing the back of my head and placing me back on his shaft. I gave Ramel head until we pulled into the driveway. Each time he would nut, I swallowed it and gave him a minute to collect himself before I continued supplying my man with the best head he ever had. Two nuts later, we were home and rushing to our bedroom. I didn't know if our rush with death had us horny, but I was finally ready to allow my man full access to my sweet spot.

Walking into the room, he picked me up, placing me on the bed softly. Starting with my pants, he slowly pulled them down and off, placing them in a corner. Taking his pants off, he did the same, placing them in the same corner. I went ahead and took my jacket and tank top off, placing them in the corner as well. It was no secret that each article of clothing would be burned by the morning.

Looking at my naked body spread out on our king-size bed, I watched my man walk over to me. Grabbing my legs, he pulled me to the edge of the bed. With his tongue kissing my sweet spot, he made a trail of kisses up to my breasts, and he devoured them. With his soft lips, he made circles with his tongue and sucked each one sensually. I arched my back, and he massaged my clitoris. My body was fuming with heat and ready for penetration.

"That feels so good, baby," I moaned. He flipped me over with my ass now up in the air. Pushing me forward and pinning my legs up, he spread my pussy lips and ass cheeks. With one swift motion, he licked my clitoris and sucked all the way back to my ass.

"That tickles." I laughed a little until he began sucking. "Oh shit, I can't take it." I moaned in defeat, and he ate my ass and played with my pussy. I had never experienced anything like this before, and the shit felt awesome. Burying my face in the covers, I moaned loudly in pleasure.

Flipping me back over with my juices all over his face, he stood and stared at my naked frame.

Holding his dick, he leaned down and began kissing my lips, which I thought was kind of weird, considering the fact that he just ate my ass. But I kissed him back even harder because I loved Ramel just that much.

Taking his time, he dipped his rod into my honey pot, slowly taking it in and out until I opened up enough for his big manhood to fit.

"Damn, this shit so tight. Fuckkkk." He moaned, going deeper as he picked up his pace. I arched my back so he could get all the way in. What was painful quickly turned into pleasure.

As he rolled his lower body, my juices began to soak his dick. Pulling me on top of him, he grabbed my waist, and I rode his stick.

"Damn, baby, this pussy feel so gooooddd. Who pussy is this?" He moaned, turning me over and putting both of my legs in the air. This shit reminded me of Tyrese and Yvette from *Baby Boy*. Going deeper and harder, he asked again. "Who pussy is this, Marcy?"

"Oh shit! It's yours, daddy. This your pussy, *papi*." I moaned.

"Say it louder," he demanded.

"This your pussy, Ramel, forever and always!" I yelled, not being able to control myself anymore. At that moment, we both locked eyes.

"I want you to cum with, baby. You gon' cum with me?" he asked, breaking the stare and long stroking my ass.

"Yessssss!" I yelled with my legs still high in the air.

Without a word, pushing deep inside of me, Ramel released his soldiers as I released mine.

Boom, boom, boom! We froze as we heard a loud knock at the door.

"Can y'all quiet down! We do have a sleeping baby in here!" Milan yelled as we burst into laughter.

"I hope y'all made twins with that loud ass fucking y'all just did!" Rome added, laughing. "I'm saying! You gon' let me get it like that?" I heard Rome ask as he and Milan walked away from the door.

Breathing heavily, we both fell beside each other.

"That shit was lit, though, baby," I said as he pulled me closer to him.

"I know," he replied, wrapping his arms around my waist and kissing my neck.

"I love you, boy."

"I love you too, girl."

20

"WHO THE FUCK KEEPS CALLING YOU?" Ramel asked as we watched the news.

"My mother. She's been calling all day, nonstop."

"Don't you think you should answer it?" he replied. The news about the gas station incident that happened last week had made top news stations, and they didn't have any leads.

"Give that girl ten grand since she kept her mouth shut."

I smiled because I planned to do just that today when I met up with her. Before I could reply, my phone rang again. Ramel took my phone, pressing the answer button, and I looked at him like I could kill him. He smiled, placing the phone to my ear.

"What do you want!" I yelled.

"Marcy, I need to speak with you. Your brother and sister are on their way. I need you here. It's an emergency," she whispered. In all my years of living, my mother never used words like this.

"No, now stop calling me," I replied. I fully intended to stop by. I just didn't want her to expect me.

"What she want?" Ramel's nosy ass asked.

"I don't know, but I'm about to go see," I said, getting up off the couch.

I texted Manuel, and he informed me that he was on his way to Mom's house, and since Milan was already out, and about I knew she would head that way.

"I'll be glad when I get another car!" I yelled out loud, taking the keys to his Audi.

"Quit letting lames take yours!" Ramel yelled back, and I laughed. Sliding on my Adidas to match my tights and shirt I had on, I walked out the door. Forgetting the most important thing, I turned around and walked back into the house to my baby sitting on the couch in the same spot. I walked over to him, and he leaned his head back and stuck his lips out, knowing that I was coming back for a kiss.

Releasing his tongue, I kissed him one last time.

"Oh, I need the ten grand to give her," I reminded him of what he just recently said. I had planned to give her ten grand of my own money, but since he offered, I planned to use his. The bitch was truly lucky. If Ramel had his way, she would be dead as well, but since she was cool in my book, he gave her a pass.

"You think you're slick. Get it out the safe," he said, followed by a slick smile.

I walked to my niece's room and moved the picture of her out the way. I pushed the wall to the left, and the safe revealed itself. Pressing the combination, 08-16, which was the month and year we met. I took the ten stacks of cash and placed them in my oversized Burberry bag and closed the safe. It had been a while since I looked inside, and from the looks of the cash in there, it was well over $500,000.

Closing and locking the safe, I exited and headed out the door. "Love you!" I yelled.

Hopping in his car, I texted Michelle to meet me up the road from my mother's house. I planned to make this trip short and sweet.

Damn near speeding down the highway, I made it to the mall's parking lot up the road from my mother's place in time. Spotting Michelle's older Honda, I parked next to her and grabbed my purse. Getting out, I opened her door and got into her car, looking her up and down. She still looked shook.

"Are you OK?" I questioned.

"Ummm, yes, just can't believe that happened," she admitted. I wasn't buying it. She couldn't believe that happened but had the nerve to be hounding me for the money I promised her.

Shaking my head, I reached in my bag and pulled out five stacks. She had just talked herself out of ten grand.

"That's five grand, as promised, and it's all there," I informed her.

"Thank you, Marcy, but can I ask you a question? Why did you do it?" she asked. I was getting annoyed with her, obviously.

"Do what?" I replied, acting dumb to her question. Her eyes began to water. It was then I knew she couldn't handle this.

"Look, Michelle, you seen what happened. He almost killed my man. And trust, you and I would've been next. What did you expect? This is life, Michelle. Either you get with it or get rolled on. I know this is a lot to handle, but you need to get it together. You'll go through worse shit than this if you allow it."

At this point, I was aggravated and a little scared that she might crack.

"Now I hope we don't have to have this conversation again, because I can guarantee you it won't be this nice next time," I threatened her as I exited her car. Taking a moment to think, I started my engine and pulled away.

I was aggravated just that quick and really not feeling having a family moment with my mother and siblings. My thoughts got the best of me, and I was pulling up to her house a few minutes later, not even noticing it.

Heading toward the door, I saw Milan's car and a black Tahoe truck. I opened then unlocked door. Cautiously walking toward the living room, I was greeted with the shock of my life.

"What the hell is going on?" I questioned as I saw my father, Manuel, tied to a chair as my grandfather, two uncles, and two bodyguards stood around him. Looking around the entire room, I saw Milan was sitting on the couch in tears as my brother looked on in confusion. The only person looking as if they could shit a brick was my mother. It was time to explain the truth.

"Awww, about time you joined us, my daughter," my grandfather greeted as he grabbed me into a hug.

"What's up, *Papi*? Why all of this? Did I miss something?" I inquired, walking into the den, looking at my father.

"Oh, you missed a lot, and until these two start telling the truth, they won't leave here alive," he angrily spat.

"Will you just untie him, please?" Milan pleaded.

"Not until they tell you guys the truth, and I don't have all day."

"Don't say a thing, Tasha!" my father yelled at my mother.

"See, that's the first lie. Her name isn't Tasha; it's Letecia Ford," my grandfather admitted.

Out of nowhere, one of the guards began choking my father.

Gasping for air, my father began fighting to keep whatever air he could in his lungs as Milan looked away. As much as I wanted to help, I knew better, and I also wanted to know the truth.

"Just fucking tell the truth!" Milan yelled at my mother, catching her attention.

"Wait, wait, wait. I'll tell them. Just please don't hurt him or my kids!" my mother yelled, finally knocking out of her daze.

"This shit is insane," my brother expressed, still watching everything play out.

"Nineteen years ago, I studied abroad in Colombia. The moment I got there, I began working at a local store. Unbeknownst to me, the owner of the store was a local drug lord who never showed his face until one night when my boss went missing, and I was personally greeted by the owner to run the store alongside another Colombian girl. After that first meeting, the owner would make frequent stops by the store, and we became fond of each other. Before I go on, let me say that I never loved him like I loved your father," my mother admitted.

"Tell the fucking truth," my grandfather encouraged.

My mother was breathing hard as if this were taking everything in her. She continued. "What turned into frequent visits became a full-blown romance in no time from taking trips to paying for my tuition.

He treated me like I was the only girl in the world. That didn't last long, because the moment I became pregnant, the truth came out.

"Not only was he older; he was also happily married. I had nowhere to go. He possessed so much power there that I couldn't even fly home to have an abortion. So not only was I left pregnant by a married man, I was also considered his other woman, and everyone knew it. My life was taken away from me.

"I would go the store and didn't have to pay for things; I didn't wait in lines, and didn't pay bills. I even got straight A's from my professors whether I did the work or not. It was all because they feared this man. I hated my life so much because I never wanted to be the woman that breaks another woman's home. Six months into my pregnancy, I met a local boy in one of my classes, which was your father, Manuel.

"He had just come back from school in California and was taking summer classes in his hometown. Instead of judging the black girl with the big belly, he befriended me. And instead of fearing the man I was pregnant by, he acted as if it wasn't a problem. We bonded over working on assignments together, and the rest just happened. I couldn't believe that the day I gave birth in Colombia would be the day I found out that Manuel was my baby's father's son.

"Imagine his shock when he found out his father had a twenty-year-old pregnant with his first baby girl. That moment created a hate in both of us for this one man. The fact that he refused to leave his daughter's side and had someone watching me twenty-four hours out of the day made me sick. So since Manuel was heading back to school soon, we decided to leave together without his father knowing.

"He admitted the truth to his mother, and she helped me leave. We changed my name and my daughter's, so when he thought he was sending his son back off to school, I was also leaving. We escaped and started a life, but the best part other than having my daughter was being able to tell *Papi's* wife sorry before she left this earth. A few months after being here, I became pregnant again, and that's where you guys came in," she explained as tears escaped her eyes.

"Damn, so we have another sister? Where is she at?" Manuel asked as everyone stood quietly.

"How did you find them?" Milan added.

"Thanks to Marcy's short visit to Colombia, we reconnected, and the rest was history. I sent her back, thinking you guys would finally tell the truth, but I see I was wrong," grandfather admitted.

"So, Mom, let me get this straight. You fucked around with our grandfather, got pregnant, and fell in love with his son? Only you didn't know it was his son, and now the mom we thought we knew real name is Letecia Ford? Now the million-dollar question is, where is our long-lost sister?" Milan asked, dissecting the entire situation.

I shook my head. This shit was crazier than I thought. I replayed my trip to Colombia in my head. Still not talking, my father, sitting in the chair, dropped his head. Picking it back up, he looked at me, confirming what I was thinking at the moment with tears forming in my eyes. I looked away from him.

"In Colombia, there was a picture of *Papi* holding a baby that looked to be me. I'm the child that was always different. I caused problems. I never felt truly loved, and I get a rush out of danger. It all makes sense that I am his daughter," I whispered, pointing at *Papi*.

Everyone's eyes were now on my mother.

"That can't be right! You're our age!" Manuel yelled.

"Not unless you had the connections my wife did. You were born in Colombia. You left at three months. She was pregnant again by the time they escaped. After having the twins and becoming lawyers, they passed you off as a triplet and created Marcy Gomez. So when they turned eighteen, you were turning nineteen shortly after," *Papi* shedded more light.

"So my whole life has practically been a lie?" I cried.

"I'm sorry. I'm so sorry. I did it to protect you, Marcy," my mother admitted, now on her knees, crying.

"So let me get this straight. Not only is Marcy our sister, she's also our aunt, and she's also our real father's sister?" Manuel asked, pointing at him and Milan.

"Marcy, I'm sorry," Manuel responded.

"Her name is Marcella, and she will be addressed as that from here on out. That is my late mother's name, and you will be proud of your real name," *Papi* added.

Everyone at this point was wrapped up in their own thoughts.

"You couldn't even trust your closest brother with this secret for years. I waited, and after a while, I searched around California to make sure you were OK and alive. I prayed every day only to find out nineteen years later that you ran away with this negro bitch!" my uncle Geraldo released, visibly hurt.

"My brother, forgive me," Manuel replied.

"Can you untie him, *Papi*?" I spoke, wanting Manuel to be released. Truthfully, I didn't blame him. If it were someone I loved, I would fight for them too.

He motioned for his men to cut him loose as Geraldo stayed in position. Milan ran to hug him. I guess she felt the same way.

"I don't ever want you to say another word to me for the rest of my life. You are dead to me. I hate the ground you walk on, and I hate you even more," I spoke as I approached my mother, crying.

Standing on her feet, she grabbed my arm, attempting to apologize. "It's not what you think. He's a dangerous man and means you no good. I did this to protect you, Marcy. Why can't you see that?"

Snatching away, I looked her deep in her eyes. "The same way you had Royal released from prison for him to come here and almost kill me!" I yelled.

"Say that's not true!" Milan and Manuel yelled at the same time.

"I did that to help you as well! I can't take you hating me. Please let me make it right," my mom pleaded.

"Man, that's fucked up," Manuel added.

"Marcy, I mean Marcella, let's go. This is enough for one day. Just as Marcella said, stay far away from us and especially my child," Milan added, grabbing my hand, pulling me away because my next step would be to kill the woman who birthed me.

"Aye, *Papi,* let me holla at you!" I heard Manuel say as we all exited the house, leaving Manuel and Letecia to live in their pool of lies. I laughed because I knew Manuel was about to pitch his shot to be put on in Papi's empire.

"Sure, grandson. How about dinner on me?" *Papi* added.

"Hell yeah. Aye, Milan, I'm chillin' with Grandpop!" his ghetto ass yelled.

"Son, just call me *Papi*, and Marcella, I will be in touch before I depart," *Papi* called out as I nodded my head, getting in my car, headed back to pour my heart out to my man.

The crazy part about this day was the fact that in my heart, I knew something wasn't right. But to think of myself being the daughter or a cartel leader made perfect sense for my gangster ass.

Arriving home with Milan right behind me, I rushed into the house. Running up the stairs, I found Ramel on the toilet and taking a shit.

I burst through the bathroom door, and he held the newspaper up like an old ass man.

"Baby, are you OK?" he asked, pulling the paper away from his face.

"No, but first, let me wipe my face because I refuse to cry anymore." Grabbing my rag, I wiped my face before I continued. "So basically, I just found out that my whole life was a lie. *Papi* is actually my real father. I'm nineteen and not eighteen. Who I thought was my father is actually my oldest brother. I was born in Colombia, and my real name is Marcella Gomez, and my entire life has been a bold-faced lie. The twins are my siblings as well as I'm their aunt. This story is so crazy that I even feel crazy for telling it. Just promise me that we won't live a fucked up life like mine, and we won't ever lie to each other or our kids. I can't take anymore lies, Ramel. I just can't," I blurted out in one breath. "So if there's anything you want to tell me, you need to say it now!" I reasoned.

"I'm good. I'm the perfect one. You're the one that needs to be questioned." He laughed.

"I'm being serious. I can't take anymore, Ramel. I need you to be honest with me. If there are any secrets that may come out later, here's your chance to tell it now so we can work through it," I added.

"I been honest from the jump, baby. You got all of me." He smiled. "But damn, baby, I'm sorry to hear that. I'm speechless. Anything you need me to do? I got your back," he replied, and I smiled.

"You know you're stank as hell, right?"

"Oh, I know, but you mean to tell me I waited all that time to fuck the shit out of you, and technically, I could've been did that? Now I'm pissed for real. Your people owe me." He laughed. I loved how he knew exactly what to say to make light of a situation.

"I love you, boy," I said, turning around to leave his stank ass to finish his business.

"I love you more, girl." He grunted.

21

WAKING UP, I felt like a whole new person; although sadness crowded my vision, I also felt like a new person with a new chance at life. I had a court day coming up, which I didn't sweat since my lawyer said she had this in the bag. Not reading me my rights before arresting me was a big red flag, so there was no doubt I'd beat this.

Rolling over, I kissed Ramel. Last night was full of lovemaking and a long talk. There was no doubt this man was the man for me, and although my life was hell, he made it feel like heaven each time.

Boom, boom, boom!

"Baby, you hear that?" I asked as he grabbed his phone. Jumping out of bed, he put his sweats and a T-shirt on as I placed my pajamas on. He looked at his outside cameras from his phone.

"Oh shit, it's the police. Why the fuck are they here?" he wondered.

"Just chill. Let me answer it," I said, pushing him back.

Walking into the hallway to head downstairs, I looked to see Rome standing by his door with his gun at his side.

"It's the police," I whispered. He shook his head. Thank God we didn't bring drugs to the house, so I knew we were in the clear.

I opened the door, and two male officers stood there, waiting for an answer.

"How can I help you?" I asked, looking them up and down.

"Yes, we are looking for Ramiel Brown," the taller one replied.

"For what?" I inquired.

"Ma'am, is Ramiel Brown home?" he asked, ignoring my question.

"Yes, I'm here. How can I help you?" Ramel said walking up behind me.

"You're Ramiel Brown?" they both asked.

"Yes, why?"

"You're under arrest for the rape of a girl named Kiona Turner."

"What? Man, I ain't rape nobody!" Ramel yelled as they reached in and handcuffed him.

That shit caught me off guard. My mind couldn't process what was going on, and who the hell was Kiona Turner? I thought hard as they wrestled, trying to arrest him.

"Y'all don't have to get physical. I'll go peacefully. Just let her get my shoes," he said, agreeing to follow their orders. "Baby, call my lawyer. This shit is a lie. I ain't rape that girl!" Ramel yelled.

Running up the stairs to get his shoes like a bolt of lightning, it hit me. The twin whose ass I whooped in her front yard months back, her name was Kiona—the same girl he claimed only sucked his dick.

He sat on the ground as the officer waited, and I walked over to him, placing his shoes on his feet.

"Can you guys please give us a minute?" I pleaded as the officers faced the other way and walked closer to the door, talking to each other.

"Is this the twin?" I asked. Nodding his head yes, he looked down. "We both know you didn't rape her, but all I want to know is if you fucked her." Without an answer, he looked away, and tears formed in my eyes. "Was it more than once?" He slowly shook his head. "I knew what happened when we broke up, but did you fuck her while we were together?" I questioned.

"I'm sorry. I only fucked that bitch twice. Once when we broke up the first time, and once right before Khyrah died. She only doing this shit because I cut her ass off and told her I was getting married to you. She bitter and trying to ruin a nigga life. I know you asked me to be honest, but I didn't want to hurt you more than you were already hurt. My job is to protect you and love you, and a nigga fucked up. I'm sorry, baby. Don't let this shit break us. We came too far. I love you, Marcella," he begged, but the fact that he was given the chance to be real and chose not to made me feel cheated yet again.

Standing to my feet, without one word, I walked upstairs to our room and got myself together. It was at that moment that I knew love didn't love anybody, and it damn sure didn't love me. After everything I'd been through—everything we'd been through—Ramel just reminded me of the one rule I lived by before I met him. Trust no one.

Even after our relationship elevated to better heights, and I gave him the green light to come clean, he refused to do so. Protecting me meant being real even if it hurt me; I could respect that more than a lie. I went back into my room and lay back in my bed. As the front door closed, he was taken to jail.

Hearing my room door open, I heard Milan's footsteps as she slid into the bed behind me.

"I'm sorry, Marcy. I know you're tired of going through shit. But one thing I learned is that you never know how strong you are until being strong is your only option. I know you're still trying to get over what Letecia and Manuel did, but this doesn't define you. What defines you is how you stand after everything around you falls. You were not meant to break, and what Ramel did was fucked up. But he's a man, and that man loves the air you breathe, and trust you've fucked up more than a little bit.

"Don't let one mistake make you lose the love of your life, because it could be a lot worse. If you're up to it, what we can do is go beat that hoe down. I'm sure she'll be ready to tell the truth then," Milan joked as my frown turned upside down. She was right, but Ramel was definitely going to pay for his little lie.

"I already beat that hoe's ass once before," I admitted, thinking about the time I pulled her out of her house. Milan didn't know since it was during the time we were not speaking.

"Who y'all going to beat up?" Rome interrupted.

"Damn, nosy ass!" I yelled.

"Milan's damn phone keeps ringing off the hook, and it's about to wake Rylee up, so I brought it in here. And shouldn't you be making some calls to get brah outta jail? Don't tell me you are salty about that old ass shit with that project hoe. You better than that," Rome advised as Milan answered her ringing phone.

"I know, I kno—" was all I said before Milan screamed.

"No, no, no, no, don't say that!" she screamed again.

Taking the phone from her, I looked at the call as she cried. "Hello, who is this!" I yelled.

"This is your mother's secretary at her office, Cathy. I came into work and found... found... found," she kept repeating as my heart began to beat fast. "I found her dead!" she cried into the phone. "She shot herself in the head. She's gone," she added, crying even more. "There's also three letters I found on her desk for you guys. They're taking her body now, so you guys may want to meet them at the police station," she instructed.

Dropping the phone from my hands, I realized that when it rained, it poured. As much pain as she caused, as many times I yelled I hated her, and as many times I never said I love you back to her, I never thought she would die. I never really wanted her to die.

I honestly didn't know how to feel, what to think, or even what to believe. In a matter of two years, I watched the strongest woman I knew crumble right before my eyes. That was one of the main reasons I grew distant from her. Instead of fighting for her marriage, she let it go. Instead of fighting for me to make the right decision, she made me get rid of it and run away. And instead of fighting for her rights and standing up to a liar and cheat, my real father, *Papi*, she found a way and ran from him. I hated that about her. And now, instead of fixing her problems she created, she ran away with death, leaving us to pick up the missing pieces.

Rome took a distraught and crying Milan out of my room to

console her, and looking to the left, I watched the empty spot grow cold. It was funny the way your darkness caught the light just in time to create enough pain before it faded back to darkness.

Grabbing my phone, I texted Manuel.

*Me: Your mother killed herself last night in her office. Call her secretary for more information.

I had no time for sympathy. Hell, life didn't even have sympathy for me. All this shit I kept going through, and I had the nerve to be pregnant. Maybe they were right; God knew best. Sitting up, I placed my feet off the edge of the bed and hung my head low. My world was spinning yet again, and I just couldn't find the strength to breathe.

Walking into our spacious bathroom, I cut the shower on and undressed myself. Making sure the water was as hot as I could stand it, I walked in and leaned against the wall. I felt numb, as if I could feel no pain, as if I were a mute. I didn't know if it was shock or what, but all I knew was that this feeling was one I couldn't shake.

"Why can't I just live a happy life? Is that too much to ask, God? Why do you make it so hard for me? Do you hate me that much that the moment I open my eyes each day is already preset to tear me down? I feel like a marked target. What have I ever done to you, God, that would have this much pain be over my head? I know you hear me! Answer me! Why do you hate me so much!" I screamed out as the hot water hit my face and body. Sliding my body down, I hit the floor. I laid my head against the wall and closed my eyes. Whatever I had to realize was that I was in control, and nobody had my back better than me.

Washing and getting out the shower, I created a new mindset. It was time to take control of my own life. If being strong was the only option I had, then I planned to be the strongest I'd ever been.

Grabbing the scissors, I began cutting my hair. Every wild piece that flowed on top, I chopped off. I just kept cutting; my hands wouldn't stop. I felt a sense of relief and control like I was creating a new woman.

Thirty minutes later, I looked to see all my hair around the sink. Rubbing my hands through my two inches of curly hair that now graced my head, I couldn't believe what I had just done. In a weird way, I liked what I saw. Heading to my closet, I looked around to see nothing that I wanted to wear. I planned to change my style for the better. It was time to become a real adult and start living my life as Marcella Gomez.

Grabbing a black pantsuit I didn't realize I had, I placed that on with my Givenchy heels. Instead of carrying an oversized bag, I grabbed my black Gucci clutch and decided to head out.

Walking to Milan and Rome's room, I peeked in to see her lying on the bed.

"Marcy, what the hell have you done? Damn," Rome shockingly said.

"Just had an epiphany. Why? Do I look stupid?" I asked.

"No, sis, I actually like it; grown woman shit. I'm glad you were able to pull it together," he admitted, rubbing Milan's back.

"Milan, pull it together. We have shit to do, or I can do this alone," I said sternly, referring to identifying our mother's body.

"You and Manuel can go. I'll stay," she whispered.

Texting Manuel to meet me at the morgue, I headed toward the safe to grab twenty stacks of cash. Running in our room, I grabbed Ramel's small briefcase and placed the stacks of cash inside.

With that, I was off. I grabbed the keys to Ramel's Audi, and I headed to my first destination. Riding with no music, I made it to Johnson & Johnson criminal law firm where Daylon Johnson resided.

Walking in the office, I bypassed the assistant. I didn't have time to wait or talk.

"Ma'am, you can't go back there! He's in a meeting!" the secretary yelled.

I walked into his office with the briefcase to see him with two young Black men. They all turned to look my way as the secretary yelled after me.

"I'm here on behalf of Ramel Brown. I need you to make them leave," I demanded.

"I'm sorry, sir. She just barged in!" the secretary yelled, running in the office out of breath.

"It's OK. I got it from here," Daylon dismissed her.

"What makes you think I can just stop what I have going on? You have to wait just like everyone else. My secretary can assist you in booking an appointment!" he barked, but I wasn't trying to hear that. Taking the briefcase, I popped it open and emptied the cash onto the desk.

"Damn, you some type of cartel leader or some shit? Whatever you doing, I want in," one of the young boys replied.

"Umm, gentlemen, I hate to cut this short, but I will have to reschedule," Daylon confessed.

They both stood to their feet in awe of what had just happened in front of them.

"What's your name?" I asked, speaking to the young boy who remained quiet the entire time.

"Damoni Smith," he replied.

"I'll be in touch," I said as they both walked out of the office. I didn't know what drew me to him, but I liked his demeanor, and I knew I could use him.

"I need his info as well as Ramel Brown released as soon as possible," I demanded, never taking a seat.

"He was picked up this morning on rape charges. He trusts you, so that means whatever you have to do, Daylon, I need it done."

"Ramel knows this will be handled with no problem, Ms...." he said, addressing the fact that he didn't know my name.

"Marcella Gomez," I replied as I turned around to exit. "I'll be in touch, Daylon." Walking out of the office I spotted the two boys waiting by the bus stop in front.

"Aye, boss lady!" the one whose name I didn't know called out. Clutching my pistol in my small clutch, I stopped.

"I'm Justin, by the way, and like he said before, he's Damoni. Not to get all up in your shit, but we are trying to make some money," he admitted.

"Looks like you're already in trouble for trying to make some money if you're sitting in Daylon's office," I reminded them.

"That's not the case. He mentors the young kids from the hood, and each Wednesday at twelve o'clock, we come up here. Since we're eighteen now, this is our last Wednesday doing this shit as a part of juvenile release, and we are ready to make some real paper. Daylon knows what's up, though; he is just as crooked as these police officers out here," Damoni added.

"Here, put your numbers in my phone. I'll be in touch," I replied, handing over my phone. After they supplied their numbers, they walked me to my car as I left. I kinda liked their style. Damoni seemed to be the hustler, and Justin was the enforcer—the one who didn't mind getting his hands dirty. I didn't know what the hell I could use them for, but when the time or opportunity presented itself, I would definitely keep them in mind.

Heading to the morgue, I received a message from Manuel that he was already there. Picking up speed, I headed to assist my brother. I pulled up to the tiny, gray building that looked as if sadness and sorrow dwelled here.

Manuel was outside of his BMW X6 rental truck smoking a blunt. Parking next to him, I got out and took his blunt from his hands, hitting it a few times. I prepared myself for whatever lay behind those walls.

"I'm kinda liking this new look, sis. You look like a grown woman. You ready for this shit?" he asked, taking the blunt from me and putting it out. Spraying some perfume on, I walked ahead to be greeted by two local police officers. After they us in after asking a few questions, we were finally about to identify her body.

Walking into the cold room, seeing multiple bodies covered in sheets, we were escorted to the back where she resided. Pulling the sheet down to reveal her flawless face, the only thing out of order was the hole in the side of her head that blew her ear off.

"Man, this shit crazy, Marcy. Even after all the shit she did, the fact still remained that she was our girl. I feel bad for not answering her calls," Manuel confessed as I remained quiet. As much time as I spent hating her all my life, there were times when I thought the world of her. And in order for me to take control, this was one issue that I would have to let die with her and never speak of again.

Leaning down, I kissed her chilled face as I took one last look at her.

"What are your plans for burial?" the morgue worker asked.

"She will be cremated," I replied as I held my clutch and walked out.

"Marcy, we need to talk about this!" Manuel yelled right behind me.

"No, what we need to figure out is how to get rid of her things, how much insurance money is out there, and what type of things she put in that will," I responded.

"You talking about money and all that other shit when our mother isn't even six feet under yet. You're cold-hearted, Marcy," he replied.

"No, I'm living in reality. She's gone, and she took the cowardly way out. Oh, and it's Marcella, not Marcy," I said as I placed my shades over my face and hopped in my car. Just making those two stops took a lot out of me. I needed some food and some rest.

Pulling over at a local fried chicken drive-through, I ordered a two-piece snack and pulled up to the window. Grabbing a hundred-dollar bill, I stuck my hand out the window as I looked for my phone.

"Ummm, ma'am, we can't change that hundred-dollar bill," the driver-through worker said. I turned to see a familiar face waiting for my response.

"Naomi?" I questioned, hoping I was right.

"Marcy?" she replied.

"Yes, how have you been?"

"As you can see, working. Shit been crazy, but I see you're looking great," she admired.

"I'm alright. Listen, take my number and give me a call we need to link up," I offered.

"OK," she said, grabbing a piece of receipt paper.

"It's 404-321-1558, oh, and I don't have any smaller bills, so just keep the change and hit me up ASAP," I replied as she grabbed my food and handed it to me, giving me an extra milkshake.

I pulled off, feeling like I accomplished a lot today. Now all I needed was Ramel to get through this shit because I planned to become his business partner whether he like it or not. Arriving home, I walked in and headed straight to our room to eat and wait for Ramel's call. First appearance was in the morning, and I needed to be ready to bond my man out of jail.

I looked around, and life felt empty without him bothering me, wanting to cuddle, and lay up talking. Laying my head down, having enough for one day, I fell asleep.

~

9:00 A.M THURSDAY MORNING...

I was awakened by my phone ringing for the third time that morning. I sat up to see it was an unknown number calling,

"Hello," I sleepily answered.

"Yes, Marcella, this is Daylon Johnson. How are you this morning?" the lawyer asked.

"I'm assuming you have news for me?" I replied, sitting up.

"They denied his bond, so right now, he's going to have to sit. I promise it won't be for long. I'm reviewing everything now. Just a heads up, for the sake of this case, the victim should be left alone. You catch my drift?" he advised. I knew exactly what he meant.

"Trust, if I planned to, we wouldn't be having this conversation right now," I shot back.

"I'll be in touch, Ms. Gomez," he replied as I ended the call. Getting up, I decided to get ready and head to visit Ramel. We needed to talk since he obviously couldn't call.

I hurried to the bathroom and did my daily hygiene routine, starting with taking a shower. Not having to worry about my hair was a relief. After applying moisturizer, my curls looked great. After that, I fixed my makeup and headed to my closet, making a mental note to go shopping.

Walking in, I scrolled through my line and found a knee-length, tight-fitted, black dress. The dress was sleeveless but still resembled an outfit ready for business. Pairing the outfit with my black and gold

Gucci pumps, I grabbed my matching clutch and got ready to head out.

Rushing, I grabbed the Audi keys and headed out. The jail was forty minutes away from our house, so I prepared for a nice ride. Cranking the car up, I began to ride, still not turning any music on. I didn't need anything to distract my mind.

Pulling up to the jail, I grabbed my license, checked myself in the mirror, and headed in. I hated to admit how much I missed my man. As mad as I portrayed it to be, I loved the hell out of him.

When I walked in, all eyes turned to me. Allowing my designer heels to hit the floor, I walked to the receptionist desk and signed in.

"Yes, I'm here to see Ramiel Brown," I spoke, handing her my license. She looked me up and down before taking them.

"Have a seat. We will call you when it's time," she replied.

I turned around to see Black and white women from all walks of life waiting to see their loved ones, from the single mothers with the bad ass kids and newborns to the young girls waiting to see their definition of love behind those walls. Looking over each woman, I knew my life could have easily been their story or worse. Twirling my engagement ring on my finger, I took a seat and began the waiting process.

"Nice ring," an older black woman holding a newborn said.

Looking up, I replied. "Thank you."

"I guess it's safe to say he loves you a lot. My man would never buy me something so beautiful like that. He would steal it before he honestly bought it," she revealed.

"You're right; he does love me, but this ring doesn't define that. It's just a token of his love. What defines his love for me is the way he looks at me as if he sees no one else. The way he keeps me on track when I make dumb decisions. The way he won't close his eyes to sleep unless I'm lying next to him. And the way he's there for me even when I'm not there for myself," I replied. I realized that regardless of his mistake, this man loved the life out of me. The sad part was that it took a complete stranger to make me remember the sacrifices he'd made since the beginning.

"That's deep. I guess you one of the lucky ones," she said, looking down.

"And you're lucky too. You'll realize that once you stop giving discounts with your love," I replied.

"Marcy Gomez!" the guard yelled. I stood to my feet, winking my eye at her as I walked away, ready to see my man.

After walking through the metal detector and being cleared, I was escorted through a steel double door. There were sections lined up that resembled cubicles in an office, only the moment you sat down, you were faced with a glass that held a phone on each side. Taking a seat, I waited for Ramel to appear.

After waiting for five minutes, he appeared with his dreads pulled back into a ponytail and a green jumpsuit on. Taking a long hard look at me, he took a seat and grabbed the phone.

Picking up on my side, I remained quiet.

"Damn, it hasn't been a whole two days yet, and you changing up?"

Forgetting all about my new outward appearance, I rubbed my hands through my two inches of hair.

"Don't worry. I like it. You look beautiful and sophisticated," he complimented.

"You see, they got me in here with no bond. This shit is crazy, baby. I'm sorry I did this to you."

"I know, but I'm not here to talk about that. This will be handled. What I do want to know is, who do you plan to leave running things if you're in here?" I asked.

"Not you. I see what you getting at, and I'm not with that shit. I told you no before, and the answer is still no. Besides, Rome is capable of handling things. Just inform *Papi* that things may slow down, but I promise the last two million I owe will be paid, and that's on my life."

He said the perfect name. That was all I needed to know, moving forward.

"So has Daylon been here to visit?" I asked, changing that subject.

"Fuck all of that. Promise me right now that you won't get

involved. We have businesses that need to be ran. The streets is no place for my woman. Promise me that shit right now!" he demanded, gripping the phone as if he could break it into pieces.

"Damn, Ramel! I promise! Are you happy?" I returned.

"Yep, and yeah, that crooked ass nigga came and seen me. At this point, I don't know what to expect. I just need you to hold it down. I know I fucked up, and I lied. A nigga not perfect, but I love you, and just like everything else, we gonna get through this," he confessed. "Damn, I should've married you right after you got out of the hospital," he stressed, looking me dead into my eyes.

"Ramel, I know we gon' get through this together. But as far as our engagement, maybe we should hold off on that," I suggested.

"So what you saying?"

"I'm just saying I still want to be with you, but this situation made me realize we may be moving too fast and need to slow things down."

"Marcella, don't do this shit—not here, and not right now," he begged.

"I'm not leaving you; I'm still your girl. I just want to start doing things the right way. I want to be married, I want to have kids, and I want to be happy with you and only you. But from the beginning, we've rushed things. I just want this to last, and I want to allow life to happen without rushing it. Do you understand? I need to become who I am so that I can be the woman you need and not the little girl you've been dealing with," I explained.

"As much as I want to protest this shit, I can't even argue with this shit, because I know I fucked up. I'm even more pissed that your mom is gone, and I can't be there to help you through this. As crazy as your relationship was with her, no one wants their parents to not be here, because there was a time when she was your everything. Do what you need to do, Marcella. Just promise me one thing: that your love for me won't fade," Ramel expressed, smiling because I knew it took a lot for him to take the higher road, and the fact that he wanted me to be happy even in his lowest moment let me know that I had a real man.

"That's one promise I'll go to my grave with. I love you, boy."

"I love you too, girl," he said, forcing a smile through his pain. Seeing such a strong and powerful man fall victim and get cased up in the lowest crime a man can commit made me know he felt defeated. I looked away, unable to keep eye contact.

"And I still mean everything I said. Get yourself together, and boss up the right way. Start your clothing line and promote that shit. Leave the street shit to my brother and my team," he repeated in a way I knew he felt that his words were falling on deaf ears, but I agreed and changed the subject.

Leaving visitation left me with an uneasy feeling as if things were about to change in a major way, especially between Ramel and me.

I grabbed my phone, dialing the one number that would change my life forever. It was time to do business.

22

TWO WEEKS LATER...

I TOUCHED the golden vase that sat above the fireplace in my and Ramel's home. The vase held my mother's ashes, and in a weird way, it made me feel as if she was here on most days.

Walking out of the house, I spotted Damoni and Justin reporting for their first day of work with the Glock Nineteen, fifteen rounds, nine-millimeter guns I provided them with to their sides.

"All I need you to do, Justin, is drive, and for you, Damoni, to ride in the back with me," I instructed as Justin opened the black Tahoe door for me to get in. Making sure my Diane Von Furstenberg two-piece, black pantsuit fitted me just right while sliding my foot down in my Chanel pumps, we were off to our first destination.

Looking to my left, I saw Damoni sitting quietly just as the first time I seen him. After telling Justin the address to our first stop, I started small talk with Damoni.

"Why are you so quiet?" I asked.

"No reason. I just don't talk if there's no need. Plus, I learned that being quiet allows you to see people for who they really are," he replied, and I was truly impressed.

"Spoken like a real man. Old people must have raised you?"

"Yeah, my grandfather did before he passed away. I was sent here from Gainesville, Florida. I used to get in trouble also, and my mother couldn't handle it anymore, so she shipped me off. He died a few months ago, and I refused to move back, so Justin's mom let me move in with them," he spoke, spilling his story. I could relate to the broken relationship with his mother and being the problem child.

"How's your relationship with your mom?" I inquired.

"It's cool; that's my world. We just realized for the sake of our livelihood, we get along better being apart from each other," he admitted. I didn't want to get too far into this discussion, so I changed the subject.

"So once we pull up here, all I need y'all to do is follow my lead. Don't speak, and when I say shoot, be ready to blast," I prepped Damoni, but I knew they needed no introduction to this lifestyle, considering the fact they were robbing before I came along. I waited and planned for two whole weeks for this day, spending day and night getting my boys ready for whatever may happen, so my first stop was Ramel's biggest trap house.

It looked suspicious, pulling up in the truck I was in, and that's why I exited the vehicle first. I could stand in clear view of the cameras. That way, they knew it was me.

After getting out, Justin and Damoni followed suit behind me as I walked through the fence to the front door. Without knocking, I twisted the knob and walked right in.

The first thing I saw was most of the boys playing games. I also saw young girls sitting around as if it were a chill spot, along with my man's money laid around in different areas. As if time stood still, all eyes were on me as my boys exposed their weapons at their sides.

"So this is what goes on here?" I questioned, breaking the sudden silence.

"Yo, Marcy, I know this shit looks crazy. Ramel being gone got shit a little off right now," Flex, the point person over this trap, admitted.

"All of your little girlfriends need to leave, now!" I demanded as they all stood and rushed out of the house. As they all exited the house, I waited to speak. "Crazy how? Are you still making money? Are you motherfuckers still getting paid around this bitch? Aren't his drugs still flowing in this bitch?" I asked, now standing by the kitchen table, looking at everyone's frozen faces.

"Yeah, but—" he attempted to say.

"Yeah, but what, Flex? From here on out, I'm in control, and shit is about to change. Just look at it as Ramel is taking a break, and his bitch is filling in for him. First things first, don't ever call me Marcy again. It's Marcella, and—"

"I'm not taking leadership from no girl. This shit not happening," Flex interrupted. "Ramel know he could've hit me up or one of the other leads in this shit. He could've even got Rome to take over. This nigga tripping. I see I'm going to have to pay him a visit," Flex expressed.

"Well, I'm sorry you feel that way, Flex, but I'll be the only one communicating with Ramel. However, you can visit him in heaven or hell one day," I replied as I pulled my pistol and shot Flex in the middle of the forehead. He was a liability the moment he said he would visit Ramel, and he signed his own death certificate.

"Anybody want to join him?" I asked as the boys wiped splatters of blood off them.

"Hell no," I heard a few voices say as they all looked shocked.

"Great! Now I'll need a new point person for this trap, and you all will be making more money because I'll need more hours put in. I got some new shit to try out. I'm about to flood the city with more dope and lower prices. If that goes well, I'll introduce y'all to heroin. That alone will cut out the competition, so we will have some angry people. Stay strapped and ready at all times. Oh, and if I ever walk back up in this bitch to see y'all living life and playing with my money, you all will die a slow death. These two boys are with me at all times. To reach me, you need to get through them, so I suggest you get to know them. A shipment will hit this trap house at midnight tonight. I expect you all here and to spread the word that there's a new bitch in town!" I spoke as I prepared myself to leave.

"Oh yeah, and clean this shit up," I demanded, looking down at Flex's lifeless body. Walking out as if I owned the world, I honestly felt great about life at that moment. As Damoni opened the door to the truck, I pulled my phone out and called Naomi. She was up next, and her main target was D-boy. "Tonight, you're up. His crew will be at club Spade, just as we planned. Take it slow and get him to fall for you. After that, I'll do the rest," I instructed.

"Understood, oh, and Marcella, thanks again," she replied. Naomi had more problems than a little bit, especially after her family became poor due to her father's medical bills from his cancer. She was the oldest of five siblings, and they lived in the roughest hood in Miami. After turning tricks and stripping, she ended with the local boss nigga who treated her like shit and used her to transport drugs. Naomi had been through a lot, and that's why after completing this little task for me, I planned to give her the biggest payday of her life.

After ending the call, my phone began to ring again, but this time, I declined the call. Speaking with Ramel would only throw my day off track, and I needed to be on point. Heading to my brother's new trap, I powered my phone off. My brother didn't want to do business with Ramel but with me. He planned to take over the game like we were destined to do.

Deciding to stop for food, I made Justin pull over to a local chicken spot, and they opened the door for me to exit. I walked in, and they trailed slowly behind, engaged in their own conversation. We walked in, and there was a wait, but I refused to stay in one spot longer than ten minutes. Walking to the front, jumping in front of a low-cut, handsome, dark-skinned man, I smiled as I began to talk.

"I'm sorry, but I have to go. Can you please take my order?" I convinced as I slid a fifty-dollar bill toward the cashier.

"Bossy and still beautiful, I see," the man behind me spoke, and I turned around to face him. I knew he looked familiar, but I couldn't place where I knew him from.

"Actually, take both of our orders, and I'll handle the rest," he spoke, moving my hand back and directing me to put my money away.

"Sampson?" I addressed, remembering his handsome face.

"Impressive. Didn't think you would remember me. How you been? I mean, you look astonishing," he complimented.

After ordering myself the same thing he ordered for himself, we both took a seat to finish talking. "I've been great. I can't complain, just making a few changes," I replied, running my hands through my two-inch curls.

"I see, and those changes look great, might I add. Look, last time when you were with your girl—I think her name was Khyrah—we sat and talked for two hours, and we parted ways. I don't plan on leaving here today without your number," he expressed.

Taking a long, hard pause, I stared into his eyes. The fact that I was lonely and missing my man didn't help that this fine brother was interested in me.

"Sampson, I want to be honest. I have a boyfriend, and although things are crazy right now, I just don't think that would be a good idea," I admitted.

"I like that you're honest, but the fact that things are 'crazy' lets a nigga know that maybe you need an extra ear. Put it like this. Get my number, and if I cross your mind, then hit me up," he replied.

I smiled as I powered my phone on and handed it over for him to put in his number. I didn't know what I was doing, but at that moment, if felt good to know I still had it.

As our order was called, I stood to my feet to shake Sampson's hand. After parting ways, I felt him staring me down as Damoni opened the door for me to enter the Tahoe.

Just as I was about to text him my number, my phone began to ring, displaying a collect call from Ramel, and I decided to finally answer.

∼

FIVE HOURS LATER...

Walking in the house, I immediately saw Milan rocking my niece to sleep. Out of nowhere, Rome appeared behind Milan and visibly pissed.

"Baby, let me holla at Marcella right quick," he spoke, dismissing Milan. Her eyes grew big, looking at me as she shook her head. That was always her way of warning me that I was in trouble. "Are you out of your fucking mind!" he yelled.

"Rome, let me explain. Your brother isn't here. What did you expect?" I questioned.

"I expected to do what he asked, and that was for me to take over for a while! Damn, Marcella, he ain't dead. The nigga just in jail!" Rome yelled.

"And I understand that, but hear me out, Rome. We can do this together. Listen, at this point, I've lost more than I've gained. Ramel is in jail, my mother is dead, and my real father is in Colombia. I need this. I was made for this lifestyle, and unlike Ramel, I know you feel it in your heart that I can handle this. All I'm asking is for a partnership. You have a family to think about. Let me handle and worry about the street shit; you just focus on the income," I reasoned.

"My brother will kill you and me, Marcella. This shit doesn't feel right at all. If you get hurt or anything happens to you, that'll be on me," he replied, walking into the kitchen. Looking around, I saw Milan's nosy ass listening from the stairs.

"That's a risk I'm willing to take. I'mma give it to you like this. Whether you work with me or not, I'm still going to push my product. Since you can't see the bigger picture in this, let me help you. I know about the debt your family owes mine. Now, I'm willing to help pay that debt and make us more money than we've ever dreamed of in a matter of months. If you're down, we can make that happen, and if not, I'll make it happen on my own, and you can find your own connect to pay my father off with. The choice is yours, but I would hate to be that vengeful to you. Just think about it. This could set my niece up for life as well as you and my sister," I reminded Rome as he just stared.

"To be truthfully honest, I never planned to get this deep in this shit. When you and Ramel came back from Colombia, I had no choice, because my brother needed me. But that little girl upstairs needs me more. Look at us. None of us are graduating high school, and none of us have shit going for ourselves but the streets. Man, listen, I'm down to let you do whatever. If I can focus on keeping my family business in order, then it's all yours. I'll tell Ramel whatever you need me to, and I'll keep records of the money coming in and out," he replied. I smiled and gave Rome a big hug before speaking.

"Thank you so much, Rome. I got this. Now you can let your little soldiers know tonight that there's a new boss lady in town," I said.

"OK, *boss lady*," he emphasized. "Just don't kill off all my boys before they have a chance to keep making us more money", he joked.

"Flex deserved that!" I yelled, walking to my room. Going up the stairs, I made eye contact with Milan, who shook her head and walked off. I knew she would be upset, which was the reason I planned to keep her far away from all of my madness.

23

"IT'S BEEN DAMN near a month at this point! If you don't handle this, then I will!" I yelled at Daylon, Ramel's lawyer. It didn't make any sense that he was still in jail—not that I was trying to speed up the process—but I missed my man.

"I got that info you needed," Damoni said, walking into my office. I learned early on not to trust anyone, which was why I rented a little house across the street from my two main trap houses. These were the places Damoni and Justin spent most of their time. I watched who came in and out, and if things looked suspicious, I had it checked out.

"Thanks," I replied, grabbing the paper from his hands.

"You know I can handle that for you," Damoni offered.

"No, this is something I personally need to handle. I'll take a flight out tonight, and Justin can pick me up from the airport in the morning," I explained as I watched the cameras hidden in the trap house.

"I need you to focus on this and the fact that my crew got this lil' nigga working for us. What pisses me off even more is the fact that he runs errands for D-boy." I pointed to the screen to show Damoni and Justin the teenager that I noticed hanging around my trap lately.

"I asked them about that shit when I walked in there the other day. Derek spoke up and said his name was Percy and that he needed to make some extra money. So they let him bring them food and shit. I followed the little nigga the other night and seen him go straight home. I also seen that his mother is a junkie, and he takes care of his little brother that's sick," Justin admitted.

"Interesting. Well, I'll look into that. Just be ready for whatever. Other than that, I have a flight to catch. I'll be in touch," I directed as I grabbed my things to leave. I had one mission in mind, and I planned on doing just that—alone.

Checking to make sure my new fake ID would pass in the airport, I headed straight there in my Altima rental car, I waited long enough for this day, and I refused to let it pass me by. Ramel may have been right about some things, but there were some areas even he had no control over.

While I rode down the road, Sampson came across my mind, which had to be the third time in two weeks. I decided to send him a text with my info, and soon after, I powered my phone off. I planned to leave it in the car until I returned. Once I reached my destination, I would purchase a throw-away phone for the day. With my mind all over the place, I reached the airport, and after parking the rental, I grabbed only my ID and cash. The rest, I kept in the car.

Walking into the airport, I checked in under Katherine Dotts. After being cleared, I found the gate to Atlanta. Taking a seat, I waited until it was time to board. The closer I came to my destination, the angrier I became.

After a five-hour flight, I was finally back to my original home. Smelling the soul food in the air and watching the hustlers on every corner trying to survive made me miss my home. If business kept going great, maybe I could push my product in my hometown.

"*Hola*, Marcy," Manuel, my father/brother, greeted. I didn't have time for pleasantries. I had one mission in mind, and he was lucky that he wasn't the target for the lies he told.

"Manuel, my name is Marcella. Now did you do what I asked?" I inquired as I got inside of his Range Rover.

"*Sí*, here's the flip phone, and here's the address to where he's been living. The landlord is a good friend of mine and will give you the extra key to let yourself in. Marcella, get in and out because Royal has been making major moves, and his crew is always with him. His main man Jack said they were going out tonight. He will try to convince the crew to relax tonight and get Royal drunk. Pay attention and get in and out. The less you say, the better, *tú comprendes?*"

Nodding my head, I agreed and laid my head back to get ready for tonight's events. What he didn't know was the fact that Royal wasn't a dummy, and he befriended any nigga that he felt was a rat or mold. He kept them close for informational purposes, so if Jack was his main man, then he didn't trust him, which was why I formed a plan B long before this day.

7 *P.M.*

I entered the small house that sat on the corner of Luther street. This place had to be a two-bedroom close to the hood just like Royal liked it. Walking into the kitchen, I turned down the hallway to see three doors. Opening them, all I found was the bathroom and an empty room with boxes all over. Opening the third door, I found a woman sound asleep in his bed.

Trying to remain silent, I looked around to see nothing but a bed, dresser, and his clothes neatly stacked. Looking at the dresser once more before I took another step, I noticed a picture sitting up against the dresser mirror. I smiled, looking at the picture of him and me when we thought the world of each other, but those were distant memories.

Walking to the bed, I shook the sleeping woman. Opening her eyes, expecting to see him, she jumped before she realized it was me.

"Wow, he let you stay in his home while he's not home? I guess he really likes you," I said.

"He says I remind him of someone he loved," Naomi replied.

"I knew it was something about you the day we met in jail." I laughed, helping her out of bed.

"But I will say this. You must have really loved that nigga. His sex game is weak, and his dick is not that big." She laughed.

"Right, maybe that's why I love Ramel." I laughed along with her.

I sent Naomi down here two weeks ago, and just like that, in two weeks, she had Royal more than interested—I guess since I prepped her on his likes, dislikes, and things that drove him crazy about me. She was in a position to win no matter what. I guess Royal missed me more than he would ever admit.

As Naomi got dressed, we both waited for the return of Royal.

"What did you tell D-boy to get away for two weeks?" I asked, making small talk.

"Actually, I had a bitch from around the way suck his dick as I walked in and caught him, so he thinks I'm in my hometown, Louisiana, taking a break. He's a real pussy nigga. You should see the text messages he's sending. I've never seen so many thug niggas so vulnerable and sensitive over a bitch. But I did tell him I would return home so we can talk, and he's been counting down the days." She laughed.

"You're a cold bitch, and I love it," I replied.

The next few hours while we waited for Royal, we talked and made sure our plan was solid. I needed her to understand that she needed to be ready.

∼

Two Hours Later...

"Naomi, I think you should leave," I said, breaking the silence. We were both waiting anxiously.

"What? No, I'm not leaving you alone," she protested.

"Oh, yes you are, because if shit goes wrong, he will kill you first. This is my fight, so let me handle it. Plus, you have shit to handle with D-Boy. I'll pay you double for your time—just leave, or I will be forced to make you leave," I replied.

"Bitch, you didn't have to threaten me! All you had to say was that you wanted the nigga all to yourself!" she joked, grabbing her things. "Marcella, please be safe," she added.

"I will. Get home. I'll be back shortly," I said as she got her things and made an exit.

❧

12 P.M.

After waiting in the closet for three more hours since I made Naomi leave, I finally heard the door open. Hearing the keys hit the kitchen counter, I knew he would be headed this way soon.

"Baby girlllll, I hope that pussy ready for daddy!" he yelled toward the back in hopes of Naomi hearing him.

Hearing his footsteps walk toward the room, I cocked my Glock, ready. He walked in and stood by his bed, confused that Naomi wasn't there. This position had his back toward the closet in the perfect position, so I stepped out and placed my pistol to the back of his head.

"This pussy belongs to someone else," I replied to his statement, and he yelled.

"You know, I knew this day would come. I just didn't think it would be this soon. I actually thought your punk ass boyfriend would have come for me. But I knew better. I raised you, so I knew you would come ready and alone," Royal admitted.

"Shut the fuck up. You didn't know shit, and that was the problem. You're petty hustling ass could never walk in my man's shoes. You're weak, and you manipulated me. You acted as if you loved me and used me to do your dirty work. I loved you. I would've died for you. All along you, were risking it all for them," I exposed, pulling a picture out of my pocket with my free hand.

He looked down at his baby's mother and their son—the family that lived in Ohio, the exact family he hid from me. I would wonder why money would come up short, or he would leave from around me to talk on the phone. Having my newfound power created the ability to get any information I needed, and after looking into Royal's history, I found them.

Pulling out two more pictures with the gun still pointed at the back of his head, I dropped them on the bed in front of him. Silence took over, and his whole demeanor changed. He dropped his head, knowing he was defeated.

"Cat got your tongue? Did you think I would let you come in, take another child from me, damn near kill me, and let you just continue to live your life!" I yelled.

"I don't give a fuck about what I did. You didn't have to kill my lil' nigga. He was only eight years old," he whispered, speaking about his son. A life for a life was my motto. He took the one thing I looked forward to receiving, and for that, his child had to die.

"Just kill me," he whispered. Royal was defeated and had given up. He was in the perfect position for what I had planned next.

"Jack, can you and the boys tie him up!" I instructed him and two other boys came and grabbed Royal. He looked as if he had mentally checked out and didn't plan on putting up a fight. They cuffed his hands and tied his feet. As he lay on the bed, ass up, Jack proceeded to strip him naked, ripping his clothes off piece by piece.

"You're sad because your precious son is dead, but you took mine from me, and for that, you will pay."

With those last words, the extra men exited the house as Jack released his manhood from his pants. With his dick in hand, he climbed on top of Royal, stuffing his penis in his backside. Royal screamed out in pain, wiggling to get loose, but there was nowhere to run. I watched as Royal's pained face cried out for help.

"I'm sorry!" Royal screamed as Jack pounded away at his backside.

I smiled, standing and watching the scene without one drop of emotion. I couldn't believe that my mother was right the entire time about this nigga. The sad part was that he would take his last breath, not knowing that his son was still alive and well. His money-hungry baby's mother gave me the idea to take pictures of their son as if he were dead. She even sent her gay cousin Jack to help set Royal up. She moved away to get away from him and his abusive ways, but she allowed him to send her money and talk to their child. Royal made a lot of enemies, but the worst thing you could do was leave a woman scorned.

"OK, that's enough," I told Jack, whose eyes were rolling in the back of his head as he enjoyed the tightness of Royal's bootyhole. Relieving himself inside of Royal, Jack placed his large dick inside his briefs and retired to the bathroom.

"Look at your shitty ass. You smell like shit, nigga," I joked with a barely conscious Royal.

"See you in hell, bitch," he barely said as blood covered his ass cheeks.

I let off two bullets in his head, silencing him forever.

"Clean this shit up," I demanded, walking out of the room. Opening my flip phone, I dialed Justin's number. He picked up on the third ring, letting me know that he knew exactly who it was calling.

"Did you get that info on the youngin?" I questioned.

"Yeah, not good at all," he replied.

"You know what to do next," I replied, ending the call, giving the green light on Percy's death.

I wasn't in this business for handouts, to give favors, or to look out for any nigga. I took risks just like all of my workers did. The only difference was the fact that my risks could create a bigger downfall. One thing I was taught was that emotions could get you killed, and whether it was your kids, grandmother, brothers, or sisters, you added them as a liability the moment you placed your foot in this game.

Leaving the house, I walked down the street to my hidden, unmarked car. I was at a point in my life where I didn't give a fuck about anything and it showed.

24

"WHAT MAKES no sense to me is the fact that you fail to answer my mutherfucking calls, Marcella!" Ramel yelled into the phone as I cruised down the highway.

"I've just been busy working on launching this clothing line. I'm just getting back from California from a meeting with vendors," I lied into the phone. It seemed as if every time he called, I was busy handling business.

"Just remember I'm in jail, not dead," he replied and ended the call before I could reply. Sitting back, thinking, I knew I was fucking up and giving him every reason to check on me through outside sources.

Directing Justin to turn around, I decided to stop and visit Ramel. I couldn't allow my business to get in the way of what we had, especially since I had been lying to him about my whereabouts and taking over his business in the streets.

Shit had been going great. I was making damn good money. Niggas actually feared me, and surprisingly, shit had been going great.

Looking at my phone, I saw a text from Sampson. We had been texting on and off for the last few weeks. When he would ask about meeting up or going on a date, I would always make up excuses. It was bad enough that we were texting. Meeting up could take things to another level. The fact remained that I loved Ramel.

Turning into the prison, Damoni opened my door, and I walked into the building. Going through the normal routine, I waited as the clerk pulled up his visitation list. Bending my head to take a peek at the list, I attempted to make sure that none of my soldiers had been paying him any visits. I saw myself, Rome, Milan, and just as I was about to take a seat, I noticed an unknown name at the bottom.

Kate Jackson was the name that I viewed and was also a name that I had never heard before. Trying to contain my composure, I looked to see the last visit day next to her name since they only get visits every Thursday, Friday, and Saturday. Today was Friday, and her last visit was on Thursday, which was yesterday. I turned to take a seat, my heart was beating fast, and the fact that I had no knowledge of this made it worse.

"Visitor for Ramel Brown!" I heard from the speaker. I stood to my feet, so deep in thought that I didn't notice I was in the back waiting for him until I saw him walk to the glass. He shook his head, and I also noticed how his once neatly twisted locks were now a low, even cut.

"Now you come and visit a nigga," Ramel stated into the phone, taking a seat.

"Don't start that shit, Ramel. You know I've been busy, but the real question is, who the hell is Kate Jackson on your visitation list?" I asked.

His face twisted up in confusion as if the words I had just asked were foreign to him. "What are you talking about? I don't know Kate Jackson," he answered, but I knew it was a lie.

"Considering the fact that the only way she can get on your visitation list is if you send out a form for her to fill out, then she sends it back in, and you get it approved. Either you're lying, or there's a glitch in the system," I replied, gripping the phone, wishing it were his face.

"Marcella, baby, listen to me. I don't know what you're talking about. I love you and only you. Even though you been slacking and not showing a nigga real love behind these bars, I'm not tripping, because I know your conquering your dreams and designing shit. I'm proud of you. I'm just missing you. This shit is for the birds, and I'm ready to come home. But even after all that shit, I still wouldn't put you through no flaw shit. True, I lied, and that's the reason I'm in here, but I really don't know who Kate Jackson is," he admitted.

I looked Ramel into his eyes, and for the first time, it was hard to tell whether he was lying or not. But one thing still remained—the fact that I loved this nigga with everything in me.

"I spoke with your lawyer. What I need to know is why the fuck do they keep continuing your court date? Is there something I'm missing? There's no way you should still be sitting here," I said.

"Right, that's why I been calling you so much lately. Need you to check into that lawyer; something isn't right," he confessed.

"So are you asking me to get my hands dirty?" I smiled.

"Nope, not at all. I'm dead serious about that shit, Marcella. Just have someone check into him. I'll have Flex handle the rest if needed," he instructed. "Baby, you got too much good shit going on. You're traveling and designing clothes, and Rome has the business on the streets doing numbers. We should be paying your people off real soon. Milan is handling the family business. Y'all handling shit, I see. When a nigga come home, we gon' have a legit mini empire." He laughed excitedly.

"You're right. You look great with your new haircut, but I won't have anything to grip when I scream your name after releasing my juices all over your face," I said, reminiscing about the nights he would wake me up out of my sleep with head.

"You definitely want a nigga dick to get hard talking like that? I miss the fuck out of you. I'mma make that pussy scream when I get out of here. A nigga trying to put twins in you soon as I walk out these bars," he confessed, laughing at his remark.

I couldn't help but look at the man I loved more than anything. We had been through so much, and I knew he was mad at the fact that I hadn't been coming to visit or answering the phone as much. But the fact that he put all that aside and enjoyed the fact that I was here made my heart smile. I had to find a balance and maintain my relationship with him and the streets.

"God knows I love you, boy," I expressed, interrupting his words.

"You know I love you more, girl. You just need to pick up the damn phone and show a nigga some love. I'm in jail, not dead, and a nigga sure don't have a life. Remember that," he replied.

The rest of the visit went great. I honestly hated getting up and leaving him there.

I walked back to the front of the waiting area, about to leave. Something in my heart wouldn't allow my feet to move. Grabbing my license, phone, and money out of the locker they provided, I walked back up to the clerk. Pulling a hundred-dollar bill out, I slid it to her.

"All I need is confirmation on a visitor and an alert the next time she comes," I whispered as the older black woman stared as if she were contemplating. I slid another hundred, and she took the money and pulled Ramel's visitor account up.

"She comes every Thursday, She's a Black girl, tall and thick, and she normally stays the entire visit," she said.

"He said he doesn't know her. Could this be a mistake?" I questioned.

"She comes every Thursday and stays the entire visit," she repeated, which confirmed that Ramel had just sat in my face and told yet another lie. I was over this shit, and I was definitely over his lies. Grabbing my things, I thanked her and walked out of the jail house. Hearing my phone beep, I looked to see a text message. For some reason, I felt like going out for drinks tonight.

∾

Six Hours Later...

My normal attire had been suits and heels, but tonight with my crew, I planned to get sexy and party. Pulling out my gold and black bodysuit with the deep V-cut, I decided to wear it. I fell in love with the fabric more than the outfit. I topped it off with my 100mm Christian Louboutin Gold Jonatina heels with the clear strap. Putting on my diamond earrings, along with my diamond-encrusted Rolex that I had recently purchased, I looked like a sexy boss bitch. Grabbing my clutch, I was ready to walk out of the house.

"Rome and Milan, hurry up!" I yelled.

They both walked down the stairs in matching all-black Gucci attire. Looking at them made me jealous that my equal wasn't around to enjoy the fun times. As Damoni opened the door for us, I checked the babysitter to make sure she was OK with my niece before we all left and entered the truck.

Justin pulled off, and we headed to South Beach to Club Black. It was a new club that was becoming very popular.

"So how's business?" Rome asked.

"Great, can't complain, and so far, no real issues," I replied.

"That's great, but I do want to inform you on an issue that Manuel spoke of. He mentioned that you have one of your boys watching his traps. Is that true?" Rome said.

"Fuck no. That's my damn brother. I trust him more than anybody. Why would I have someone watching his trap? Even if my brother came up short with my profit, I wouldn't trip, so that makes no sense. The worst part is the fact that he expressed that shit to you and didn't just ask me," I expressed, pissed off.

"Marcella, you act like you're the easiest person to reach these days. Shit, I have to make an appointment just to see you. Manuel has reached out to you on more than one occasion, and even if you are around, your attitude sucks as if you're on top of the world," Milan added.

"Wait a minute, that's not fair. I would never treat my family any different. But what all of you do need to understand is the fact that I am running shit, and in order for y'all continue your glamorous little lives, this is how it will be. You can either get with it, or get lost. I really don't give a fuck," I bluntly stated without one flinch.

"We don't want any problems, Marcella. We get it, boss lady," Rome surrendered. I knew he was being sarcastic, but truthfully, I was just that the boss.

Milan rolled her eyes, and I ignored her. We pulled up to the club, and Damoni let us out. Of course, the promoters were waiting for us at the door, walking us straight to the upstairs VIP. I was ready to have some fun. I grabbed Milan's hand, and we walked to the area together where I spotted a few dudes from my crew. Even gay ass Jack hung around and got money with me after we handled Royal.

I looked around to see a semi-packed club. To my crew, I was known as Marcella, but to the looking eye, I was addressed as Boss Lady, and as far as the streets knew, that was my birth name.

I loved to have fun, but I required more soldiers than normal when I stepped out to club events. I rented out the entire top floor of the club for my crew and me to enjoy our night hater-free.

I felt good and free for the first time in a long time—as if I were in control of my life and everyone around me. As much as I loved Ramel, I couldn't wrap my head around the fact that he was still lying to my face even after all we'd been through. He had my head in more places than one.

"Shout out to boss lady and her crew in the building!" I heard the DJ say as the bottle girls brought us lit-up bottles of Don P, Cristal, and Belaire, along with Patrón, Hennessy, and Don Julio 1942. My crew became excited and ready to blow off some steam, but I also needed them to be on point as well. Looking around, I saw Damoni and Justin kicking it with some girls. As I made my way over to them, I received a text message.

*Message: I'm here

Smiling, I stopped in my tracks to reply:

*Me: Come up to the top

"So you guys going to introduce me to your girls?" I asked, catching Damoni and Justin off guard.

"Oh, what's up, boss lady? This is Brielle and Sasha," Justin replied.

"Hello," the ladies both said in unison as if they were nervous.

"No need to be scared. I don't bite unless you make me." I laughed as they loosened up.

"Fellas, never allow your ladies to drink nothing but the best in my presence," I said, grabbing a bottle of Cristal and two wine glasses. Handing the ladies their drinks, I noticed Damoni hadn't said a word. I was also confused because as much as we talked about life, he never mentioned having a girlfriend.

Grabbing Damoni away from their crew, I decided to make sure he was OK.

"Is everything fine? You seem a little quiet?" I asked.

"I'm good, just not feeling tonight that's all," he said.

"Why am I just finding out about your love interest? As much as we talk, I would have loved to know that you were in love. I think that's great, especially in the field of work we do," I replied, speaking more to myself and the fact that I was heartbroken.

"Because it's not what it seems," Damoni replied. For some reason, I felt as if he were hiding her for a reason.

"You're the most beautiful woman in the room," I heard a voice whisper in my ear before I could reply to Damoni. Looking up, I saw Sampson's handsome milk-chocolate face looking at me with admiration. Turning around, I hugged him and couldn't do anything but lust for him. At that very moment, he looked and smelled so damn good.

"Oh, Damoni, this is Sampson," I introduced as he looked on in confusion. Sampson held his hand out to greet as Damoni looked at it as if it were a foreign object and walked away.

"I'm sorry. I don't know what his problem is tonight," I spoke, walking out of the VIP area. I knew my soldiers were on high alert for this new face, and I needed them to enjoy their night. I texted Rome, informing him that this was a new business associate concerning his brother so he wouldn't think otherwise.

When I got Sampson closer to the bar, we began small talk. He sported an all-black Gucci sweatshirt and pants to match, along with black Gucci drivers and belt. His Diesel cologne added the right touch to his ensemble.

"I felt like I was about to get shot walking out of that VIP with you," Sampson admitted. "What's up with all them niggas in there? You must be an important lady."

"Not at all. I'm just kicking it with my brother and his crew. So you know they all treat me like their little sister," I lied.

"I definitely understand, so tell me about yourself?" he replied, looking into my eyes.

"Not much to tell. I'm into fashion, I love my family, and I want a house full of kids one day," I replied, thinking of the future I would've wanted for myself if life hadn't taken a turn for the worse.

"I like that. I'm a huge family man myself. Well, I'm twenty-six, and I'm a music producer here in Miami." He smiled.

"Wow, music? That's big. I love that. I'm thinking of opening up a music studio myself and letting all the local artists record for cheap," I revealed.

"Wow, really? So you're into music?" he inquired.

I took a moment to think; music was a passion of mine that I slept on. Not many knew of my singing talent. I didn't think I ever told Ramel of my talent. But other than fashion, I loved to sing in private since my mother expressed early on that singing wasn't a real career.

Coming back into reality, I began to speak. "Actually, I love music. I can't believe I'm about to say this, but singing is what I would call my hidden talent," I said.

"Why is that a hidden talent? You're too young and beautiful to forget your dreams. Take my hand," he replied. For some reason, I was feeling him and this conversation. It had been a while since I thought about my real hopes and dreams. It seemed as if the closer I got to them, the further away life would pull me. Wrapped up in the moment, I followed him as the DJ played an old slow jam—"Slow Motion" by Juvenile. Pulling me close, he turned me around and wrapped his arms around my waist.

"Just move to the music," he instructed, and I began to grind my hips on his pelvic area. At that moment in time, I forgot that I was a big-time drug dealer, that I had a crew that watched my every move, and that I lived my life corrupting others. At that moment in time, I was Marcy, a young girl with the world at her fingertips.

The next thing I knew, I was pulled to the ground, and before I could speak, shots were fired.

Pow! Pow! Pow! rang out through the club as more gunfire challenged back.

I grabbed my arm as everyone began to run in fear as I searched for my crew. Spotting a few members with their guns drawn, I began to head in their direction until I was scooped off my feet and carried out the club. Outside the club, I was hysterical. I needed to find my sister, brother, Rome, and my boys.

"Put me down! I need to find my family!" I yelled.

"Check this, baby. You could have gotten yourself killed in there. One moment, you were dancing, and the next thing I know, a nigga got a gun out, walking toward us. Now either they were headed toward someone standing by us, or they were aiming at you," Sampson spoke.

Grabbing my phone out of my breast, I called Milan first. Standing in the crowd of people, I walked toward the back entrance of the club, but she wasn't answering. I became scared, and along with the fact that my crew was nowhere to be found, I became frantic.

"We have to go. I'm parked over here!" Sampson yelled, pulling me toward his car.

Dialing Milan again, I began to walk.

"Hello, Marcella, where are you?" I finally heard her answer on the other end of the phone. Opening the car door to his red Ferrari, I took a seat. I needed to be in a concealed area because I knew those shots were intended for me.

"I'm fine. I'm in the car with Sampson. Is everyone OK? Where are you guys?" I questioned frantically.

"We are all OK. We're in the car with Manuel. Everyone's OK. Your boy Damoni is on point. A guy from D-boy's crew tried to sneak you, and the man you're with pulled you down, but your boy Damoni peeped everything from the door and was behind y'all on the dance floor," Milan said.

"So Damoni and Justin are cool as well?" I inquired.

"Yes, but I need you to be safe, Marcella. I can't take losing you as well," Milan added. After saying our goodbyes, I turned on the Find My iPhone link so my location could be tracked by Domani and Justin. I was relieved to see that everyone was OK and headed home. I also knew that playtime was over.

I watched Sampson as he whipped in and out of traffic and headed north.

"Ummm, Sampson, I'm going to need you to get off on the next exit," I instructed.

"Where we headed?" he replied.

"To my spot," I said. Without one word, he followed each of my directions until we were pulling up to my house. Looking around, I made him pull around back so my crew in the back wouldn't get suspicious since they never saw activity around the house.

"So this is your little spot, huh?" Sampson asked as he turned off his ignition.

"Yep," I replied, admiring the tiny two-bedroom home that I purchased just to watch my trap house across the street. The only people who knew of this place were Damoni and Justin.

"You can come in if you like," I invited, opening the door, stepping out of his car. I didn't know what the fuck I was doing, but living this lifestyle made me lonely and angry most of the time. If Ramel wanted to have his little fun even behind bars, then so would I.

Without one word, opening his door, Sampson followed as I opened the back door to my private home, which was equipped with a sectional, table, and bed. I didn't have or require anything else since the only time I spent here was for business purposes.

We walked in the door, and before I could cut the light on, I felt Sampson turn around to face me. Before I knew it, he grabbed my neck and pushed me against the counter. I immediately went into alert until I felt his lips crash into mine. Not being one to back down, I kissed back. He lifted my body onto the counter as his hands and lips explored different areas.

"Mmmm." I moaned as he pulled my bodysuit down, exposing my bare breasts. He pulled the rest off, and I was now bare ass naked on the counter, and he began kissing me. He parted my legs with his left knee, and his kisses began to trail down to my sweet spot. Spreading my lips with his right fingers, he targeted my clitoris and began sucking and licking as if it were his last meal.

Grabbing the back of his head, I pushed him deeper as his tongue twirled, licked, and sucked each area of my pussy. Arching my back, I rode his face as wetness filled my sweet spot.

"You taste so good," he whispered as his face and mouth filled with my creamy juices.

Picking me up, he released himself out of his Gucci jeans. Pinning me up against the refrigerator, he inserted himself inside of me. Wrapping my legs around his back, I allowed him the ability to push all of himself inside of me.

He began to hump away, and what I expected to be rock-hard meat had me feeling as if I were feeling a rock-hard Vienna sausage.

"Ohhhh, this pussy is so good! Say my name!" Sampson yelled as I tried not to laugh. The fact that he ate my pussy like steak on a silver platter had me feeling as if his dick would possibly kill my insides. I was actually cheating on my man for this little ass dick.

"Yesss, daddy, right there," I replied to play along. I'd be damned if I would call his name.

Sliding me down, he pulled me back to the counter and bent me over to hit it from the back. I closed my eyes to keep from laughing at the fact that his little dick fell out with each pump. Grabbing the back of my neck, since I didn't have hair to pull, he humped away until he released his little babies on my back.

He was breathing hard, and I knew he felt as if he had just won an Olympic race. Slapping my ass, he began to talk.

"Damn, you got some good ass pussy. Sorry I had to give it to you so rough like that, but I been wanting to fuck the shit out of you since I met you," Sampson admitted, looking into my eyes. He was a nice guy, but in reality, I had a man, and my rules were simple. If I planned to cheat, I at least wanted the shit to be worth it.

But since he was such a nice guy, I decided to play along. "Yeah, you tore it up, baby, but I'm actually kind of tired, and I have an early-morning client to style. How about I call you once I wake up tomorrow?" I suggested.

"Ummm, yeah, that works. Wouldn't want to keep you up all night and have you sleepy at work," he replied, caught off guard. I guess he figured he would be putting that little sausage to use all night. He had me and all the real bitches of America fucked up. Barely giving him enough time to properly get dressed, I kicked him out and locked the door. Heading to the shower, I texted Justin and Damoni to head my way. I needed to get to the bottom of what happened tonight.

After washing my entire body over and over for fifteen minutes, I finally got out of the shower and wrapped the only towel I could find in the house around my body. Walking out of the bathroom, I spotted Damoni and Justin looking my way.

"One second. I'll be out," I replied, heading into the master bedroom to grab the jean shorts and tank top I left over here when Damoni and I were watching the trap one late night. He was the only person besides my family that had seen me out of my normal business attire.

I walked into the living room, and the boys both sat with serious looks on their faces. "So what happened?" I asked, breaking the silence.

"What happened was you almost got killed, and I saved your ass," Damoni said first.

"Correction, getting myself killed will never be an option because I pay you two damn good of money to make sure that doesn't happen. Now let's try this again. Congrats for doing your job, but let's get down to real business. It's time to take D-boy out," I replied. I didn't know what Damoni's problem was, but he needed to chill.

"I'm already ahead of you. I hit up your girl Naomi. What I think is that we should hit their spots from the inside. Since your girl is a known face, let her start taking shit right under that nigga nose from the drugs to the money and make it look good. We can set up a crew to hit their trap houses to make it look legit," Justin suggested.

"That's a little too risky for Naomi, but I'll think it over. In the meantime, I want a body watching each of D-boy's traps day and night. And as for our traps, if you're not a part of the crew, I don't want a single soul stepping foot on either of my traps' lawn," I stressed, visibly pissed that D-boy had finally made his contact. Knowing that he would only try harder let me know that it was time to tighten up security and sleep with one eye open. "At the end of the day, I just need everyone ready for war if it comes to it," I added, looking at my young soldiers' faces.

"You knew that the day you picked us to protect you. Don't wait until now to question us about shit. We are riding with you, but we need to know if your head still in the game because you played your-self with that wack ass nigga tonight," Damoni boldly stated.

"My head is always on business, but I am allowed to have fun. I mean, what's going on, Damoni? Is there a problem that I'm unaware of? Because you have been acting real shitty lately. What? You working for D-boy or something?" I replied, knowing that my last statement questioning his loyalty would piss him off.

Taking a long, hard look at me, he shook his head and walked away. Not being the type of person that allowed anyone the pleasure of dismissing me, I grabbed my gun and followed as Justin took a seat, shaking his head.

Walking out of the house, I called out to Damoni, but he ignored me and kept walking. This was too much shit for one night. It was four in the damn morning.

"Damoni, I'm going to say it one more time! Stop!" I yelled, cocking my gun and pointing it.

He stopped walking and turned around. Walking back toward me, reaching me face to face, he stood with the gun pointed toward his head. Looking into his eyes, I lowered my gun to finally speak. I couldn't have my number one, most-trusted worker mad at me. That shit wasn't good for business, considering the fact that he knew so much.

"Damoni, just talk to me. What's up with you? We don't handle things like this, and lately, you been tripping, but tonight, I saw a whole other side to you. Forget that you work for me, forget that you sell drugs and protect me, forget all that shit, and just be real. If there's anybody that I can be real with, it's you. Now I'm asking for the same in return," I reasoned with my gun at my side.

Still not talking, Damoni stepped forward, and before I knew it, his lips crashed into mine. Before I realized it, I was kissing him back. Breaking the kiss, I stood back in confusion.

"My bad. I shouldn't have done that, but Marcella, that's the problem. A nigga done fell in love with you. And I don't know what to do about the shit. I try to keep it professional, but having a nigga like Ramel and entertaining that clown ass nigga tonight made that shit uncontrollable. Tonight made me realize that all you need is real love, and I know that because I need that shit too," he expressed.

"This can't be happening, Damoni. You work for me, and I'm in a relationship. That wack ass nigga you seen tonight wasn't shit. I could care less about him, but I care to much about you to ruin what we have going on here. We make a lot of money. I don't want to ruin our great work relationship," I admitted.

The truth was, I loved Damoni, and he was cool. We talked about a lot of things and spent more time together than any of my workers simply because I trusted him. Never in a million years would I ruin that, and it was true I loved him but only as a friend.

"I can understand that, Marcella. A nigga just had to express that before I began expressing it in other ways. You're right; we do make a lot of paper together, and I don't want to fuck that up. Just promise me that if you do bring another nigga around, make sure they can hold their weight when standing next to you. That nigga was out there dancing like a Pretty Ricky ass nigga on the dance floor. I should've popped his ass for being so lame," he joked, lightening the mood. If I did a million things wrong in my life, I could honestly say the one thing I did right was choosing someone like Damoni to watch my back.

"That's not the only department that nigga was lame in." I laughed.

"That's why it's best to fuck with only real niggas," Damoni added as we both walked back into the house. My night was more than eventful, but I had one more task before I ended this month.

25

THREE WEEKS LATER...

WITH MY PRADA shades covering most of my face, I took a seat in the waiting area. I was here strictly for business. I looked around, and there were four other women in the area. One black girl dressed in a suit with long hair, two white girls with kids, and another black girl that looked to be younger. Neither of them interested me.

"Visitor for Ramel Brown!" the guard yelled. My man and I were on great terms, and by the way everything was looking, he wouldn't be getting released until trial.

Completing the usual routine, I was finally in the back, ready to see the excitement on my man's face. Walking to our normal sitting spot, I saw her. Even in her seated position, she looked tall and thick with long hair. She was actually pretty. I saw why Ramel would want her, but it hurt to see her smiling at what was supposed to be my definition of love.

For the first time in my life, I wanted to run. I wanted to back down and allow them to continue whatever made them happy. But I had to let it be known that there was a new boss in town, and this shit would never fly. Walking behind her, I watched as Ramel's eyes grew big. Kate then turned around and looked at me.

"No need to stand. This will only take a moment," I recited with my Louboutin pumps pressed to the ground. As I grabbed the phone from her hand, she stayed seated, looking on in confusion.

"Just know that your lies made this happen," I spoke into the phone as Ramel began to yell.

"It's not what you think! Let me explain!" he yelled. "Marcy! Marcella, baby!" he yelled as the guards began to circle around him.

"You need to quiet down and take your seat!" a guard yelled.

I watched as they tackled him to the floor since he ignored them and continued to yell after me. I walked away, shaking my head as Kate stood still as if a cat had her tongue.

"Marcella, let me explain," she finally said as I reached the door

"Explain what? That you in love with my nigga?" I asked, stopping in my tracks as she approached me.

"I do love him, bu—" was all that escaped her lips before my closed fist met her face.

Immediately, she fell backward as I turned to exit the building before the situation landed me in jail. Quickly exiting the building, I walked to the parked Tahoe in the front and entered the vehicle. Pulling off from the curb, Justin, Damoni and I were gone.

"You aight?" Damoni asked.

"I will be," I replied, placing my Prada shades back on.

Picking up my phone, I made a call to my realtors. I had my eyes set on a sky-high condo overlooking the beach. Today was the day that I left the home I shared with Ramel and anything to do with him besides Rome.

I also changed my phone number; although I fucked up and did sheisty shit, we always somehow got through things. But today was different. Today I made the choice to move on.

Hearing my ringing flip phone, I answered on the third ring.

"Speak," I said into the receiver.

"Boss lady, we have a problem," Zane replied. I immediately hung up the phone.

"Head to trap number two," I demanded. Each of my traps had a number indicating how important they were concerning the money they brought in.

Justin made a U-turn as we headed to the trap. I expected to be graced with nothing but bullshit. And with the day I was having, blood would be shed.

Pulling up to the house, I immediately saw most of my workers standing outside. Damoni opened the door for me as I pulled my nine millimeter out immediately. Walking to the door, I motioned for everyone to follow me inside. Walking in, I saw a body on the floor.

"There's two more in the room, all the dope and money gone as well," Zane spoke, knocking me out of my shocked state.

"This house requires at least eight niggas at all times, so why the fuck are three of my niggas dead and five of you are still breathing and in perfect health?" I spat, now facing my entire crew.

"Umm, being straight up and honest, I wasn't here because my baby was being born. So I left early in the day," Zane admitted, which was the first person to call me.

"And," I spoke, waving my gun toward the other guys

"We went to get some food," Tip replied.

"So y'all niggas was hungry?" I replied. "That's understandable. Get rid of the bodies, and I want you four to stay here the entire night and tomorrow! Get my fucking money back!" I yelled.

"Zane, I want you to head home to your family. That's where you belong," I added as I walked out of the house.

Reaching the truck, I turned to Damoni and Justin.

"I want this bitch burned to the ground tonight, and I want all of them inside with no way to escape," I instructed, and they agreed.

Opening my phone, I texted Manuel to meet me at the spot. Playtime was over.

Moving quickly, I arrived at his stash house within minutes to see him pulling up in his new Benz truck.

Getting out of my truck, I walked in the house with him on my heels. Not being one to wait, I immediately began speaking.

"One of my main trap houses got hit. They took over $40,000 and the rest of the drugs. I know it was D-boy, and I'm done playing. I want him dead!" I relayed to my brother, Manuel.

"I understand, but we want this shit to happen the right way. You can't just go sending shots. You'll kill our crew and his, then who gone make money?" Manuel reasoned. "I agree it's his time to go, so continue to use Naomi right now," Manuel said.

"How the hell do you know about Naomi?" I questioned, looking at Justin and Damoni, who shook their heads, indicating that it wasn't them.

"Come on, Marcella. You know don't shit happen unless I have a hand in it. It's just fucked up that you're keeping secrets from me all of a sudden," he added.

"I'm just handling business like you should've been doing. Need I remind you that he shot and almost killed you. There's no reason D-boy should still be walking the streets and even making money with the position you're in now," I challenged.

"Because I have the one thing you will never have, and that's patience. You're living your life out here as if you can't die tomorrow, Marcella. The key for you is to stay low-key, get money, and chill until Ramel comes home," Manuel reminded me.

"I'm living my life like the boss bitch I am, and in my position, I call the shots. I brought this situation to you, thinking we were on the same page, but now that I see we aren't. I will proceed to handle shit on my own terms," I replied as I gathered myself to leave. Since I stepped into this position and started making more money than the average nigga, it seemed as if everyone had a problem with it. I couldn't help that I produced more income than Ramel in just a few short months. I couldn't help that my real father, *Papi,* made me pay next to nothing for the bricks I gt, and Manuel paid full price. I couldn't help it that D-boy was losing out on money due to my traps and product being the cheapest and rawest in the city. I was even working on opening up a clothing store and studio. I snapped my fingers, and niggas fell to my feet. That was why it puzzled me that D-boy would make a hit so soon, and conveniently, nothing but three workers were present at the time. Something was up, and I planned to find out very soon.

Walking away from Manuel before I forgot our connection as

family and got into a confrontation, I walked to my truck and hopped inside.

Two Weeks Later...

It was eleven o'clock at night, and not a creature was stirring, not even a mouse, I thought to myself as we entered the dark two-story home. Looking out the window, I watched as the outside watchman was thrown inside my oversized black van before it drove off.

Walking behind Damoni, he led me straight to the upstairs master bedroom. The house had an old but glamorous feel to it from the many crystals, glitter, and fur that decorated the house. Grabbing my hand, he led me up the stairs. I stopped and looked at Damoni's leading me and couldn't help but smile.

Reaching the closed master-bedroom door, I heard a phrase that almost made me lose it.

"I heard old bitches got some good ass pussy," Nate spoke.

"And if you touch her down there, you'll die right along with her," I spoke, breaking up my three workers' session. All they were responsible for was tying her up and waiting. I walked to the side of the older woman that was tied to her bed with a scarf securing her lips. Tears stained the side of her face as fear took over her body.

"All I want to know is one thing. Where's your son?" I questioned, and she shook her head.

"I'm going to remove this scarf so you can talk. If you scream, my men will take pleasure in blowing your head off. But if you cooperate, we will make sure you only wear a black dress to your son's funeral and not your own," I stated as she shook her head with more tears falling down her cheeks.

Nate removed the scarf as my crew stood with their weapons in hand, ready for whatever.

"I swear I don't know where he is. I haven't talked to him in a few weeks," she whispered.

"You know, my mother always told me if a person speaks fast, then it's most definitely a lie," I replied, pulling Nate's gun and shooting her in the knee.

"Ahhhh, ohhhh, God! Oh, God!" she screamed, crying even more as the blood leaked from her knee and soaked the covers.

"Now I'm going to ask you one more time. Where is your punk ass son!" I yelled. Since word spread around town that my trap had been hit, neither Naomi nor anyone had heard from D-boy. But after tonight, I was sure he would come looking for me, which was all I needed. Feeling sick to my stomach all of a sudden, I stepped back. I had a stomach virus that I couldn't shake, but that didn't stop my show.

"I swear I don't know where he is!" she cried out as her phone began to ring next to her. All of our eyes diverted toward the phone as her eyes shot open.

"Didn't your mother ever teach you that it's not good to tell lies?" I asked as I put my gloves on and answered her phone.

"Well, to what do I owe this pleasure?" I spoke into the receiver as I heard D-boy's loud breathing.

"Don't do this. You're making a mistake. A nigga had nothing to do with your traps getting hit. I make my own fucking money. I don't need your shit," he explained. Lies were the only thing that I didn't tolerate anymore, and he was for sure telling a lie.

With him still on the phone, I placed the gun and fired one single shot into his mother's head, silencing her forever. Pressing the end button, I tossed her phone to Justin to get rid of it, and I exited the house.

"Boss, we didn't get that nigga location!" one of my workers yelled out as I continued to leave.

"Don't worry. He'll find us soon," I replied as I made my exit as quickly as I came. Killing his mother was about more than him stealing from me. I had long-standing beef with D-boy, and he knew it; my best friend killed herself, and my brother almost lost his life at the hands of him. One thing I learned about the streets was everyone in them had an expiration date the moment they stepped foot in this lifestyle, and D-boy's was approaching fast.

"I gain more and more respect for you every day," Damoni blurted out, out the blue.

"Well, thank you. I couldn't have picked better men to stand beside me," I replied.

"I love you, Marcella. I mean, not like in love, but I respect you like I got love for you," Damoni added as I laughed at his choice of words.

"No worries, Damoni. I love you too," I replied, no longer being able to hold in the fact that I liked him. Since the night he shared his true feelings a few weeks ago, I'd been looking at Damoni differently. He was a handsome yet serious man that loved from the heart but didn't trust many.

We both shared a smile and turned away. I truly loved him, but we both knew that business and pleasure never mixed.

"If anything ever happens to me, Damoni, I want you to take over," I said.

"That will never happen as long as I'm by your side," he expressed as he leaned over and kissed my lips. *Fuck it*, I thought as I extended what he intended to be a short, sweet kiss. Our tongues danced in each other's mouths as we searched for air to pull apart. Breaking the kiss, I smiled again.

"You can't keep doing this to me," Damoni said as we both joined each other in laughter.

"Justin, take me to my sister's place," I said, referring to Ramel's house that was occupied by my sister and Rome since I moved out. Milan had been calling me for two days to stop by because she had a surprise for me, but business made me forget.

Pulling into the driveway and seeing Ramel's trucks and Audi outside brought back memories. He called constantly until I changed my number. None of my family or friends besides Damoni knew what I endured that day at visitation, and I planned to keep it that way.

Damoni opened the door as he and Justin followed behind me. I knocked on the front door, and Rome answered quickly. Walking in, I looked around for my niece.

"She's in the kitchen. Follow me," Rome spoke, knowing exactly who I wanted to see first. My niece was my heart, and I would lay down my life for her. After walking into the kitchen, I immediately stopped in my tracks when I saw my niece in the arms of the woman who I recently had contact with.

"What's going on?" I questioned, ready to spit fire.

"Oh, Marcella, this is Kate, and after tonight, I found out that she's Ramel's and I older sister. Apparently, my father had more than a few secrets he left behind," Rome added.

"Then I'm sure your sister informed you that we've met," I replied, still looking her straight in her eyes.

"Yeah, but that's water under the bridge. She's a lawyer, and she found Ramel in the system when he got locked up. He was trying to surprise everyone with our new-found family member. But Ms. Mike Tyson ended that." Rome laughed as Milan shook her head.

"Let me properly introduce myself. My name is Kate, and I'm Ramel and Rome's sister. How are you?" She stuck her hand out for me to shake. At that instant, I felt like the worst person in the world.

"Why would Ramel want to hide that type of information? And from me?" I questioned, never shaking her hand.

"That, I can't answer. In the situation, all I could do was respect his wishes even after that left hook you gave me. I would've done the same due to the circumstances of the situation, but I did come here to spread good news. Ramel will be getting released within a week, and all charges against him will be dropped. Apparently, she confessed to lying about the rape, so as soon as I turn this over, he will be a free man," Kate replied.

"So she just confessed with no problem?" I asked.

"I can be a little persuasive in such matters," Kate replied. It was then that I stuck my hand out to give her a proper handshake. It was something about this bitch that I now liked, and I knew she would be a great addition to this family.

"Well, I must go. It's already two in the morning," I spoke as I prepared to leave.

Everyone said their goodbyes as Justin and Damoni escorted me out of the house. I was tired, and I had fucked up big time. I knew there was no explanation I could give concerning my actions, and I also knew that Ramel was done with me. Hell, I would be done with me.

Heading to my condo, I fell asleep on Damoni. Sleep was the only thing I could use that would help me to not think about my life and how it was about to change again drastically.

Arriving home, I was too tired to even walk into my place, and with the fact that my feet were killing me due to my high heels, I needed support.

"Grab my hand," I instructed Damoni. Although I was on high alert for my safety, I had men guarding the inside and outside of my place. I entered through the back doors of the building, but to the average person, the only way in was through the front lobby and the elevator.

Holding onto his arm for support, I felt secure and ready to hit my bed. Damoni and Justin were staying at my place to keep a watchful eye just in case we had initiated a war from killing D-boy's mother.

My mind was everywhere at the moment, but the key was to stay on track. A boss never ruled with emotions even if you were dealing with someone that you loved more than anything. But the longer I stayed away from Ramel, the quicker the streets began to take over my life. They say there's no love in these streets, but my heart was beginning to yearn more and more for this life. The money, the cars, and the clothes meant nothing to me. I yearned for the power, the respect, and the love. And the more moves I made, the more powerful I became. I made a name for myself in just a few months and at a young age. True enough, my real father played a major role in my fast rise to the top, but he also gave me something that stood apart from the rest. I was born for this life, and it flowed through my bloodstream daily.

Walking into my spacious condo, I walked straight to my bedroom. Placing my Glock Forty on my nightstand and making sure my second pistol remained under my pillow, I walked into the huge closet. I pulled out my all-black Chanel sweatsuit and black tennis shoes to match. Rubbing my hands through my short hair, I changed my clothes in the middle of the closet. Grabbing my bag and the keys to the used Impala I just bought, I prepared myself as I looked around before I made my exit.

"You ready?" Damoni asked as he and Justin stood by the door, waiting. There was no way I could get away with killing my enemy's mother and think my life would presume as normal. Even with around-the-clock guards and soldiers ready to lay their lives down, I still needed to take precaution, so my day-to-day schedule was about to change drastically.

Walking into the garage, I handed Justin the keys to the Impala, and the three of us loaded in and left to our temporary home on the outskirts. I bought an upscale cabin that provided comfort and safety, not to mention the cameras surrounding it.

I thought about informing Manuel about my plans, but due to his recent outburst, I decided I should move alone. At first, when Rome informed me of Manuel's anger about me sending someone to watch him and his trap, I was offended. I trusted my brother and loved him more than anything, but given his recent actions, I now went about things differently with him. At times, I felt as if I were suffocating, like the family I once knew was no longer the same. The friends I once encountered were now gone, and the love I once showed was now hidden. It was no secret that this was the price I was paying for the life I dreamed of having.

"Are you OK?" Damoni asked.

"Yes, I'm fine," I replied.

"You know you got us," he said as if he could read my thoughts.

I smiled in agreement, I knew I had him and Justin the moment I met them, but I'd be lying if I said my heart didn't beat for Ramel. But I fucked that up, and what was worse was the moment he came home and witnessed the very thing he told me to step away from, he'd probably want to kill me. I closed my eyes to collect my thoughts. At that moment, I needed to clear my head in more than one way.

26

Within a few days, I'd lost more soldiers than I could imagine. D-boy and I took hit after hit at each other. There was definitely a war going on. I knew with the amount of bodies dropping on both sides, the police were hot on our trails, and we were losing major profit.

Looking at the doors that separated me from my soldiers as they waited to meet with me, I grabbed my ringing phone, ignoring my father's call yet again. I was a big girl. I could handle this all on my own. Folding and quitting was not an option; plus, the only regret I had at this point was not sharing the throne with the man that I loved.

Walking in on my men standing around, I took in their faces. It was as if they'd seen a ghost.

"I know shit looks crazy," I opened. "I know this war is costing you guys more than myself or you even expected, and trust me, I prepared for days just like this," I added.

"With all due respect, boss, you just need to step down and handle this clown. We lost our lead runner the other night, the nigga that all the rich basers fucked with, so on top of that, you are damn right. We are losing money. This shit needs to be handled, or I'm taking my ass back to the west side," Brice, one of my young hitters, said.

"Is that a threat?" I asked, and all eyes diverted to me and Brice.

"Take it how you want to take it. When Ramel was out here, we didn't have to worry about shit like this," Brice insulted.

Grabbing Damoni's gun at his side, I pointed it at Brice's head.

"Guess what, nigga? Ramel ain't here, and if you don't like how I'm running shit, you know the way out, but you won't be left breathing," I replied. Out of nowhere, I heard a loud clap as my men departed to different sides as the person clapping made their way to Brice and me.

Taking the hoodie off his head, Ramel revealed himself. Immediately, shock and rage filled my body as he looked me dead in my eyes. Ramel wasn't set to get out for another week, and I needed more time. I wasn't ready for this shit.

Some expressions revealed the same as mine, while others smiled.

"You might want to do what she says. She'll kill you right where you stand," Ramel added as Brice backed down.

Justin and Damoni stood next to me and stared Ramel down as he looked around.

"Tell your little boyfriend and minion to stand down. They're outnumbered," Ramel stated as most of my soldiers now had their guns pointed our way. As expected, they stayed in position.

"Suit yourself," Ramel stated as he pulled out his gun and shot Justin between the eyes, killing him instantly. Damoni, left defenseless since I had his gun, stood solid and refused to let them see him sweat, but I knew otherwise.

"How did you expect this shit to go?"

"Did you think you were just going to lie to me and run my empire without me knowing shit?" Ramel asked, now pointing his gun at me. Remaining silent, I was at a loss for words, but I also knew my words would make it worse.

"To make matters worse, you falling for this young ass nigga. Your time's up, Marcella," Ramel stated as he shot a single bullet through my chest.

"Marcella! Marcella! Marcellaaaa!" Those were the only words I heard before I opened my eyes to see Damoni over me. "You're dreaming; wake up!" Damoni shook me as I jumped up out of my sleep, feeling my body for bullet holes. Scared wasn't the word for my feelings right now. Without one word, I got up and retired to the shower. Against everything in me, I grabbed my phone, informing the family that I would be picking up Ramel from jail today.

I looked at the time and had an hour to get ready. I informed Damoni and Justin of my plans today. I knew Damoni's feelings were hurt, but I had to make things right with Ramel whether we ended up together or not.

Grabbing my Delmi off-the-shoulder Scuba Maxi Dress by The Row and my Valentino ankle strap heels, I retired to the bathroom and took a shower. After the dream I just had, it was clear as day what needed to be done. On a normal day, I would stay in the house I purchased away from the city, but today, I had to show my face. It was no secret that D-boy had a bounty out on my head, and in return, I had one on his.

There was no secret that a war was going on, but up to this point, money was still being made. The streets had a choice; either you were down with my crew, or you were dead out here. I changed locations for some of my spots, and the main trap was turned into an exit only, which meant the only way to enter the trap was if someone let you in, and only three men were assigned to run that trap. To the watching eye, it looked as if business was no longer there, but the drugs were transported through a small tunnel built under the house that led into the living room.

I refused to miss out on money, especially when there were a million ways to make it. The best part was the fact that my crew was on board as well. I allowed the cold water to drown my body as I took the African Shea butter soap and massaged my body. Cleaning myself from head to toe, I took a thirty-minute shower. Turning the water off, I stepped out of the shower. Grabbing my towel and tooth-brush, I did my normal hygiene routine.

Finally, ready to get dressed, I slid the dress up my body, and it squeezed every curve I carried, even the new ones I'd been recently gaining. Grabbing my heels, I exited the bathroom and grabbed my purse. I planned to take this trip alone, and the Impala would fit just right. I didn't want to be too flashy.

"I'll be in touch soon. If you need me, you know how to reach me," I instructed, referring to my burner phone. I knew Damoni was upset and confused by my actions, but after the dream I just had, I knew this was something I needed to do alone. Getting in the car, I pulled away, not knowing what to expect of my day.

I had a forty-five-minute drive ahead of me, and my plan was to not think. Turning on some old Drake, I allowed his truth to flood my speakers and my mind.

~

FORTY-FIVE MINUTES LATER...

I pulled up to the jail and parked my car outside the station in the front. Walking to the front counter, I saw the same lady who helped me find out about Kate, Ramel's new sister.

"What time is Ramel Brown being released?" I asked.

Looking at her records, she typed his name in before speaking. "He was released at 8:00 a.m., and it's now 9:30 a.m., so he's gone," she replied, and I looked around, confused. Not wanting to draw attention to how I felt, I walked out of the precinct, ready to grab my phone and call Rome.

"Aye, sexy, wassup!" I heard someone yell at my backside while I continued to walk fast to my car. I was pissed. "Damn, boss lady, I was just trying to tell you how beautiful you've gotten and how I dreamed about this day every night!" I heard the man yell, and I instantly turned around.

With his muscles peeking through his tank top and his baggy jeans sagging, Ramel looked great. His dreads were now cut off, and his waves were dancing in the sunlight. As if time stood still, we looked each other up and down, not able to speak one word. My emotions got the best of me, and I took off running. The bag he held in his hands was now on the ground as he opened his arms to scoop me up.

Planting kisses all over my face, his lips attacked every area as if this were a dream. It felt as if it had been years since I felt his touch when, in reality, it was months. But after the way life hit both of us hard, the time apart from each other felt like forever.

"Damn, a nigga missed you so much," he admitted, breaking our kiss as I smiled.

"I missed you too. I'm so sorry, Ramel. I—"

Before I completely broke down, he placed his hand to my mouth, silencing me. "Let's go," he replied as he grabbed my hand, and we walked toward the car. Walking me to the driver side, he opened the door for me, and I sat in the car. He then walked to the passenger side to get into the car. My emotions were everywhere at the moment, but I was glad he was finally home.

"Where you wanna go?" I asked.

"Your new spot on the beach," he replied, laughing.

"Why we gotta go to my place?" I inquired.

"Because I want some pussy and alone time," he truthfully stated as I smiled like a kid in a candy store.

Taking a left, I headed toward the condo I purchased when I decided to leave Ramel's house. Although it was risky due to the war with D-boy, before anything happened to me, they had a whole army to go through.

I glanced over to see Ramel watching me the entire time I drove.

"You see something you like?" I asked.

"I see something I want to marry actually," he said. I felt good because what I thought would be challenging and hard seemed to come so easy right now. I guess it was my proof that love conquered all, no matter what happened.

"Seriously, the hardest part about all that shit was being away from you. But after seeing you today, I know that you felt the same way. I didn't know who was picking me up, but I prayed to God that if our love was real, it'd never let us part no matter what," he confessed.

"So you prayed for us?" I replied, never hearing Ramel speak of God in this way.

"Of course—day and night. I prayed that he protected you and my family. All a nigga had was walls and God, so I developed a deeper understanding," he admitted. "I'm not like them other niggas that find God only in prison. I just established a relationship and believe in praying more. Maybe one day you could too." He smiled. This man always knew how to speak not only to me but through me. With each word, he spoke to my mind, body, and soul.

The rest of the ride consisted of us making small talk about people in the streets and life. As much as I wanted to reveal to Ramel about my position in the empire he built, I decided to keep the good vibes going.

Pulling up to the condo, I parked in the garage where I normally entered. Texting the doormen and surrounding people that I was in the area and at home, I put an alert out for my safety.

Ramel exited the car and walked over to let me out the car.

"Come on, baby. It's OK now. Daddy's home," he stated as I deleted my text thread. Grabbing his hand, I followed his lead as I directed him where to go.

We made it into my condo in no time. He pulled me right into the bathroom. Turning the shower on, he stripped from his clothes, exposing his rock-hard penis and tight abs.

"I guess somebody missed me," I expressed, slipping out of my dress.

"Damn right, he did," Ramel said, pulling me into the shower as the almost warm water hit our skin. Crashing his lips into mine, I challenged back as my heart beat with every kiss. I missed Ramel more than I could breathe. This life meant nothing without someone to share it with, but I also knew my man would not take a back seat to his woman running shit.

His large frame picked me up, and he press my body against the shower wall. As I wrapped my legs around him, he inserted his penis into my wet spot, taking all of my breath away. He slowly stroked in and out of my wetness.

"Damn, this pussy so wet. Shit," he expressed as I tried to match his rhythm. "Get down and let me hit it from the back." Ramel changed positions because he knew he would cum quickly in that positions.

Getting down, I turned around as he entered me from the back and began pounding my tight pussy. I clawed the wall at the pain and pleasure he served with each stroke.

"Damn, I can't hold this shitttt! Fuckkkkk." He moaned as he released his cum inside of me. I couldn't trip at how quick it was. I knew it had been awhile. I was just glad to have him inside me.

Taking a minute to gather ourselves, he washed himself and me before we exited the shower. Grabbing my towel, he pulled it away from me as my wet naked body stood at attention.

"You won't be needing that," he said as he pulled me to the bathroom counter and rubbed his finger up and down my clit.

~

TWO DAYS LATER...

Swallowing every bit of cum Ramel shot into my mouth, I stood to my feet and fell back onto the bed. We had been going at it nonstop for two days, not leaving the house. I barely answered calls, so I could only text. We made love in every area of my home, and now it was time for an official break. We hadn't had time to talk to each other.

"Damn, baby, I don't think I can go anymore. I'm sore and tired," I admitted, lying on the bed, looking up at him in defeat.

"I know, baby. You turn over and get some rest. I'mma shower and go get us something to eat and get me some clothes," he replied as I waved him off. I couldn't even muster up the energy to reply to him. Grabbing my black and gold Versace comforter, I snuggled up with my pillows before falling asleep. I felt at ease for the first time in a long time as if I had no worries.

. . .

THIRTY MINUTES LATER...

"Wake the fuck up," I heard a voice as someone shook my body, and I sat straight up with my weapon drawn. I knew better than to be anywhere without my gun.

Pulling my gun down to my side after realizing who it was, I covered my bare chest with my covers.

"Damn, I understand you have a key, but a warning would be nice!" I yelled at Damoni.

"We are not going to talk about nice. While you up here playing wifey, shit been going down. A nigga been hitting up your burner phone like crazy. I got word that D-boy has a shipment coming through in three days. This is a big shipment, and he plans to be around for the drop. It's coming through on a Good Year semi-truck. The drop is supposed to be at this address. It's a big-time mechanic shop in the Fort Lauderdale area. If we gone move, then we need to know something quick," Damoni expressed.

"I need to think about this. Where would you get such sweet information from out of the blue anyways?" I inquired.

"If you would answer your phone, you would know that Naomi gathered all this shit for you. I took the liberty of sending her away. She's leaving tonight on a flight to Mexico for a few days until all this shit blows over. All I need to know is if we need to gear up. This means a major payday and the revenge you've been waiting for," Damoni added.

"I don't care about the money. I'm good, and my team is good, but you're right. I won't be able to sleep peacefully until D-boy is gone," I released, shaking my head. Just when I began to find my happy place, reality hit just like that. I heard keys juggling in the front door, and my eyes shot open.

"Get in the closet now. Ramel is back," I whispered, getting up, exposing my fully naked body.

"A nigga don't care about that," Damoni replied, and I grabbed him up and pushed him inside my walk-in closet, cracking the door.

"Wassup, baby? I thought you were getting some rest. You ready for another round?" Ramel jokingly asked.

"Real funny," I replied, kissing his lips and grabbing my food. He had changed into a Nike sweatsuit and carried a large duffle bag.

Taking a seat on the bed, he watched me eat the baked chicken.

"I guess now that we have time to talk, what's been up, beautiful?" he inquired.

"Nothing much since the last time I spoke with you. Still designing and looking into music as well."

"Music? So you sing? Why am I just hearing this?" he spoke.

"I don't know. I thought I mentioned it before. But life just happened too fast with us. A lot of shit detoured us. By now, Ramel, we should be married and working on our second child," I expressed, somewhat sad.

"I know, baby, and that shit going to change. I blame myself completely for all the shit that happened with you almost getting killed, losing our baby, and myself going to jail. Shit so fucked up, but I promise daddy's here, and I'll never leave your side again unless it's in a body bag."

Water lined my eyes as I saw the seriousness in his tone, body language, and eyes.

"So where do we go from here?" I asked.

"I don't know, but I do want to do this shit all over again. The day you asked me if I had any secrets, to let it all out. I'm here to bear it all. I have no more secrets except that I'm out the game, and your father granted me that. He said all debts were paid, and he has someone bringing him more money than I did. So we legit, baby, so I'mma ask you the same—to lay it all out there. Is there anything I should know that may affect our future?" Ramel asked.

Taking a long, hard look at him, I wanted to scream that not only did I take over his operation, but I also wanted to tell him that I fucked another man and had feelings for one of my workers. I wanted to say I lied, betrayed, killed, and completely disrespected him. But my words were mute. I didn't know if it was because I knew Damoni was in the closet and could hear me or if I was scared to lose the one person I felt I needed in this world.

"There's nothing to tell, baby. You're the only man I ever loved the way I do, the only man that makes my heart beat fast and slow at the same time. No matter how hard I try, no man, person, etcetera will make me feel the way that you do. I love you, Ramel Brown, and when the time is right, I can't wait to be Mrs. Brown," I expressed as tears rolled down my face.

"A nigga not waiting for that day like we did before."

Grabbing my ring he bought me before he went to jail, he placed the ring back on my finger.

"I want to do this shit ASAP. Start planning and getting shit together. We gon' buy a new house and start our lives with each other, Marcella. And I love you too, baby girl." Ramel laughed as we kissed. My mouth was greasy and sticky from the chicken, but we didn't care. Shit finally felt right, and after I got my revenge on D-boy, I planned to live my life with Ramel and step out of the game for good.

Remembering that Damoni was in the closet, I grabbed Ramel and led him to the bathroom. Although I was tired of sex, his words had me fiending for him right then and there. That created the perfect opportunity for Damoni to escape.

27

I SAT ACROSS FROM ROME, my niece, Milan, Manuel, Kate, and Ramel as we all ate dinner together. This was Ramel's welcome home dinner with just family, per his request. Everything was going great although I caught a few casual stares from my brother. I guess he was still salty about our last conversation and my actions afterward.

"A nigga missed y'all like crazy," Ramel expressed.

"We missed you too, brah. What's crazy is we even missed Marcella. It seems funny, actually being able to catch up with her without her two new best friends," Manuel blurted out as I allowed a simple smile to grace my lips. Milan looked his way as if she could shoot fireballs at him right then and there. We all knew he spoke of Justin and Damoni, and that's where I draw the line.

"Best friends? You never told me of any new girls you're hanging with, baby," Ramel added.

"You'll meet them eventually, but Manuel, if my absence made you upset, maybe you should work a little harder, and you can vacation like me," I shot back, referring to the fact that I made more money than him and did what the fuck I wanted too.

"Point taken. Well, family and Marcella, I have to get up with a friend and handle a few things. I'll get up with y'all later." He grinned as he stood to walk away. I knew I hurt his pride and feelings on many occasions, but there was no love in these streets.

Looking at my phone, I read the message from Damoni that everything was set and ready to go for tomorrow. I didn't know how I would get away from Ramel, but at this point, if fucking him to sleep didn't work, then I would have Rome help to call him away.

"Well, I guess that's our cue to leave as well. I have a surprise for you anyway, baby, and it's 6:00 p.m. We have to be there at 8:00 p.m.," Ramel spoke.

I grabbed his hand, and we said our goodbyes as we exited the house we once shared that now held Rome, Milan, and their child.

Getting into his Audi, we sped off and made our way to my big surprise. To Ramel, he was free and home, living life carefree. But with every stoplight and corner, I was on alert, watching every angle. I felt bad, leaving him clueless, but it would all be over after tomorrow.

"Are you OK?" Ramel asked, knocking me out of my trance.

"Yes, I'm fine. Just glad you're home, and we are back on track," I admitted.

"Yeah, me too," he said, grabbing and kissing my hand.

We talked and laughed the entire time until we reached a destination. There was a well-kept building with a fence around it. We entered the gate after Ramel entered a code and parked the car.

"What's this?" I inquired, feeling nervous.

"This is my surprise. Now let's go. My homeboy only has two hours to spare," Ramel expressed as he hopped out and opened my door.

We were let into the building by a bodyguard that let us down the hallway. The walls were filled with pictures of great musicians that were no longer here. Finding a room in the back, we entered another door that held couches, chairs, and a soundboard with digital equipment. It was clear that I was in a studio, and for the first time, I felt as if Ramel was focused on me and making my dreams come true. Grabbing his hand and squeezing it from excitement, I smiled. My baby had outdone himself.

"Baby, this is my homeboy, Sampson, aka Sammie Sam. He's a big-time producer in this area and my childhood homie," Ramel introduced, and the moment Sampson got up from his seat and turned around to greet me, my heart jumped out of my chest. As if our silence was speaking, his eyes grew big. Trying to think quick, I stuck my hand out.

"Nice to meet you. I'm Marcella," I replied, throwing a slight smile in hopes we were on the same page.

Grabbing my hand, he fell in line and greeted me as if he didn't know who I was.

"This is the fiancé you've been telling me about? OK, let's see what she's working with. This is one of my new tracks from an up-and-coming artist that needs a female touch to it. Grab this paper, read over the few lines, and just sing. I'll do the rest," he instructed.

Ramel smiled, seeming pleased that he was helping me finally live out one of my dreams. On the other hand, I had to also watch out for the dirty looks Sampson threw my way. I changed my number and acted as if he didn't exist after the night we shared. Thinking back to that night, I wanted to throw up all over again.

Nervous and sweating, the first few takes were hard. My voice shook so bad because I had my man and his childhood friend who I had fucked a month prior looking at me.

"Brah, give us a minute. Let me talk to her and get her on track. This happens with a lot of new artists, and you may be making her nervous. Step out and let me get her comfortable," Sampson suggested.

Ramel asked me if that was OK, and after agreeing, he made his exit. Standing to his feet, Sampson entered the booth with me.

"I don't even want an explanation, because I know shit happens, but out of all the people in the world, you fucked around on my boy. That's a solid nigga in there with a good heart, and now you got me in a fucked-up position," Sampson said.

"You don't think I know that? How was I supposed to know y'all were friends? We weren't together at the time we had our little fling. It wasn't shit and ended even quicker, so I say we drop it," I suggested in a somewhat harsh way.

"Damn, glad to know how you feel. I actually thought highly of you. But after the night we spent and you not answering my calls, I did a little research myself, *boss lady*. I bet my boy doesn't know about all the shit you've been doing out here." Sampson laughed.

"And if you really did your homework, you would know that if he were to find out, you or anyone else will never breathe another day on this earth. I'm not to be fucked with. Now get back on that sound-board and do your job before I do it for you!" I demanded, not feeling Sampson's childish reaction at all.

Turning around, he gave me one last look. "Every dog has its day," he recited as he walked out and took his position. "Start from the top," he said as I took the headphones and placed them on. I planned to give it all I had, so I sang like my life depended on it, until the song was over.

"Damn, baby, a nigga never knew you could sing like that. Brah, when the shit gets mastered, send the final copy over to me. We may have something on our hands with Marcella," Ramel expressed, happier than me.

"We might have a little more than something with her, but I got you, brah. I'll send it all over as soon as possible. Thanks for stopping through and trusting me with your goldmine there. She's done... I mean, she's gonna make you a lot of money with that voice," Sampson spoke, throwing shade, but he knew better. I rolled my eyes as I kissed Ramel's lips, thanking him again and pulling him out of the studio so we could leave.

That night, I went home and made love to Ramel as if it would be our last time. I ran his bath water, washed him, applied lotion to his body, and massaged every inch of him. I took my time and pleased him the entire night because tomorrow, I planned to leave early.

∾

5 A.M.

> *My love,*
>
> *Don't be alarmed, but just like you, I have a huge surprise. I'm heading out early, because I have a few things to get in order to secure our future as well. Ramel, I want you to know that no matter what I love you more than I've ever loved anyone. I just need you to trust me on a few things to handle on my own. No worries, I'll be home by tonight lying next to you in your arms loving you for life. I will call you to check in throughout today.*
>
> *Love,*
>
> *Your future wife, Marcella Brown*

I kissed the letter and placed it next to him in the bed as I said a silent prayer. Since Ramel came home, he had been making it a routine that we pray together at night, and today was the first day that I prayed without him.

Leaving the apartment, I made my exit while Damoni and Justin waited for me. We sent a soldier three days ago to scope out D-boy's drop-off area. The drop was going down later tonight, and that left me with eighteen hours to play with. I had all the traps shut down last night and moved soldiers around the city.

I planned to return home, so the plan changed. I would witness my soldiers seize his whole operation, but D-boy would die at the hands of someone else.

Riding around in deep thought, we made our rounds, checking on my soldiers and making sure the spots were closed down properly. We went over the plan a thousand times, but tonight, almost my entire crew would be with me.

I thought about Manuel and Milan. Once I made it home, I planned to make things right with my brother/nephew. I still laughed to myself when I thought about how fucked up my family was. The fact that I missed my mother also played a part in many things. Maybe she was right for making the choice she did.

Although *Papi* was my real father, he definitely wasn't the nurturing type. Since finding out about him, our relationship had strictly been about business and nothing more. Royal taught me a lot, but Ramel turned me into a woman. The road for me was still unclear, but one thing was for sure. I would always be the head bitch in charge.

Now it was time to play the waiting game.

~

THIRTEEN HOURS LATER...

"You need to turn that phone off; all that ringing is a distraction," Damoni spoke as I declined Ramel's call again.

"You need to remember who's in charge," I replied, silencing my phone. He had been calling all day since waking up and finding my letter. He even sent text messages that I refused to read. I hated doing him like this, but I had to be prepared.

I couldn't eat or drink. Thinking about what was about to go down and spending the rest of my life with Ramel gave me some ease —that what I was doing was for the best. D-boy had cost me money, my best friend, and almost my brother, and in return, I took his mother. If I didn't take him out, I would never be able to live a peaceful life.

Powering my phone off, I informed Justin to take me to the drop spot early. I planned to wait the last five hours out, watching the spot. I had a feeling that I couldn't shake, so after going with my gut feeling, I decided to stake the spot out before the drop.

"Both of y'all leave all of your phones here with mine. We don't need anything linking us to the area," I directed.

~

THREE HOURS LATER...

"Everyone on post?" I questioned Damoni, who had a mean mug on his face.

"Yeah, they're straight," he replied.

"When this is over, my offer still stands. I want you to take over," I stated.

"Is that your brother?" he replied, ignoring my statement. I followed his eyes from where we were parked in the cut across from the building.

"Yes, it is. what the fuck is he doing here?" I spoke out loud as I watched him walk inside the building. I witnessed a few other cars from his crew pull up, but no one else in sight.

"He probably got the information that D-boy would be here and came for the same reason you did," Damoni suggested.

"But that doesn't make sense. Why would he just pull up in plain sight, get out like he doesn't have a worry in the world, and walk in the building?" I pondered.

"There's only one way to find out," Damoni added. Cocking his gun, he opened his door. I signaled for the crew to stay alert as Justin followed as well. In my heart, I felt as if I should've waited a little longer to see what was going on. But the big sister in me couldn't allow anything else to happen to my brother on my watch. No matter how bad of terms we were on, I had my brother's back no matter what. Changing my entire plan, I walked across the street, ready for whatever.

Following Justin and Damoni, we walked on the side of the building, attempting to look in to see what was going on. I looked around to see my crew lurking around the building, waiting for me to enter. With complete silence surrounding us, I decided to walk inside the building, entering from a door we spotted on the side.

I crept in with my nine-millimeter in hand. The smell was horrible, and the building was old but still standing. As Justin and Domani walked in front, I spotted Manuel talking to someone. As I walked closer, I noticed it was D-boy. Confused and not understanding what the hell was occurring, I stood in place behind some boxes, watching the two interact like old friends.

"Remember when you just stated that you wanted me to take over when this was over?" Damoni whispered as we both watched in confusion.

"Now is not the time, Damoni," I stated, still trying to see the interaction before I made my move.

"My bad, boss lady. I just wanted to inform you that I already began taking over," Damoni stated as I turned to look back at him.

With his gun drawn on me, he and Justin stood in visible sight, grabbing my nine.

"Walk," he demanded with his weapon now pressed against my head.

I was pissed and obviously outsmarted. He escorted me to the middle of the floor where D-boy and Manuel smiled at my presence. Looking around, I noticed both of their crews as well as mine with all eyes on me. It was evident that this was a set up, and I was the main target. What hurt the most was the fact that the two men I introduced to the game had now turned on me along with my crew.

"Wow, you needed all these niggas to kill little ole me?" I joked.

"Not at all. I needed all these niggas to show you how powerless you are when it comes to men. But I do have a question. How did you think this would end? Did you really think we would allow your pretty ass to come in our hoods and take over our shit just like that?" D-boy confessed.

"Am I sensing some type of jealousy? Because that's exactly what I did," I replied, unfazed at this point. I had nothing to lose, so if I died tonight, I definitely wasn't going out like a sucker.

Still quiet and staring a hole in me, Manuel stood solid.

"Do what y'all have to do. At this point, the only thing that hurts is the fact that my own flesh and blood couldn't handle me at the top," I spat as Damoni pushed me.

"No, you couldn't handle being at the top. You got vicious and messy. You questioned my loyalty and even had niggas watching me. You even betrayed the one nigga that brought you in the game and lied to me about money and product we were splitting up 50/50."

"That's what your weak ass is mad about? The fact that you allowed your feelings to crowd your judgement and side with the enemy says enough. Just kill me. Hell would be better than watching this unfold."

"You heard boss lady! Kill her, Manuel!" D-boy yelled, but Manuel hesitated.

"Oh, and Manuel, you forgot one thing. '*La Familia* over everything'," I recited as doors burst open, and more men appeared with guns drawn.

"Meet the Gomez Cartel," I replied as Damoni's brains were blown across my body. Without one blink, I looked up and saw Ramel holding the gun a few feet away. We shared a smile as bullets began to ring throughout the building. Running over to me and grabbing my hand, he placed a gun in it. We ran for cover behind some boxes, taking turns shooting.

"Took you long enough," I replied.

"You know I got you, baby. I'll cover for you. Find D-boy and handle your business so we can get out of here," I replied.

"Hey, I love you, boy," I said.

"I love you too, girl," he replied as we shared a kiss and stood back in the war zone.

It took a lot to come clean to Ramel about my affiliation in the streets against his wishes. But after Damoni popped up with that information, things didn't make sense anymore, and I knew I needed Ramel more than ever. I didn't think my brother had any dealings with all of this, but in the end, sometimes money was thicker than blood, and for some people, that was enough to betray your entire bloodline. Manuel and I both knew his real issue was the fact that I out hustled him and rose to the top becoming, richer and more powerful than him.

The spot began looking like a war zone. Bullets and bodies were flopping everywhere. Ramel rang out shots in every direction as I ducked and dodged, looking for D-boy. Spotting a few of his crew members guarding his body, I slid from behind Ramel and used my pistol to get closer to him.

I even shot members from my crew. After doing more research, I found out about my crew's betrayal and the ones that refused to follow Damoni and Justin's plan. I made sure they stayed home, using them to guard the traps, when in reality, I was sparing their lives.

I spotted my Colombian family shooting nonstop. I guessed my father was good for more than just business purposes even after spilling the truth to him. He offered to handle the situation for me, but I refused, so in turn, he offered a crew to ensure my safety.

Getting closer, I noticed that D-boy's crew wasn't guarding him. They were guarding Manuel. Confused and trying to avoid gunfire, I hid behind boxes again, trying to scan for D-boy, but he wasn't in sight.

Standing again, I looked to see Ramel shooting his way toward me. I stood again to find Manuel. Spotting him, I began opening fire on anyone in sight. While shooting, I lost sight of Manuel. The shooting began to die down as more bodies began to drop, and I began to look for an exit. Before I could take a step, I heard someone yell my name. I turned around and came face to face with D-boy, who was about ten steps away from me with his weapon pointed at my chest.

Before I could think to begin firing, D-boy's gun let off rounds of bullets, and one pierced my shoulder. The last thing I remembered was getting tackled to the ground as bullets rang out in front of me.

As the stinging sensation traveled through my shoulder, I yelled out in pain. Finally taking a look, I felt a heavy body on top of mine. Pulling them to the side as I scooted from under their big frame, I saw Ramel.

Noticing the blood soaking him and me, I began to panic as blood filled his mouth. Thinking quickly, he must have seen D-boy and ran to cover me, taking the rest of the bullets that didn't pierce my body.

Grabbing his body as blood seeped from every area, I cried out for help, forgetting my own pain.

"Helpppppppp!" I yelled as I looked to see Manuel standing over D-boy's body. Hearing me cry for help, he turned and ran toward me, dropping to his knees to help with Ramel.

"Get away from me! I don't need your help!" I yelled, pushing him away. I guess Manuel had his own plan, but the way he went about shit wasn't cool.

"Man, shut the fuck up! I wasn't gon' let them kill you. Apply pressure to his wound," Manuel instructed as he went for help. In the blink of an eye, there were bodies surrounding us, and for the ones that weren't dead, they were long gone from the scene.

"Baby, please hold on. I need you, Ramel. Please fight for me. I can't do this without you. Don't leave me, baby!" I cried as he grabbed my hand tightly, struggling to speak.

"I'm sorry," he spoke as blood drained out of his mouth.

"Don't say that. Don't speak like that, baby. You're going to make it, and were going to go home and build the perfect life together. We're going to have about ten babies running around, and you're going to be the George Jefferson of the neighborhood," I tried to joke as he began coughing, attempting to breathe.

"Remember when we first met? I knew you were the one for me, and you promised that you would always be there for me, Ramel. So you can't leave. Not like this and not right now. I can't live without you, baby," I whispered in his ear as I held onto him. As his grip became lighter, the next few seconds became a blur. He let my hand go as his eyes closed.

"No, no, no, no, no, no, no!" I yelled in pain as tears clouded my vision. My soulmate, my world, and my man were gone. I guess that wasn't enough, because soon after, I witnessed Manuel being carried back in toward me in handcuffs. As if time stood still, a SWAT team flooded the building as officers approached me holding Ramel's body.

"Well, well, well, we finally caught up with the infamous Marcy Gomez, AKA Boss Lady, AKA Marcella," a tall, white officer with glasses spoke.

"Marcy Gomez, you are under arrest for the murder of Viola Green and Anthony Dell. For money laundering, trafficking, smuggling, and distributing heroin and cocaine. You have the right to remain silent..." he trailed off as I sat numb and unfazed. Nothing was worse than the pain I felt looking down at Ramel's lifeless body.

The officers grabbed me up and handcuffed me as Manuel shook his head.

Taking one last look at Ramel, I spoke my last words.

"I'm sorry," I said as tears streamed down my face even more.

"You sure are sorry, and where you're going, you're going to be sorry for life," another officer replied to the words I spoke to Ramel.

The end...

EPILOGUE

FIVE MONTHS LATER...

"It's been a long road, Marcy, and as hard as it seems, we are going to go for option two. I was able to get the information and verify your birth in Colombia. They are going to try to throw the book at you since D-boy was an informant and had the recording on you from his mother's murder. Although the witness is dead, he was considered state property. The day you called, he was around the cops, releasing information. That will fall against us.

"Also, the murder from the gas station with you and Ramel, there was a girl that witnessed it, and she's taking the stand. She even recorded you paying her off to keep quiet. The drug charges will be dropped, but the state is offering you life without parole due to your affiliation to gangs and street ties. I'm going to do the best that I can, but I can't make any promises," Kate explained, but at this point, I didn't care. I would have rather been dead than living this nightmare without Ramel.

Without speaking or reacting to her news, I remained quiet just as any other day.

"Hey, Marcella, I know you're hurting, but you have to pull it together. One thing I know is that my brother loved you and wouldn't want you living like a zombie with his daughter inside you. That is the only piece of my brother that Rome and I have. Please give her a chance to make it to see her family," Kate reasoned.

In my mind, I knew she was speaking the truth. It was hard to connect with a child I would never have the chance to raise—to even raise a child that would never get the chance to meet one of the best men God allowed to grace this earth. Her father. It was funny, thinking back to the day Ramel told me that when we did have another child after losing the first one, it would be a girl. He even told me that we would name her Razelle Brown. A tear slid down my face as I stood to leave. Even seeing Kate brought memories of Ramel to my mind, and I needed to be out of her presence.

A Month Later...

"We, the state of Florida, find Marcy Gomez guilty of first-degree murder of Viola Green and Anthony Dell. Any last words?" the judge asked.

I remained quiet. Manuel's charges were reduced since I took the blame for his drug charges; he would be out within four years.

"Well, OK, you are sentenced to life in prison with no chance of parole." I looked at Kate and smiled.

"Judge, one more thing. My client isn't technically a citizen of the U.S. She was born in Colombia after being kidnapped and given a false identity. There's no trace of her identity besides the made-up one provided by the woman that took her, Trina Gomez, which doesn't match the name of her mother, Letecia Ford, on the birth certificate. So she's to be deported back to Colombia," Kate spilled, which caused the prosecution to all become pissed.

Since my mother decided to run from my birth father, she also lived under an alias name, and since she was no longer here, this all worked in my favor. I began digging the day my mother died, and I found the truth about her growing up in the foster system. Letecia Smith was her birth name. She adopted the last name Ford from one of her foster parents. I knew that with my background, prison would never be in the question since technically, I was a citizen of Colombia.

I planned to live my life and raise my child the way I was supposed to be—in Colombia—and I knew *Papi* would ensure that we had everything we needed. I learned a lot in my short years here on earth, especially that the streets didn't love anybody.

But if you ever come across a real thug that loves you, always remember he'll sacrifice it all for you, even his life. Rest in peace, my love, Ramiel Brown.

FOUR MONTHS LATER....

"LET me find out the big bad Marcella Gomez can't take pain" Milan laughed

"GET this damn baby out of me! this shit hurts I can't take it" I cried

"OH NO LA HIJA, you are strong like your papa this pain is nothing." Papi added

"ROME GET HIM OUT OF HERE!" I yelled as Rome grabbed my father by the shoulder escorting him out of my room.

IT WAS bad enough I was in Colombia and delivering my first child in a room at my father's mansion. I had around the clock care with the best midwives present, but the pain was unbearable.

AFTER BEING TRANSPORTED HERE to serve my time three months ago I was instantly released. The moment I received a life sentence In Flor-ida, I knew I would never serve that sentence. I was transported back to my birthplace where my father ran everything from the govern-ment all the way down to the small business owners.

"JUST BREATHE and on the count of three push" One of the midwives instructed

"YOU GOT THIS!" another voice said

"OK, ONE, TWO, THREE" Everyone yelled

I PUSHED AS HARD as I could having my family come all the way here for the birth of my daughter meant the world. The only missing piece was Manuel, I loved my brother with everything in me and the moment he walked out of those gates I planned to bring him here with his familia. But Milan planned to send him plenty of pictures of this day.

"OH MY GOD look at how beautiful she is, she looks just like my brother." Kate yelled as tears instantly crowded my vision.

THE MIDWIFE PULLED her as she handed the scissors over to cut the umbilical cord. At that moment I realized that everything I had been through was worth it to experience this moment. I was beyond happy and I now felt completed.

"WHAT ARE you going to name her?"

.   .   .

"RAZELLE BROWN" he spoke out of nowhere, up until this moment he had been silent. I guess watching me endure all of this pain and the reality of being able to witness it had him in a state of shock.

"OH, you're still here for a moment I thought you clocked out on us," Milan said, making everyone laugh.

"I LOVE YOU MARCELLA BROWN" Ramel said as he motioned for the midwife to hand over our daughter. He instantly began placing little kisses all over her as he admired her beauty.

THREE MONTHS ago I came to Colombia still in a state of sorrow and pain. I knew I had to move forward because of the life I had growing inside of my body. I just couldn't believe that after losing everything that I lost Ramel too.

THOSE FEELINGS WERE short lived because the moment I was released in Colombia, I was taken to the home of a nurse that was helping Ramel get his strength back. Guess it's safe to say the moment I thought he took his last breath in my arms wasn't true. I have my father to thank for that because the moment he realized Ramel was still breathing and fighting he helped him. And had him transported to Colombia, the damage was heartbreaking. Ramel does therapy to regain his strength to be able to walk again. But my baby is a fighter, he just recently began taking steps on his own and he's officially using a cane and wheelchair to get around.

WE WERE MARRIED the day after I arrived and the last few months of my pregnancy has been pure happiness.

.   .   .

As everyone finally left out of the room and the midwives took Razelle to make sure she was a healthy baby. Ramel and I were left alone.

"Ramel, I have something to tell you" I said breaking his stare

He smiled and pulled his wheelchair closer to my bedside.

"What's up Mrs. Brown?"

"I know this is an awkward time but we promised no more secrets and well papi is retiring. He wants to vacation and travel the world with your sister Kate" I chuckled, we all knew papi loved black women and the second he came in contact with Ramel's sister he's been head over heels.

Staying silent I knew for a fact he knew my next words.

"He wants me to take over his empire, just until Manuel is released to continue the Gomez legacy" I admitted waiting to hear him yell, fuss or get upset. To my surprise he remained quiet.

"I see, and what did you tell him?" he finally spoke

"I told him, I couldn't make this decision without you." I expressed

. . .

"Is this what you want and don't bullshit me Marcella I know you?" he asked

"YES" I admitted putting my head down I knew with that answer I could possibly lose Ramel forever.

"THEN LET'S DO IT, but we are doing this shit together. I'm tired of fighting with you about this lifestyle when it's clearly a part of you, which makes it a part of me. I got your back, plus I knew this day would come the moment I found out he was your father. I'm rocking with you baby let's get this money." Ramel replied

SHOCKED WAS an understatement for how I felt. I knew God loved me after all he sent a man like Ramel to be in my life. I leaned over and grabbed his face kissing all over it.

"BUT ONE SMALL THING, we move as a unit the moment you start that bullshit again, by making decisions on your own and keeping secrets, I'm out and I'm taking Razelle with me!"